CLASSIC SUMMER STORIES

Edited and introduced by
BECKY BROWN

MACMILLAN COLLECTOR'S LIBRARY

This collection first published 2026 by Macmillan Collector's Library
an imprint of Pan Macmillan
The Smithson, 6 Briset Street, London EC1M 5NR
EU representative: Macmillan Publishers Ireland Ltd, 1st Floor,
The Liffey Trust Centre, 117–126 Sheriff Street Upper,
Dublin 1, D01 YC43
Associated companies throughout the world

ISBN 978-1-0350-6949-1

Selection copyright © Macmillan Publishers International Ltd. 2026
Introduction copyright © Becky Brown 2026

The permissions acknowledgements on p. 323 constitute
an extension of this copyright page.

All rights reserved. No part of this publication may be reproduced, stored in
a retrieval system, or transmitted, in any form, or by any means (including,
without limitation, electronic, mechanical, photocopying, recording or
otherwise) without the prior written permission of the publisher.

1 3 5 7 9 8 6 4 2

A CIP catalogue record for this book is available from the British Library.

Endpaper pattern by Andrew Davidson
Typeset in Plantin by Six Red Marbles UK, Thetford, Norfolk
Printed and bound in China by Imago

This book is sold subject to the condition that it shall not, by way of
trade or otherwise, be lent, hired out, or otherwise circulated without
the publisher's prior consent in any form of binding or cover other than
that in which it is published and without a similar condition including this
condition being imposed on the subsequent purchaser. The publisher does not
authorize the use or reproduction of any part of this book in any manner
for the purpose of training artificial intelligence technologies or systems.
The publisher expressly reserves this book from the Text and Data Mining
exception in accordance with Article 4(3) of the European Union
Digital Single Market Directive 2019/790.

Visit **www.panmacmillan.com** to read more about
all our books and to buy them.

Contents

Introduction vii

E. M. DELAFIELD 1
Holiday Group

VIRGINIA WOOLF 29
In the Orchard

ANTON CHEKHOV 35
Not Wanted

F. SCOTT FITZGERALD 47
Three Hours Between Planes

O. HENRY 59
A Midsummer Knight's Dream

ELIZABETH BOWEN 69
The Contessina

WILLA CATHER 93
The Enchanted Bluff

ARTHUR CONAN DOYLE 111
The Adventure of the Devil's Foot

EDWARD THOMAS 157
The Flower-Gatherer

A. A. MILNE 165
A Summer Cold

THOMAS HARDY 171
An Imaginative Woman

SELMA LAGERLÖF 215
The Musician

GUY DE MAUPASSANT 229
The Fishing Hole

ALGERNON BLACKWOOD 241
The Olive

KATHERINE MANSFIELD 261
At the Bay

Permissions Acknowledgements 323

Introduction
BECKY BROWN

The best short fiction often feels like a window into a moment, something brief but resonant with a power that defies its length. It is little surprise, then, that so many of the great masters of the form – from Anton Chekhov to Katherine Mansfield, Conan Doyle to Guy de Maupassant – have been drawn to the summer months, in all their dazzling, fleeting brilliance, a precious moment between spring and autumn. Each summer, redolent with nostalgia, is capable somehow of holding every summer we ever lived within its evocative sensations and smells; heat on the skin, salt in the air, the sun dancing on a wall, the scent of roses or the lapping of cold water over tentative feet. And in all those sights, sounds and scents is *holiday*, a longed-for moment carved out from the summer months, and a gift for every storyteller – the ideal catalyst and crucible for change, revelation or even destruction.

The fifteen stories in this selection span four continents and almost one hundred years, yet their themes and preoccupations are remarkably similar. The overwhelming beauty of nature at her finest is near-omnipresent. In Virginia Woolf's 'In the Orchard', sound, texture and colour all swamp the half-sleeping Miranda, who thinks she hears 'life itself crying out from a rough tongue in a scarlet mouth, from the wind, from the bells, from the curved green leaves of the cabbages'.

A younger child, Edward Thomas's eponymous Flower-Gatherer, is drawn irresistibly through the fragrant countryside under trees blossoming 'in rounded clusters as of bubbling snow, and close as honeycomb', while Willa Cather's narrator looks back on the sun-baked summers of his Nebraskan childhood, camping on an islet 'beautifully ridged with ripple marks, and strewn with the tiny skeletons of turtles and fish', in 'The Enchanted Bluff'.

In each of these stories there is a tone of childish magic and escape that is amplified to an adult madness in Algernon Blackwood's 'The Olive', in which an encounter with a young woman in a hotel dining room descends into a midnight bacchanale, 'untamed, wild as the wind', and to greater heights still in Selma Lagerlöf's fairytale of 'The Musician', who is alone in the woods and hears 'everything thinkable and unthinkable . . . rioting and clamoring in the depths of the stream', and takes up his violin to challenge its beauty, with terrible and supernatural consequences.

INTRODUCTION

There is a sense in many of the tales of a crucible, a catalyst, where relationships – transplanted on family trips, or newly made in the lobby of a hotel or on a beach – are forged or undone in the strange, transient state of *holiday*. Thomas Hardy and Anton Chekhov narrate the disintegration of stable family units, eroded by the uncertainties and changing cast of summer colonies, with infidelities (real or imagined) and no small amount of drama.

Katherine Mansfield and E. M. Delafield muse in that same direction, depicting a holiday as a prism through which 'normal' life is refracted into new shapes and colours. Both the former's 'At the Bay', with its patchwork of New Zealand holidaymakers navigating the temporary micro-society of a 'summer colony', and the latter's 'Holiday Group', in which a drab family of four desperately wring small pleasures from a chilly English July, is almost entirely free of incident – but somehow all of human life seems to sit within them. Such is the summer-bright brilliance of the short stories in this collection, which cherish brevity above all else.

CLASSIC SUMMER STORIES

E. M. Delafield

Holiday Group

I

The Reverend Herbert Cliff-Hay's legacy had been paid at last. It seemed almost incredible, they had waited for it so long, talked about it so much, and alas! borrowed money upon it twice already. It reached them, indeed, in a terribly diminished form, what with death duties, and mysterious stamps, and fees of which they had had no previous cognisance.

The Reverend Herbert paid back all the borrowed money, and paid the premium on little Martin's Educational Annuity Policy a whole month before it was actually due, and took out a brand new Educational Annuity Policy for little Theodore, who had reached the age of nineteen months without his parents' having been able to afford this so necessary outlay on his behalf.

Their second child, Constance, being a girl, Herbert had not thought it necessary to do more than open a Post-Office Savings Account for her. Constance, as a matter of fact, would have been his favourite child, if he had considered it right to have a favourite child—which he didn't—but with boys, one had to think about education. The legacy paid their debts, enabled him to put a tiny nest-egg into the bank, and caused Herbert to make an announcement to his wife.

"We are going to have a holiday," he said. "A real holiday, Julia."

Julia looked startled.

"A second honeymoon!" he cried.

"Except for the children . . ." hinted Julia, rather tactlessly, and almost indelicately.

"Naturally," said the Reverend Herbert, frowning. He told her his plan.

He had kept twenty pounds out of the legacy, in cash—in his desk. It was there at this very moment. And it was all to be spent on a holiday, at the sea.

Herbert's living was a country one, and so they hadn't felt justified in going away every summer. It was, in fact, three years since they had been away—before Theodore was born, said Julia reminiscently.

Constance, aged four, had never even seen the sea.

"When did you think of going, darling? It's the end of June now—shall we be able to get in anywhere?"

"Oh yes, I think so," said the Reverend Herbert

brightly and firmly, meaning really that he hoped so. "Of course, we shouldn't care for one of the fashionable, expensive, crowded places, should we, dear?"

"No. But even—"

"Cornwall, now, or North Devon—and that wouldn't be too long a journey, which would mean less expense. We needn't feel bound to any one date. Smith will take duty for me any Sunday I like, and we can get away on a Monday, and stay till the following Saturday week."

"What about Ethel?"

Ethel was their general servant. It was very difficult for Mrs. Cliff-Hay to find a servant, and still more difficult for her to keep one. Ethel had been with them six months, and Julia's great preoccupation in life, after the welfare of Herbert and the children, was how to make certain that Ethel would never leave.

"Ethel will look after the house, of course."

"Dear, she won't sleep here alone, I'm perfectly certain. You know what girls are."

"Well, well, we can settle about Ethel later, surely," said the Reverend Herbert rather peevishly. "Here am I, full of a surprise plan which I hope will be a joy and a pleasure to you, and all you can talk about is the wretched Ethel!"

It did indeed seem ungrateful, looked at in that way.

"I didn't really mean it like that," said Julia—although she had really meant it exactly like that. "Of course it's a glorious idea, Herbert, and so kind of you to think of it all. I'd love it, naturally."

"It would do you good, dear," said Herbert, mollified at once. "We'll cast off all responsibilities, for once, and simply enjoy ourselves. After all, we're still young," he added wistfully. And Julia, in quick response to the wistfulness, answered at once: "Of course we are!"

She, as a matter of fact, was thirty-five, and Herbert eight years older. But she had a suspicion that they both looked more—Herbert because he was getting fat, and she because her hair was turning grey so very quickly. (It wouldn't have shown, though, if her hair had only been fair instead of dark brown.)

Julia wrote to various places about rooms, and found, as she had expected, that everything was full up already, until the middle of October.

"If one was on the spot . . ." said Herbert thoughtfully. "I think, dearest, the only thing would be, if you didn't very much mind, for you to go yourself to one of these places—say Bewlaigh, which is the shortest journey—and go round the town, and find a lodging or one of the less expensive hotels or boarding-houses. It'll really save you time and trouble in endless writing, in the long run, and you're sure to find something."

Julia was rather astonished. He had never suggested that she should go away anywhere by herself, before, but it just showed how much his mind was set upon this plan of a holiday.

Julia went to Bewlaigh, a journey of about two-and-a-half hours by train. It was a nice hot day, and the sea looked very blue, and there were people bathing, and children playing on the sands and climbing over the rocks, and Julia thought of Martin and Constance and Theodore, and made up her mind then and there that she *wouldn't* go home until she'd found rooms for them.

The place was small—only one cinema, no Pierrots, no bathing machines, and only a very tiny pier. It couldn't really be full up.

The station was in the middle of the little town, and she walked slowly up the parade, not looking much at the white, shining, square houses with green shutters, and striped sun-blinds, and gardens, that lined the roads, because she knew that these would be the most expensive of all the lodgings.

Anything not directly overlooking the blue, sparkling sea would be cheaper.

She turned up a little side road, called Prospect Road. The Prospect, if taken literally, referred to a number of small, grey stone villas, all exactly alike, duplicated in two long rows. Almost every window had a card in it, bearing the word: *Apartments*.

Julia tried the first one.

"Full up till the end of September," said the woman pleasantly.

The next one was full up till October. So were the third and the fourth and the fifth. The fifth doubted very much if there was anything to be had anywhere in Bewlaigh so late in the day. Rooms were generally booked in the winter, or the early spring—sometimes the year before, if people wanted to return to the same house.

But Julia could *try* Mrs. Parker, in York Terrace—the last house but one on the left as you went down.

Julia said that she was much obliged, and went to York Terrace. She had expected to have great difficulty in finding what she wanted, and was neither surprised, nor very much discouraged.

With three children and not much money, it was never easy to get in anywhere.

She passed a pink house, with "Board-Residence" placarded on the balcony, on her way to York Terrace, and went in, just in case, and asked for the manageress.

The manageress thought she *might* have rooms, when would it be for?

"Any date in July or August," said Julia. "Two rooms, and a double bed and a single one in each, or else three single beds in one room, for the children—"

"Oh," said the manageress, differently. "Oh, I'm sorry, but we don't really care about taking children. How old would they be?"

"Five and four and nearly two," said Julia, conscious that these were, of all ages, the most damning.

"I'm sorry," said the manageress firmly.

They wished one another a good morning, and separated.

York Terrace was on the top of a hill. It would be a terrific climb up from the sands, but it needn't take more than fifteen minutes even with the pram.

"The last house but one on the left, as you went down . . ."

It was called, poetically, "Eventide." It reminded Julia vaguely of some hymn, which seemed suitable. Perhaps a good omen, or was that being superstitious?

"Mrs. Parker?"

"Yes."

"I was wondering if you had any rooms vacant

any time in July or August—" glibly began Julia, in the formula that she had now used seven times within an hour.

"Any time in July or August," said Mrs. Parker. "*Any* time."

"I've the middle of July practically vacant, owing to a party having failed. How long would you be wanting the rooms, and for how many?"

Julia gave particulars, not slurring the ages of the children.

Her heart leapt when Mrs. Parker asked if she would care to see the rooms.

One front bedroom—one back one on the same floor, the requisite number of beds, and a small sitting-room downstairs.

"What are your terms for these rooms?"

"Six guineas a week, after the first week in July. I have to try and make up, in the season, for all the rest of the year, when I may get no let at all," said Mrs. Parker mournfully.

Six guineas wasn't too bad. But Julia knew about landladies.

"Does that include cooking and attendance?"

"Yes."

"Lighting—if any?"

"Lighting is an extra. It varies so much."

"Baths?"

"Baths is naturally an extra. Sixpence, a hot bath is."

"And what about early-morning tea?" said Mrs. Cliff-Hay, having learnt all the moves in the game by painful experience three and a half years ago at Ilfracombe.

She could see that Mrs. Parker, while resenting this catechism, at the same time respected her for it. She replied curtly, but not unkindly, that early-morning tea would be sixpence—without bread and butter.

"Just the two cups," said Mrs. Parker.

Julia engaged the rooms.

"In time for tea on the 15th," said Mrs. Parker. "Shall I order in some bread, and milk, and butter, and what quantity of milk shall you be requiring, and will you want cake, or jam, for tea?"

Julia gave the required information.

"Plain or fancy?" Mrs. Parker further demanded, referring to the cakes for tea.

It was evident that she had been keeping lodgings for years, Julia thought, and said, "Plain, please. Buns. Six penny ones would do. We shall be bringing the baby's pram."

"That'll be all right. At the back."

All being thus made clear between them, Julia Cliff-Hay promised to send a postcard confirming the time of their arrival, and walked back to the station again.

As there wasn't a train for an hour and a half, she had time to go slowly, and to have a cup of tea on the way.

Herbert, hearing of her success, was delighted, and said twice in the course of the evening that it would be a second honeymoon, and although Julia—who had been young, ignorant, and frightened, at the time—had not enjoyed her honeymoon at all, she had long ago succeeded in forgetting this with her conscious mind, and now agreed with him quite happily, and looked forward eagerly to the holiday.

The question of Ethel was settled about a week later, after a good deal of difficulty. She was to go home to her mother and take the Cliff-Hays' cat with her, and the Rectory was to be shut up, and the gardener would keep an eye on it.

"But Ethel's mother always puts some nonsense into her head, and goodness knows if we shall ever get her back," thought Julia. "And if Ethel isn't here, and the house is empty, we can't very well have in the sweep, as I should have liked. It'll have to wait till we get back."

When twelve o'clock on the 15th of July came, the packing was done, the suit-case and portmanteau belonging to Herbert, and a small tin trunk containing the effects of Julia and the three children, were locked and labelled, the basket, with sandwiches and bananas in it, stood ready. Ethel, with the protesting cat in a little hamper, waited at the back door, the village Ford that was to take them to the station was due in twenty minutes—and Herbert, Julia and their two elder children waited anxiously for the infant Theodore to wake from his morning sleep, so that the pram could be put into its sacking and get its label tied to the handle.

"You know how it'll upset him if we do wake him. I'd wake him in a minute, if it didn't mean that he'll be so cross all the way down," said Julia for about the seventh time.

"That's all very well, dear, but I can't tie the covering on to the pram all in a minute, and we do *not* want to miss the train."

"Miss the train!" echoed Martin, aged five, in great dismay.

"Shall I have a spade, Daddy?" said little Constance.

"If you're good, dear."

"I can't think why he's sleeping so late this morning—it's always the way when one doesn't want them to—"

Julia made a hasty trip to the front door, outside

which stood the pram. Theodore, inside it, still slept peacefully.

"Daddy, shall I have a spade?" Constance said, earnestly.

"Yes, darling."

"A real spade, Daddy?"

"Yes, yes, certainly, when we get there. I say, Julia, you must really wake the child. This is nonsense."

"I'd wake him in a minute, if it didn't mean that he'll be so cross all the way down. I can't think why he's sleeping like this—he never does as a rule, but it's always the way—"

Ethel appeared in the hall.

"The car is just coming up the lane, 'm. Didn't we ought to wake Baby?"

"He'll be so cross—there! isn't he moving?"

"Mummie," said Constance in a voice of passionate and uncontrollable anxiety, "*can't* I have a spade?"

"Certainly, my pet, you shall have a spade. I promise you. Well, if that's the car, Ethel . . ."

Ethel darted towards the pram.

Theodore was awakened, and cried pitifully, and Julia hurried him into the house, and changed all the clothes he had on for other, similar clothes, that were clean instead of dirty, and Herbert tied up the pram and helped the driver to put the luggage on the car.

"Martin dear, run and tell Mother that we shall miss the train," said Herbert, who had all his life suffered from train-fever.

Martin rushed in, shrieking: "We shall miss the train, we shall miss the train!" And Julia said, "Oh no, darling", soothingly, and finished off Baby as quickly as she could, and ran out with him to the car.

"Can I sit in front?" said Martin.

"No, me," said Constance.

"Daddy will sit in front."

"With me on his lap—"

"No, me!"

"It's Martin's turn," said Julia, who had to remember these things. "Constance darling, come and sit with Mother and Theodore in the back."

"Tell me a story, Mother!" cried Constance.

Julia immediately said, "Once upon a time there was a little pig who lived in a wood and—wave goodbye to Ethel, darling—Baby wave his little hand—ta-ta, Ethel! Are you all right, Herbert?"

"Quite, thank you, dear. Have you any room for your feet?"

"Yes, thank you . . . Lived in a wood and went out every day to look for acorns . . ."

The story lasted until they reached the station, when Julia said: "Get out carefully, my pet, and wait for Mother."

"Am I going to have a spade for the sands?"

"Yes, you shall all have spades."

On these lines, the journey proceeded. Herbert was very kind, and took his turn in amusing the fractious Theodore, and Julia told stories, and reassured Constance about her spade, and from time to time smiled her pleasure at the holiday having really begun, and received Herbert's equally pleased and sympathetic smile in return. And it was a fine day, even if not a very warm one.

Everything was ready for them at "Eventide," down to the six plain buns upon the tea-table; and the moment tea was finished, they went out.

"To the shops, please, dear," Julia said. "I've got to order the things for our meals to-morrow. It's Sunday, you know, and she's got nothing in for us, except just the milk and the bread."

"And shall we get my spade now, Mother?" said Constance in a trustful, uncomplaining voice.

"Yes, of course. Poor little thing, you have been patient!" cried Julia, really believing this, owing to the fabulous number of times that she had heard her daughter's request.

"Will you let me have some money, Herbert?"

"I'll come with you," said the Reverend Herbert, and he took Martin's hand.

"Is the pram undone, darling? Because of Baby. It's too early to put him to bed, and besides, I couldn't leave him alone, in a strange room, anyway—but we ought to hurry, because the shops shut at six."

They unwrapped the pram, and set out. Julia had a list, and they went—as fast as the pram, the narrow streets, the people, their unfamiliarity with the locality, and the short legs of Martin and Constance—would permit from the butcher to the grocer, and the grocer to the greengrocer, and the greengrocer to the baker. Everything seemed to be a little more expensive than the same things would have been at home, but one expected that, on a holiday.

When the shopping was done—and it included spades, buckets and sand-shoes for all the children—it was time for Julia to go back and put Theodore to bed.

Herbert took the other two down to the sands. He was so good about the children, Julia reflected thankfully. Even at home, where he was busy, he often helped her with them on Ethel's afternoon out. Theodore was good, and went to sleep quickly, and Julia had done nearly all the unpacking before

Herbert and the elder children came back, and she had to put Martin and Constance to bed.

At half-past seven Mr. and Mrs. Cliff-Hay had supper. Mrs. Parker had made it perfectly clear that when she said "No cooking" in the evenings, she included things like potatoes, or even cocoa. But Julia had brought a spirit lamp, and boiled water herself, which made them independent.

After supper Herbert wanted to go for a walk, and Julia, who didn't like leaving the children, and was very tired besides, reluctantly went with him. She was but an abstracted companion, and Herbert, disappointed, was quite ready to come in again by nine o'clock. By ten, Julia, who could scarcely keep her eyes open, having seen that Martin and Constance and Theodore were all sleeping, went to bed herself.

"You won't be quite so tired, I hope, at nights, after a few days' holiday," said the Reverend Herbert, when he in his turn got into the double bed.

He tried to make his voice sound only kind, and not resentful, but the effort was wasted upon Julia, who was sleeping like the dead.

II

The days sped by, only too quickly.

The order of them was always the same.

Between six and half-past six, Theodore woke, and was taken into his parents' bed so that he might not disturb the other two children, who seldom opened their eyes till seven o'clock. At half-past seven Mrs. Parker brought the early-morning tea—without bread and butter—and Julia got up, and washed and dressed and brushed the three children.

At half-past eight they had breakfast.

Then the sands—Julia doing the necessary shopping on the way. There was always something to be ordered, or bought, for the children.

The weather wasn't too bad, for an English July. Julia thought it rather chilly, but then she had to adjust her pace to that of the baby, who could only toddle about, or sit on the sands scooping holes with his fingers.

While Theodore had his sleep in the pram, the others bathed.

Julia, years ago, had liked swimming, and Herbert was "very good at it." It brought home to her the fact that she was no longer very young, when she found herself secretly rather dreading the daily treat of the bathe. Perhaps it was the difference between being able to swim with Herbert, and having to remain close to the edge of the water, encouraging Martin, who was inclined to be nervous, and calling out "Yes, I see, darling," to Constance, who was under the impression that she was swimming if she stuck her fat arms straight out in front of her, and kicked the water with her feet.

Herbert, as usual, was goodness itself.

He tried, although not successfully, to teach the two elder children to swim, and he squeezed out their wet bathing-dresses while Julia hurriedly dried and dressed them in the bathing-machine, and then he generally struck out to sea again, so as to give her time to dress herself before he sought the bathing machine. Still feeling damp and mottled, Julia would hasten out into the rather fitful sunshine, and distribute buns to the children, and try to warm her slightly discoloured hands by rubbing them in the sand. At least she kept her hair dry, for it was no longer the sort of hair that one rather enjoyed wetting, for the sake of letting it dry in the open air afterwards . . .

Her thoughts went back to other holiday-times, which, strangely enough, seemed not at all remote, when she hadn't been "Mother," but only Julia, and Mamma had been "Mother"—the omniscient, all-powerful and ever-present universal provider.

Was it possible that Mamma, who had been dead ten years, had then felt exactly as Julia felt now?

She could certainly remember a reluctance, at

the time incomprehensible, on the part of Mamma to join in delightful hill-climbing expeditions, or early-morning swims, at Weymouth.

Every year they had gone to Weymouth, Papa and Mamma and Julia.

One hadn't realised, in those days, that one was lucky to be taken to a nice hotel, where nobody bothered about "extras," and there was a real meal at the end of the day as a matter of course—not just a slice of cold ham, and bread and cheese, and cocoa made over a spirit lamp.

("Oh, what a pig I am, to think about the food like that!" thought Julia. "Though really it's on Herbert's account—except the cocoa, which is such a comfort when one's cold or tired . . .")

Had Papa and Mamma really been well off? Julia, who had inherited their small savings, knew that they hadn't, although, of course, the value of money had altered altogether since the War. It had just been that, in the past, she hadn't had the responsibility of any of it—hadn't known or cared how the holiday was paid for, how the plans were made, how the meals were ordered, or anything else.

She had gone on being blissfully irresponsible until she was quite grown-up. She could remember the last Weymouth holiday before Papa's death, when she had just left school, and she had wanted to go every night to the concert on the pier, with the school friend who was staying with her. Papa had taken them, and Mamma, to their incredulous astonishment, evening after evening, had declared that she preferred to go to bed.

"But she was much older then, than I am now," reflected Julia.

"Mother, look at me!" screamed Constance.

"I see, darling. Wonderful!"

"But did I turn head-over-heels?"

"Well—very nearly. Next time it'll be quite."

"Mother, may I have the last bun?"

"No, Martin dear. It's really too near dinner-time."

"Then will you help me to build a castle exactly like the one we made yesterday?"

Julia got up, feeling stiff.

"Did I nearly turn head-over-heels?"

"Very nearly."

Herbert emerged from the bathing-machine.

"Daddy, I turned head-over-heels."

"Nearly," Julia inserted automatically.

"I nearly turned head-over-heels."

"Did you, dear? Well, Julia, did you enjoy the water? You look cold, my dear. If you didn't stay in the shallow water so much, but went right out of your depth at once, you wouldn't feel cold."

"The walk up the hill will warm me."

The steep ascent to York Terrace was not much liked by Martin and Constance with their short legs, and Julia always told them a story while they climbed.

Herbert pushed the pram.

After dinner, the two elder children were sent to rest for an hour on their beds, and Julia amused the baby downstairs, and Herbert read the paper.

Then they all went on the sands again, or once or; twice, for an excursion by charabanc but, the children were too young to enjoy these, and rendered the whole family unpopular with their fellow-passengers, except, indeed, with those who had with them children of the same age.

But Julia, unreasonably, didn't like being told that "the little ones were all alike," and never let this opening lead to anything further.

Tea—the day fell naturally into the categorical division of time that separated one meal from another—was generally taken at their lodgings. The café in the High Street, where there was a small string band, was amusing, but it cost money, and little Theodore was really too young for that sort of place, and Constance, who was easily made bilious, was sure to eat something that would disagree with her later.

Very soon after tea Theodore was put to bed, and the other two children played in the sitting-room, since it would be too much for them to walk down to the sea and back once more.

Julia came downstairs, read about "The Story of Peter Rabbit," and then took Constance and Martin upstairs. When she came down again it was usually nearly seven o'clock, and there was only time to do the mending that always seemed to be required on one garment or another.

At half-past seven, supper—that cold and skimpy meal that was disposed of in rather less than twenty minutes.

"How the time flies, doesn't it? I can't believe we've been here so long already. What about a little walk this evening?"

"Yes—only I don't much like leaving the children—if Baby did happen to wake—"

"Surely, with two women in the house—"

"Dear, I can't possibly ask Mrs. Parker to go to him, and it wouldn't be any good if she did, either—"

"I suppose not. Well. You're not tired, are you, Julia?"

"Did I yawn? It must be the air. It's much stronger than the air at home."

"It'll do us all good. The children look quite different."

"Yes, don't they?" she said eagerly, and then immediately yawned again.

"Julia!" exclaimed the Reverent Herbert. The truth was, as they both knew too well, that Julia was intolerably sleepy. She was often sleepy at home, too, since she had never been without a baby in her room after the first year of her marriage, and was always awakened early in the mornings—but at home she sat at her desk in the evenings, or sometimes played the piano, and kept herself awake that way.

At home, also, Herbert was busy, and took it for granted that she should go to bed before he did, but on a holiday—a second honeymoon—things should have been different.

He was kind, as ever—but he evidently didn't understand it.

Julia tried going to bed very early indeed, and getting some sleep before Herbert came up, on the understanding that he should wake her, when she would then be fresh and lively and ready for conversation.

But she wasn't fresh or lively, and indeed it proved to be almost impossible to wake her without the employment of real physical violence.

"And yet," said the Reverend Herbert, rather

reproachfully, "if one of the children so much as turns over in the night, you're awake directly."

Julia wondered, but did not like to ask, if that was perhaps the reason she was so sleepy now. She said feebly that she thought there was an Instinct which woke mothers on behalf of their children. "When we get home," she said hopefully, "and I know that Martin and Constance are in their own nursery with Ethel next door, I shan't wake so early in the mornings, and then I shan't be so tired at night. Besides, it's this wonderful sea-air. It's—doing—wonders."

Julia's eyes grew fixed and watery, the muscles of her jaw became strangely set, and she tightly compressed her lips, in the suppression of an enormous yawn.

"Go to bed, my dear," said her husband forbearingly. And she looked so miserable that he added, entirely to try and comfort her for her inadequacy. "It's the sea-air."

Right up to the very last day of their fortnight at "Eventide" the sea-air continued to demonstrate its effects upon Julia.

The final evening was marred by the usual discrepancy between the visitors' attitude towards their bill, and that of the landlady.

"Of course, I knew she'd stick it on at the end, as they always do," said Julia, "but really! When it comes to cruet, sixpence—and neither of us touches mustard or pepper, and I'm sure the poor children haven't eaten six-pennyworth of salt, the whole time they've been here."

"Absurd! But still, if that's the only extra—"

"The only extra!" cried Julia. "Why, the whole thing is extras. And she's put down that hideous glass vase that Baby smashed in our room as valued at three-and-eightpence."

"Shall I have her in?" said the Reverend Herbert wearily. "It's no use letting that sort of person think that one doesn't know one's being robbed."

"No, of course it isn't."

They both of them dreaded the interview with Mrs. Parker, and knew that they had no possible chance of getting the better of her, but they felt, confusedly and miserably, that in some mysterious way they owed it to their caste to show Mrs. Parker that her extortions were resented by them.

Julia, in a deprecating, apologetic voice, called Mrs. Parker.

An interview on lines exceedingly familiar to Mrs. Parker ensued.

At the end of thirty-seven minutes, the sum at the foot of Mrs. Parker's bill, reduced by half-a-crown, had been paid by the Reverend Herbert, and the bill duly receipted by the landlady.

"Thank you, sir," said Mrs. Parker, her voice suddenly pitched in a more natural key. "I'm sure I hope you've all enjoyed your stay?"

"Very much indeed, thank you. It's done us all so much good."

"A thorough rest," said Herbert, not without a glance at Julia.

"Perhaps we shall come again another year."

"I hope so, sir, I'm sure. Good night, sir, good night, 'm."

"Good night, Mrs. Parker," they replied together with amiable smiles.

The door shut behind Mrs. Parker.

"I suppose they're all alike," said Julia tolerantly. "After all, they've their living to get."

"It must be a dog's life. And extortionate though she's been, she's let us down pretty lightly over the damage the children did. I saw that ink-stain on the counterpane myself."

"And naughty little Constance's hole in the wall, over the bed—"

"It isn't everywhere where they'll take children at all."

"No, that's true. One might do a great deal worse than come here another year. I mean, supposing we're able to afford another holiday one year."

"Now that we've got this legacy, Julia dearest,

and that our debts are all paid, I want to afford a holiday every year," said the Reverend Herbert, adding, with unwonted effusiveness, for he was a reserved man, "You and I, and little Martin and Constance and the baby—and perhaps other little ones, if we should be blessed with them. To get right away from home cares and worries and responsibilities, and have a thorough rest and change. I value it on your account even more than on my own."

Julia laid her thin hand upon his plump one, and her eyes—her tired eyes—filled with the easy tears of utter contentment. She thought, as she had often thought before, that she was a very fortunate woman. Her heart swelled with gratitude at the thought of her kind husband, her splendid children, and the wonderful holiday that they had all had together.

Virginia Woolf

In the Orchard

Miranda slept in the orchard, lying in a long chair beneath the apple-tree. Her book had fallen into the grass, and her finger still seemed to point at the sentence "Ce pays est vraiment un des coins du monde où le rire des filles éclate le mieux . . ." as if she had fallen asleep just there. The opals on her finger flushed green, flushed rosy, and again flushed orange as the sun, oozing through the apple-trees, filled them. Then, when the breeze blew, her purple dress rippled like a flower attached to a stalk; the grasses nodded; and the white butterfly came blowing this way and that just above her face.

Four feet in the air over her head the apples hung. Suddenly there was a shrill clamour as if they were gongs of cracked brass beaten violently, irregularly, and brutally. It was only the school-children saying the multiplication table in unison, stopped by the teacher, scolded, and beginning to say the multiplication table over again. But this clamour passed four feet above Miranda's head, went through the apple boughs, and, striking against the cowman's little boy who was picking blackberries in the hedge when he should have been at school, made him tear his thumb on the thorns.

Next there was a solitary cry—sad, human, brutal. Old Parsley was, indeed, blind drunk.

Then the very topmost leaves of the apple-tree, flat like little fish against the blue, thirty feet above the earth, chimed with a pensive and lugubrious note. It was the organ in the church playing one of Hymns Ancient and Modern. The sound floated out and was cut into atoms by a flock of field-fares flying at an enormous speed—somewhere or other. Miranda lay asleep thirty feet beneath.

Then above the apple-tree and the pear-tree two hundred feet above Miranda lying asleep in the orchard bells thudded, intermittent, sullen, didactic, for six poor women of the parish were being churched and the Rector was returning thanks to heaven.

And above that with a sharp squeak the golden feather of the church tower turned from south to east. The wind had changed. Above everything else it droned, above the woods, the meadows, the hills, miles above Miranda lying in the orchard asleep. It swept on, eyeless, brainless, meeting nothing that could stand against it, until, wheeling the other way, it turned south again. Miles below, in a space as big as the eye of a needle, Miranda stood upright and cried aloud: "Oh, I shall be late for tea!"

Miranda slept in the orchard—or perhaps she was not asleep, for her lips moved very slightly as if they were saying, "Ce pays est vraiment un des coins du monde . . . où le rire des filles . . . éclate . . . éclate . . . éclate . . ." and then she smiled and let her body sink all its weight on to the enormous earth which rises, she thought, to carry me on its back as if I were a leaf, or a queen (here the children said the multiplication table), or, Miranda went on, I might be lying on the top of a cliff with the gulls screaming above me. The higher they fly, she continued, as the teacher scolded the children and rapped Jimmy over the knuckles till they bled, the deeper they look into the sea—into the sea, she repeated, and her fingers relaxed and her lips closed gently as if she were floating on the sea, and then, when the shout of the drunken man sounded overhead, she drew breath with an extraordinary ecstasy, for she thought that she heard life itself crying out from a rough tongue in a scarlet mouth, from the wind, from the bells, from the curved green leaves of the cabbages.

Naturally she was being married when the organ

played the tune from Hymns Ancient and Modern, and, when the bells rang after the six poor women had been churched, the sullen intermittent thud made her think that the very earth shook with the hoofs of the horse that was galloping towards her ("Ah, I have only to wait!" she sighed), and it seemed to her that everything had already begun moving, crying, riding, flying round her, across her, towards her in a pattern.

Mary is chopping the wood, she thought; Pearman is herding the cows; the carts are coming up from the meadows; the rider—and she traced out the lines that the men, the carts, the birds, and the rider made over the countryside until they all seemed driven out, round, and across by the beat of her own heart.

Miles up in the air the wind changed; the golden feather of the church tower squeaked; and Miranda jumped up and cried: "Oh, I shall be late for tea!"

Miranda slept in the orchard, or was she asleep or was she not asleep? Her purple dress stretched between the two apple-trees. There were twenty-four apple-trees in the orchard, some slanting slightly, others growing straight with a rush up the trunk which spread wide into branches and formed into round red or yellow drops. Each apple-tree had sufficient space. The sky exactly fitted the leaves. When the breeze blew, the line of the boughs against the wall slanted slightly and then returned. A wagtail flew diagonally from one corner to another. Cautiously hopping, a thrush advanced towards a fallen apple; from the other wall a sparrow fluttered just above the grass. The uprush of the trees was tied down by these movements; the whole was compacted by the orchard walls. For miles beneath the earth was clamped together; rippled on the surface with wavering air; and across the corner of the orchard the blue-green was slit by a purple streak. The wind changing, one bunch of apples was tossed so high that it blotted out two cows in the meadow ("Oh, I shall be late for tea!" cried Miranda), and the apples hung straight across the wall again.

Anton Chekhov

Not Wanted

Between six and seven o'clock on a July evening, a crowd of summer visitors—mostly fathers of families—burdened with parcels, portfolios, and ladies' hat-boxes, was trailing along from the little station of Helkovo, in the direction of the summer villas. They all looked exhausted, hungry, and ill-humoured, as though the sun were not shining and the grass were not green for them.

Trudging along among the others was Pavel Matveyitch Zaikin, a member of the Circuit Court, a tall, stooping man, in a cheap cotton dust-coat and with a cockade on his faded cap. He was perspiring, red in the face, and gloomy . . .

"Do you come out to your holiday home every day?" said a summer visitor, in ginger-coloured trousers, addressing him.

"No, not every day," Zaikin answered sullenly. "My wife and son are staying here all the while, and I come down two or three times a week. I haven't time to come every day; besides, it is expensive."

"You're right there; it is expensive," sighed he of the ginger trousers. "In town you can't walk to the station, you have to take a cab; and then, the ticket costs forty-two kopecks; you buy a paper for the journey; one is tempted to drink a glass of vodka. It's all petty expenditure not worth considering, but, mind you, in the course of the summer it will run up to some two hundred roubles. Of course, to be in the lap of Nature is worth any money—I don't dispute it . . . idyllic and all the rest of it; but of course, with the salary an official gets, as you know yourself, every farthing has to be considered. If you waste a halfpenny you lie awake all night . . . Yes . . . I receive, my dear sir—I haven't the honour of knowing your name—I receive a salary of very nearly two thousand roubles a year. I am a civil councillor, I smoke second-rate tobacco, and I haven't a rouble to spare to buy Vichy water, prescribed me by the doctor for gall-stones."

"It's altogether abominable," said Zaikin after a brief silence. "I maintain, sir, that summer holidays are the invention of the devil and of woman. The devil was actuated in the present instance by malice, woman by excessive frivolity. Mercy on us, it is not life at all; it is hard labour, it is hell! It's hot and stifling, you can hardly breathe, and you wander about like a lost soul and can find no refuge. In town there is no furniture, no servants . . . everything has been carried off to the villa: you eat what you can get; you go without your tea because there is no one to heat the samovar; you can't wash yourself; and when you come down here into this 'lap of Nature' you have to walk, if you please, through the dust and heat . . . Phew! Are you married?"

"Yes . . . three children," sighs Ginger Trousers.

"It's abominable altogether . . . It's a wonder we are still alive."

At last the summer visitors reached their destination. Zaikin said good-bye to Ginger Trousers and went into his villa. He found a death-like silence in the house. He could hear nothing but the buzzing of the gnats, and the prayer for help of a fly destined for the dinner of a spider. The windows were hung with muslin curtains, through which the faded flowers of the geraniums showed red. On the unpainted wooden walls near the oleographs flies were slumbering. There was not a soul in the passage, the kitchen, or the dining-room. In the room which was called indifferently the parlour or the drawing-room, Zaikin found his son Petya, a little boy of six. Petya was sitting at the table, and, breathing loudly with his lower lip stuck out, was engaged in cutting out the figure of a knave of diamonds from a card.

"Oh, that's you, father!" he said, without turning round. "Good-evening."

"Good-evening . . . And where is mother?"

"Mother? She is gone with Olga Kirillovna to a rehearsal of the play. The day after tomorrow they will have a performance. And they will take me, too . . . And will you go?"

"H'm! . . . When is she coming back?"

"She said she would be back in the evening."

"And where is Natalya?"

"Mamma took Natalya with her to help her dress for the performance, and Akulina has gone to the wood to get mushrooms. Father, why is it that when gnats bite you their stomachs get red?"

"I don't know . . . Because they suck blood. So there is no one in the house, then?"

"No one; I am all alone in the house."

Zaikin sat down in an easy-chair, and for a moment gazed blankly at the window.

"Who is going to get our dinner?" he asked.

"They haven't cooked any dinner to-day, father. Mamma thought you were not coming to-day, and did not order any dinner. She is going to have dinner with Olga Kirillovna at the rehearsal."

"Oh, thank you very much; and you, what have you had to eat?"

"I've had some milk. They bought me six kopecks'

worth of milk. And, father, why do gnats suck blood?"

Zaikin suddenly felt as though something heavy were rolling down on his liver and beginning to gnaw it. He felt so vexed, so aggrieved, and so bitter, that he was choking and tremulous; he wanted to jump up, to bang something on the floor, and to burst into loud abuse; but then he remembered that his doctor had absolutely forbidden him all excitement, so he got up, and making an effort to control himself, began whistling a tune from "Les Huguenots."

"Father, can you act in plays?" he heard Petya's voice.

"Oh, don't worry me with stupid questions!" said Zaikin, getting angry. "He sticks to one like a leaf in the bath! Here you are, six years old, and just as silly as you were three years ago . . . Stupid, neglected child! Why are you spoiling those cards, for instance? How dare you spoil them?"

"These cards aren't yours," said Petya, turning round. "Natalya gave them me."

"You are telling fibs, you are telling fibs, you horrid boy!" said Zaikin, growing more and more irritated. "You are always telling fibs! You want a whipping, you horrid little pig! I will pull your ears!"

Petya leapt up, and craning his neck, stared

fixedly at his father's red and wrathful face. His big eyes first began blinking, then were dimmed with moisture, and the boy's face began working.

"But why are you scolding?" squealed Petya.

"Why do you attack me, you stupid? I am not interfering with anybody; I am not naughty; I do what I am told, and yet . . . you are cross! Why are you scolding me?"

The boy spoke with conviction, and wept so bitterly that Zaikin felt conscience-stricken.

"Yes, really, why am I falling foul of him?" he thought. "Come, come," he said, touching the boy on the shoulder. "I am sorry, Petya . . . forgive me. You are my good boy, my nice boy, I love you."

Petya wiped his eyes with his sleeve, sat down, with a sigh, in the same place and began cutting out the queen. Zaikin went off to his own room. He stretched himself on the sofa, and putting his hands behind his head, sank into thought. The boy's tears had softened his anger, and by degrees the oppression on his liver grew less. He felt nothing but exhaustion and hunger.

"Father," he heard on the other side of the door, "shall I show you my collection of insects?"

"Yes, show me."

Petya came into the study and handed his father a long green box. Before raising it to his ear Zaikin could hear a despairing buzz and the scratching of claws on the sides of the box. Opening the lid, he saw a number of butterflies, beetles, grasshoppers, and flies fastened to the bottom of the box with pins. All except two or three butterflies were still alive and moving.

"Why, the grasshopper is still alive!" said Petya in surprise. "I caught him yesterday morning, and he is still alive!"

"Who taught you to pin them in this way?"

"Olga Kirillovna."

"Olga Kirillovna ought to be pinned down like that herself!" said Zaikin with repulsion. "Take them away! It's shameful to torture animals."

"My God! How horribly he is being brought up!" he thought, as Petya went out.

Pavel Matveyitch forgot his exhaustion and hunger, and thought of nothing but his boy's future. Meanwhile, outside the light was gradually fading . . . He could hear the summer visitors trooping back from the evening bathe. Someone was stopping near the open dining-room window and shouting: "Do you want any mushrooms?" And getting no answer, shuffled on with bare feet . . . But at last, when the dusk was so thick that the outlines of the geraniums behind the muslin curtain were lost, and whiffs of the freshness of evening were coming in at the window, the door of the passage was thrown open noisily, and there came a sound of rapid footsteps, talk, and laughter . . .

"Mamma!" shrieked Petya.

Zaikin peeped out of his study and saw his wife, Nadyezhda Stepanovna, healthy and rosy as ever; with her he saw Olga Kirillovna, a spare woman with fair hair and heavy freckles, and two unknown men: one a lanky young man with curly red hair and a big Adam's apple; the other, a short stubby man with a shaven face like an actor's and a bluish crooked chin.

"Natalya, set the samovar," cried Nadyezhda Stepanovna, with a loud rustle of her skirts. "I hear Pavel Matveyitch is come. Pavel, where are you? Good-evening, Pavel!" she said, running into the study breathlessly. "So you've come. I am so glad . . . Two of our amateurs have come with me . . . Come, I'll introduce you . . . Here, the taller one is Koromyslov . . . he sings splendidly; and the other, the little one . . . is called Smerkalov: he is a real actor . . . he recites magnificently. Oh, how tired I am! We have just had a rehearsal . . . It goes splendidly. We are acting 'The Lodger with the Trombone' and 'Waiting for Him.' . . . The performance is the day after to-morrow . . ."

"Why did you bring them?" asked Zaikin.

"I couldn't help it, Poppet; after tea we must rehearse our parts and sing something . . . I am to sing a duet with Koromyslov . . . Oh yes, I was almost forgetting! Darling, send Natalya to get some sardines, vodka, cheese, and something else. They will most likely stay to supper . . . Oh, how tired I am!"

"H'm! I've no money."

"You must, Poppet! It would be awkward! Don't make me blush."

Half an hour later Natalya was sent for vodka and savouries; Zaikin, after drinking tea and eating a whole French loaf, went to his bedroom and lay down on the bed, while Nadyezhda Stepanovna and her visitors, with much noise and laughter, set to work to rehearse their parts. For a long time Pavel Matveyitch heard Koromyslov's nasal reciting and Smerkalov's theatrical exclamations . . . The rehearsal was followed by a long conversation, interrupted by the shrill laughter of Olga Kirillovna. Smerkalov, as a real actor, explained the parts with aplomb and heat . . .

Then followed the duet, and after the duet there was the clatter of crockery . . . Through his drowsiness Zaikin heard them persuading Smerkalov to read "The Woman who was a Sinner, and heard him, after affecting to refuse, begin to recite. He hissed, beat himself on the breast, wept, laughed in a husky bass . . . Zaikin scowled and hid his head under the quilt.

"It's a long way for you to go, and it's dark," he heard Nadyezhda Stepanovna's voice an hour later. "Why shouldn't you stay the night here? Koromyslov can sleep here in the drawing-room on the sofa, and you, Smerkalov, in Petya's bed . . . I can put Petya in my husband's study . . . Do stay, really!"

At last when the clock was striking two, all was hushed, the bedroom door opened, and Nadyezhda Stepanovna appeared.

"Pavel, are you asleep?" she whispered.

"No; why?"

"Go into your study, darling, and lie on the sofa. I am going to put Olga Kirillovna here, in your bed. Do go, dear! I would put her to sleep in the study, but she is afraid to sleep alone . . . Do get up!"

Zaikin got up, threw on his dressing-gown, and taking his pillow, crept wearily to the study . . . Feeling his way to his sofa, he lighted a match, and saw Petya lying on the sofa. The boy was not asleep, and, looking at the match with wide-open eyes:

"Father, why is it gnats don't go to sleep at night?" he asked.

"Because . . . because . . . you and I are not wanted . . . We have nowhere to sleep even."

"Father, and why is it Olga Kirillovna has freckles on her face?"

"Oh, shut up! I am tired of you."

After a moment's thought, Zaikin dressed and went out into the street for a breath of air . . . He looked at the grey morning sky, at the motionless clouds, heard the lazy call of the drowsy corncrake, and began dreaming of the next day, when he would go to town, and coming back from the court would tumble into bed . . . Suddenly the figure of a man appeared round the corner.

"A watchman, no doubt," thought Zaikin.

But going nearer and looking more closely he recognized in the figure the summer visitor in the ginger trousers.

"You're not asleep?" he asked.

"No, I can't sleep," sighed Ginger Trousers. "I am enjoying Nature . . . A welcome visitor, my wife's mother, arrived by the night train, you know. She brought with her our nieces . . . splendid girls! I was delighted to see them, although . . . it's very damp! And you, too, are enjoying Nature?"

"Yes," grunted Zaikin, "I am enjoying it, too . . . Do you know whether there is any sort of tavern or restaurant in the neighbourhood?"

Ginger Trousers raised his eyes to heaven and meditated profoundly.

F. Scott Fitzgerald

Three Hours Between Planes

It was a wild chance but Donald was in the mood, healthy and bored, with a sense of tiresome duty done. He was now rewarding himself. Maybe.

When the plane landed he stepped out into a mid-western summer night and headed for the isolated pueblo airport, conventionalized as an old red 'railway depot'. He did not know whether she was alive, or living in this town, or what was her present name. With mounting excitement he looked through the phone book for her father who might be dead too, somewhere in these twenty years.

No. Judge Harmon Holmes – Hillside 3194.

A woman's amused voice answered his inquiry for Miss Nancy Holmes.

'Nancy is Mrs Walter Gifford now. Who is this?'

But Donald hung up without answering. He had found out what he wanted to know and had only three hours. He did not remember any Walter Gifford and there was another suspended moment while he scanned the phone book. She might have married out of town.

No. Walter Gifford – Hillside 1191. Blood flowed back into his fingertips.

'Hello?'

'Hello. Is Mrs Gifford there – this is an old friend of hers.'

'This is Mrs Gifford.'

He remembered, or thought he remembered, the funny magic in the voice.

'This is Donald Plant. I haven't seen you since I was twelve years old.'

'Oh-h-h!' The note was utterly surprised, very polite, but he could distinguish in it neither joy nor certain recognition.

'– *Don*ald!' added the voice. This time there was something more in it than struggling memory.

'. . . when did you come back to town?' Then cordially, 'Where *are* you?'

'I'm out at the airport – for just a few hours.'

'Well, come up and see me.'

'Sure you're not just going to bed?'

'Heavens, no!' she exclaimed. 'I was sitting here – having a highball by myself. Just tell your taxi man . . .'

On his way Donald analysed the conversation. His words 'at the airport' established that he had retained his position in the upper bourgeoisie. Nancy's aloneness might indicate that she had matured into an unattractive woman without friends. Her husband might be either away or in bed. And – because she was always ten years old in his dreams – the highball shocked him. But he adjusted himself with a smile – she was very close to thirty.

At the end of a curved drive he saw a dark-haired little beauty standing against the lighted door, a glass in her hand. Startled by her final materialization, Donald got out of the cab, saying:

'Mrs Gifford?'

She turned on the porch light and stared at him, wide-eyed and tentative. A smile broke through the puzzled expression.

'Donald – it is you – we all change so. Oh, this is remarkable!'

As they walked inside, their voices jingled the words 'all these years', and Donald felt a sinking in his stomach. This derived in part from a vision of their last meeting – when she rode past him on a bicycle, cutting him dead – and in part from fear lest they have nothing to say. It was like a college reunion – but there the failure to find the past was disguised by the hurried boisterous occasion.

Aghast, he realized that this might be a long and empty hour. He plunged in desperately.

'You always were a lovely person. But I'm a little shocked to find you as beautiful as you are.'

It worked. The immediate recognition of their changed state, the bold compliment, made them interesting strangers instead of fumbling childhood friends.

'Have a highball?' she asked. 'No? Please don't think I've become a secret drinker, but this was a blue night. I expected my husband but he wired he'd be two days longer. He's very nice, Donald, and very attractive. Rather your type and colouring.' She hesitated, '– and I think he's interested in someone in New York – and I don't know.'

'After seeing you it sounds impossible,' he assured her. 'I was married for six years, and there was a time I tortured myself that way. Then one day I just put jealousy out of my life forever. After my wife died I was very glad of that. It left a very rich memory – nothing marred or spoiled or hard to think over.'

She looked at him attentively, then sympathetically as he spoke.

'I'm very sorry,' she said. And after a proper moment, 'You've changed a lot. Turn your head. I remember father saying, "That boy has a brain."'

'You probably argued against it.'

'I was impressed. Up to then I thought everybody had a brain. That's why it sticks in my mind.'

'What else sticks in your mind?' he asked smiling.

Suddenly Nancy got up and walked quickly a little away.

'Ah, now,' she reproached him. 'That isn't fair! I suppose I was a naughty girl.'

'You were not,' he said stoutly. 'And I *will* have a drink now.'

As she poured it, her face still turned from him, he continued:

'Do you think you were the only little girl who was ever kissed?'

'Do you like the subject?' she demanded. Her momentary irritation melted and she said: 'What the hell! We *did* have fun. Like in the song.'

'On the sleigh ride.'

'Yes – and somebody's picnic – Trudy James's. And at Frontenac that – those summers.'

It was the sleigh ride he remembered most and kissing her cool cheeks in the straw in one corner while she laughed up at the cold white stars. The couple next to them had their backs turned and he kissed her little neck and her ears and never her lips.

'And the Macks' party where they played post office and I couldn't go because I had the mumps,' he said.

'I don't remember that.'

'Oh, you were there. And you were kissed and I was crazy with jealousy like I never have been since.'

'Funny I don't remember. Maybe I wanted to forget.'

'But why?' he asked in amusement. 'We were two perfectly innocent kids. Nancy, whenever I talked to my wife about the past, I told her you were the girl I loved almost as much as I loved her. But I think I really loved you just as much. When we moved out of town I carried you like a cannon ball in my insides.'

'Were you *that* much – stirred up?'

'My God, yes! I—' He suddenly realized that they were standing just two feet from each other, that he was talking as if he loved her in the present, that she was looking up at him with her lips half-parted and a clouded look in her eyes.

'Go on,' she said, 'I'm ashamed to say – I like it. I didn't know you were so upset *then*. I thought it was *me* who was upset.'

'You!' he exclaimed. 'Don't you remember throwing me over at the drugstore.' He laughed. 'You stuck out your tongue at me.'

'I don't remember at all. It seemed to me you did the throwing over.' Her hand fell lightly, almost consolingly on his arm. 'I've got a photograph book upstairs I haven't looked at for years. I'll dig it out.'

Donald sat for five minutes with two thoughts – first the hopeless impossibility of reconciling what different people remembered about the same event – and secondly that in a frightening way Nancy moved him as a woman as she had moved him as a child. Half an hour had developed an emotion that he had not known since the death of his wife – that he had never hoped to know again.

Side by side on a couch they opened the book between them. Nancy looked at him, smiling and very happy.

'Oh, this is *such* fun,' she said. 'Such fun that you're so nice, that you remember me so – beautifully. Let me tell you – I wish I'd known it then! After you'd gone I hated you.'

'What a pity,' he said gently.

'But not now,' she reassured him, and then impulsively. 'Kiss and make up –'

'. . . that isn't being a good wife,' she said after a minute. 'I really don't think I've kissed two men since I was married.'

He was excited – but most of all confused. Had

he kissed Nancy? or a memory? or this lovely trembly stranger who looked away from him quickly and turned a page of the book?

'Wait!' he said. 'I don't think I could *see* a picture for a few seconds.'

'We won't do it again. I don't feel so very calm myself.'

Donald said one of those trivial things that cover so much ground.

'Wouldn't it be awful if we fell in love again?'

'Stop it!' She laughed, but very breathlessly. 'It's all over. It was a moment. A moment I'll have to forget.'

'Don't tell your husband.'

'Why not? Usually I tell him everything.'

'It'll hurt him. Don't ever tell a man such things.'

'All right I won't.'

'Kiss me once more,' he said inconsistently, but Nancy had turned a page and was pointing eagerly at a picture.

'Here's you,' she cried. 'Right away!'

He looked. It was a little boy in shorts standing on a pier with a sailboat in the background.

'I remember –' she laughed triumphantly, '– the very day it was taken. Kitty took it and I stole it from her.'

For a moment Donald failed to recognize himself

in the photo – then, bending closer – he failed utterly to recognize himself.

'That's not me,' he said.

'Oh yes. It was at Frontenac – the summer we – we used to go to the cave.'

'What cave? I was only three days in Frontenac.' Again he strained his eyes at the slightly yellowed picture. 'And that isn't me. That's Donald Bowers. We did look rather alike.'

Now she was staring at him – leaning back, seeming to lift away from him.

'But you're Donald Bowers!' she exclaimed; her voice rose a little. 'No, you're not. You're Donald *Plant*.'

'I told you on the phone.'

She was on her feet – her face faintly horrified.

'Plant! Bowers! I must be crazy. Or it was that drink? I was mixed up a little when I first saw you. Look here! What have I told you?'

He tried for a monkish calm as he turned a page of the book.

'Nothing at all,' he said. Pictures that did not include him formed and re-formed before his eyes – Frontenac – a cave – Donald Bowers – 'You threw *me* over!'

Nancy spoke from the other side of the room.

'You'll never tell this story,' she said. 'Stories have a way of getting around.'

'There isn't any story,' he hesitated. But he thought: So she was a bad little girl.

And now suddenly he was filled with wild raging jealousy of little Donald Bowers – he who had banished jealousy from his life forever. In the five steps he took across the room he crushed out twenty years and the existence of Walter Gifford with his stride.

'Kiss me again, Nancy,' he said, sinking to one knee beside her chair, putting his hand upon her shoulder. But Nancy strained away.

'You said you had to catch a plane.'

'It's nothing. I can miss it. It's of no importance.'

'Please go,' she said in a cool voice. 'And please try to imagine how I feel.'

'But you act as if you don't remember me,' he cried, '– as if you don't remember Donald *Plant*!'

'I do. I remember you too . . . But it was all so long ago.' Her voice grew hard again. 'The taxi number is Crestwood 8484.'

On his way to the airport Donald shook his head from side to side. He was completely himself now but he could not digest the experience. Only as the plane roared up into the dark sky and its passengers became a different entity from the corporate world below did he draw a parallel from the fact of its flight. For five blinding minutes he had lived like a madman in two worlds at once. He had been a boy of twelve and a man of thirty-two, indissolubly and helplessly commingled.

Donald had lost a good deal, too, in those hours between the planes – but since the second half of life is a long process of getting rid of things, that part of the experience probably didn't matter.

O. Henry

A Midsummer Knight's Dream

> "The knights are dead;
> Their swords are rust.
> Except a few who have to hust-
> Le all the time
> To raise the dust."

DEAR READER: It was summertime. The sun glared down upon the city with pitiless ferocity. It is difficult for the sun to be ferocious and exhibit compunction simultaneously. The heat was—oh, bother thermometers!—who cares for standard measures, anyhow? It was so hot that—

The roof gardens put on so many extra waiters that you could hope to get your gin fizz now—as soon as all the other people got theirs. The hospitals were putting in extra cots for bystanders. For when little woolly dogs loll their tongues out and say "woof, woof!" at the fleas that bite 'em, and nervous old black bombazine ladies screech "Mad dog!" and policemen begin to shoot, somebody is going to get hurt. The man from Pompton, N. J., who always wears an overcoat in July, had turned up in a Broadway hotel drinking hot Scotches and enjoying his annual ray from the calcium. Philanthropists were petitioning the Legislature to pass a bill requiring builders to make tenement fire-escapes more commodious, so that families might die all together of the heat instead of one or two at a time. So many men were telling you about the number of baths they took each day that you wondered how they got along after the real lessee of the apartment came back to town and thanked 'em for taking such good care of it. The young man who called loudly for cold beef and beer in the restaurant, protesting that roast pullet and Burgundy was really too heavy for such weather, blushed when he met your eye, for you had heard him all winter calling, in modest tones, for the same ascetic viands. Soup, pocketbooks, shirt waists, actors and baseball excuses grew thinner. Yes, it was summertime.

A man stood at Thirty-fourth street waiting for a downtown car. A man of forty, gray-haired, pink-faced, keen, nervous, plainly dressed, with a harassed look around the eyes. He wiped his forehead and laughed loudly when a fat man with an outing look stopped and spoke with him.

"No, siree," he shouted with defiance and scorn. "None of your old mosquito-haunted swamps and skyscraper mountains without elevators for me. When I want to get away from hot weather I know how to do it. New York, sir, is the finest summer resort in the country. Keep in the shade and watch your diet, and don't get too far away from an electric fan. Talk about your Adirondacks and your Catskills! There's more solid comfort in the borough of Manhattan than in all the rest of the country together. No, siree! No tramping up perpendicular cliffs and being waked up at 4 in the morning by a million flies, and eating canned goods straight from the city for me. Little old New York will take a few select summer boarders; comforts and conveniences of homes—that's the ad. that I answer every time."

"You need a vacation," said the fat man, looking closely at the other. "You haven't been away from town in years. Better come with me for two weeks, anyhow. The trout in the Beaverkill are jumping at anything now that looks like a fly. Harding writes me that he landed a three-pound brown last week."

"Nonsense!" cried the other man. "Go ahead, if you like, and boggle around in rubber boots wearing yourself out trying to catch fish. When I want one I go to a cool restaurant and order it. I laugh at you fellows whenever I think of you hustling around in the heat in the country thinking you are having a good time. For me Father Knickerbocker's little improved farm with the big shady lane running through the middle of it."

The fat man sighed over his friend and went his way. The man who thought New York was the greatest summer resort in the country boarded a car and went buzzing down to his office. On the way he threw away his newspaper and looked up at a ragged patch of sky above the housetops.

"Three pounds!" he muttered, absently. "And Harding isn't a liar. I believe, if I could—but it's impossible—they've got to have another month—another month at least."

In his office the upholder of urban midsummer joys dived, headforemost, into the swimming pool of business. Adkins, his clerk, came and added a spray of letters, memoranda and telegrams.

At 5 o'clock in the afternoon the busy man leaned back in his office chair, put his feet on the desk and mused aloud:

"I wonder what kind of bait Harding used."

She was all in white that day; and thereby Compton lost a bet to Gaines. Compton had wagered she would wear light blue, for she knew that was his favorite color, and Compton was a millionaire's son, and that almost laid him open to the charge of betting on a sure thing. But white was her choice, and Gaines held up his head with twenty-five's lordly air.

The little summer hotel in the mountains had a lively crowd that year. There were two or three young college men and a couple of artists and a young naval officer on one side. On the other there were enough beauties among the young ladies for the correspondent of a society paper to refer to them as a "bevy." But the moon among the stars was Mary Sewell. Each one of the young men greatly desired to arrange matters so that he could pay her millinery bills, and fix the furnace, and have her do away with the "Sewell" part of her name forever. Those who could stay only a week or two went away hinting at pistols and blighted hearts. But Compton stayed like the mountains themselves, for he could afford it. And Gaines stayed because he was a fighter and wasn't afraid of millionaire's sons, and—well, he adored the country.

"What do you think, Miss Mary?" he said once. "I knew a duffer in New York who claimed to like it in the summer time. Said you could keep cooler there than you could in the woods. Wasn't he an awful silly? I don't think I could breathe on Broadway after the 1st of June."

"Mamma was thinking of going back week after next," said Miss Mary with a lovely frown.

"But when you think of it," said Gaines, "there are lots of jolly places in town in the summer. The roof gardens, you know, and the—er—the roof gardens."

Deepest blue was the lake that day—the day when they had the mock tournament, and the men rode clumsy farm horses around in a glade in the woods and caught curtain rings on the end of a lance. Such fun!

Cool and dry as the finest wine came the breath of the shadowed forest. The valley below was a vision seen through an opal haze. A white mist from hidden falls blurred the green of a hand's breadth of tree tops half-way down the gorge. Youth made merry hand-in-hand with young summer. Nothing on Broadway like that.

The villagers gathered to see the city folks pursue their mad drollery. The woods rang with the laughter of pixies and naiads and sprites. Gaines caught most of the rings. His was the privilege to crown the queen of the tournament. He was the conquering knight—as far as the rings went. On his arm he wore a white scarf. Compton wore light blue. She had declared her preference for blue, but she wore white that day.

Gaines looked about for the queen to crown her. He heard her merry laugh, as if from the clouds. She had slipped away and climbed Chimney Rock, a little granite bluff, and stood there, a white fairy among the laurels, fifty feet above their heads.

Instantly he and Compton accepted the implied challenge. The bluff was easily mounted at the rear, but the front offered small hold to hand or foot. Each man quickly selected his route and began to climb. A crevice, a bush, a slight projection, a vine or tree branch—all of these were aids that counted in the race. It was all foolery—there was no stake; but there was youth in it, cross reader, and light hearts, and something else that Miss Clay writes so charmingly about.

Gaines gave a great tug at the root of a laurel and pulled himself to Miss Mary's feet. On his arm he carried the wreath of roses; and while the villagers and summer boarders screamed and applauded below he placed it on the queen's brow.

"You are a gallant knight," said Miss Mary.

"If I could be your true knight always," began Gaines, but Miss Mary laughed him dumb, for Compton scrambled over the edge of the rock one minute behind time.

What a twilight that was when they drove back to the hotel! The opal of the valley turned slowly to purple, the dark woods framed the lake as a mirror, the tonic air stirred the very soul in one. The first pale stars came out over the mountain tops where yet a faint glow of—

"I beg your pardon, Mr. Gaines," said Adkins.

The man who believed New York to be the finest summer resort in the world opened his eyes and kicked over the mucilage bottle on his desk.

"I—I believe I was asleep," he said.

"It's the heat," said Adkins. "It's something awful in the city these"—

"Nonsense!" said the other. "The city beats the country ten to one in summer. Fools go out tramping in muddy brooks and wear themselves out trying to catch little fish as long as your finger. Stay in town and keep comfortable—that's my idea."

"Some letters just came," said Adkins. "I thought you might like to glance at them before you go."

Let us look over his shoulder and read just a few lines of one of them:

MY DEAR, DEAR HUSBAND: Just received your letter ordering us to stay another month . . . Rita's cough is almost gone . . . Johnny has simply gone wild like a little Indian . . . Will be the making of both children . . . work so hard, and I know that your business can hardly afford to keep us here so long . . . best man that ever . . . you always pretend that you like the city in summer . . . trout fishing that you used to be so fond of . . . and all to keep us well and happy . . . come to you if it were not doing the babies so much good . . . I stood last evening on Chimney Rock in exactly the same spot where I was when you put the wreath of roses on my head . . . through all the world . . . when you said you would be my true knight . . . fifteen years ago, dear, just think! . . . have always been that to me . . . ever and ever,

MARY.

The man who said he thought New York the finest summer resort in the country dropped into a café on his way home and had a glass of beer under an electric fan.

"Wonder what kind of a fly old Harding used," he said to himself.

ELIZABETH BOWEN

The Contessina

The Contessina arrived at the hotel one Friday evening, with an aunt and uncle from Milan. It seemed so odd to everybody else to meet Italians staying on Lake Como; their arrival created quite a stir, and fanned many smouldering conversations into life again at tables where married couples and family parties sat. Even honeymoon couples were set gently bobbing as the ripples of interest widened and spread. The Contessina sat looking very demure, and ate her dinner like a little cat between the matt black mountain of her uncle and the glazed black mountain of her aunt.

There was general though unexpressed disappointment when the new arrivals, filing duck-like from the salle à manger, compressed themselves into the lift forthwith, and were shot bedwards without so much as a glance about the lounge.

Next morning the uncle and aunt made no appearance, but the Contessina sauntered through the lounge at about eleven o'clock carrying a cerise parasol; stood a moment hesitating in the doorway, then stepped across the road to the hotel terrace that overhung the lake. Here four young English ladies, all in white, were seated in a row along the parapet watching Mr Harrison and Mr Barlow going out for a row. Their backs were turned to the road, and they dangled eight beautifully shod white feet over the reflecting water that rose and fell in the shadow of the parapet as evenly and gently as a bosom.

The Contessina, leaning over, looked for some time thoughtfully at the row of feet, then down at her own, which were by three sizes smaller than any of them. The four young ladies, all unconscious, waved their hands and called out jolly things as the boat with the orange awning slid away across the water. Mr Harrison and Mr Barlow rowed beautifully; every second day they took a boat out, and the other mornings they played golf. They took each other on at tennis at five o'clock every evening on the hotel court, while people from the other hotels watched admiringly through the railings. The Contessina seated herself also on the parapet, shaking out her fluffy skirts round her; her parasol unfurled magically as though it had been wings. When Mr Barlow turned his head for the last time she was not even looking at the boat, but away beyond it to the opposite hills, cold purple in the shadow. Mr Barlow observed this with annoyance.

Two of the girls went off together, arm in arm, and the other two, producing their embroidery, moved back on to an iron seat under the shade of a chestnut tree. These trees, clipped low till they spread out into umbrellas, followed for some distance the line of the shore. The Contessina, now their *vis-à-vis*, eyed the couple unabashedly with the naked curiosity of childhood. She studied their dresses and their attitudes, and took in the embroidery they were doing stitch by stitch. Conversation between the two was desultory; they had known each other for three days, and were entering upon that interesting phase in a hotel acquaintanceship where small talk dies, commonplaces falter, and confidences begin. The Italian girl disturbed them; her very sitting there was calculated to disturb them, even had they been quite certain that she understood no language but her own.

In this they would have been mistaken. 'Good – *morning*,' said the Contessina.

'Oh? Good morning.'

'Ah speak English,' she continued, nodding encouragingly at them. Two dimples flickered, dints of rosy light in the warm twilight of her parasol. Her eyes, usually of amber, caught here and there a glint of red that danced between the disconcerting flickers of her lashes. A queer little face, so foreign.

'Really?' said Ursula; and Jenny, smiling, said, 'How nice!'

The Contessina once again nodded, gathering her forces. She was about sixteen evidently, and this was odd, because no English girls of sixteen had figures like that. She revealed herself against the sunny water, a thing of neat assured little curves. She had wrists and she had ankles, her waist had already decided itself, and it would have been evident to the discerning eye that there were many more dimples. Jenny and Ursula hated to seem rude and – well – *English*, but she really would be very difficult to talk to. Their next move should have been, traditionally, 'How do you like Italy?' But they could not ask her that.

'Have you been to England?' Ursula inquired.

'Oh, no-o!' tittered the Contessina, and tittered again in scorn. *England* – the very idea!

Jenny, who was very intellectual, suggested, 'Then you read English, I expect?'

'Oh, yes. Marie Corelli.'

'Oh, yes.'

'She is fa-ine.'

'Oh, yes. Do you play tennis?'

'Oh, no, I think it is terrible. Do you like Italian men?'

'I don't know any,' said Jenny, with indifference. After a moment's pause she smiled kindly at the Contessina, funny little thing. Ursula said that she had once had a most interesting friendship with an Italian lady; she had been really charming. The Contessina looked at her in wonder. 'But do you like ladies at *all*?' she asked.

They were spared further of this, for a voice behind them from the other side of the road shrilled out abruptly, '*Serafinetta, vien' qui!*' To the first call, and its repetition, the Contessina remained blandly deaf. As these persisted and were reinforced and bound together by a positive Niagara of sound, the Contessina at length responded, '*Vengo subito*,' and did not stir. '*Adesso*,' the voice implored, and the aunt, immensely canopied by a parasol of sombre lace, appeared in full sail from the hotel followed by the uncle. She did not look angry nor at all excited; foreigners simply could not help talking like that. The Contessina rose and shook her skirts out, smiled, sighed, shrugged, and nodding to her new acquaintances, went off to meet her aunt, her parasol tilted quite ineffably.

After lunch, the aunt, the uncle, and the Contessina got into the hotel boat, assisted by the concierge, and were rowed up and down for an hour by the two hotel boatmen, not far out and parallel with the shore. The Contessina could be seen leaning out from under the awning to trail her fingers in the water. At five o'clock, people began to gather round the tennis-court, and by the time Mr Harrison and Mr Barlow had at last appeared, the aunt, the uncle, and the Contessina were there too, sitting close together on a seat. The uncle had sunk deep down into his stomach, the aunt deep down into her bosom, and the Contessina's glances flitted about like butterflies, never pausing long. All three looked happy and contented, and the aunt was smiling with the most profound indulgence at the English ladies dressed for tennis with their large, flat feet. Mr Barlow, down the Contessina's end of the court, walked springily about on the balls of his feet, while his opponents took their places; hacking, slashing, and under-cutting with his racquet at the air with science and ferocity. He bit his lip, the air whistled through his teeth, his head, as he recovered from a lunge, jerked sideways and remained there, for he caught the eyes of the Contessina looking up at him. Her parasol was not up, for she was sitting in the shade, and her eyes, now merely amber, studied with a mild inquiry the foolishness of Mr Barlow.

He played quite brilliantly that evening; everybody sat alert to watch him, and the crowd beyond the railings thickened. His partner, a lady of a disenchanted spirit, reported afterwards that he was poaching more than ever, and had made three foot-faults. When the final set was over he pulled on his sweater over his shirt, buttoned his blazer over his sweater, and strolled, just casually, past the seat where the Italian family were sitting. They were still there; the aunt was slumbering like a lady of lineage, and the uncle had disappeared behind the *Popolo*. The Contessina was looking sideways at the view: the evening light upon the hills was indeed very beautiful, but perhaps she had not been looking at it long. Mr Barlow dropped his racquet – most annoying – at the Contessina's feet.

The Contessina looked down at the racquet in surprise, as though it had fallen from heaven. Mr Barlow's hand, arm, shoulder, and flushed bent neck came within her field of vision; she started violently. 'Thank you,' he said, rising, though she had done nothing to assist him. She bowed, and he beheld the dimples. 'Do you play tennis?' he asked softly.

'But no. But I do *wish*, I *wish*' . . . It was inexpressible; she caught a sharp breath. Her whipped-cream ruffles shifted, swelled, and sank.

'It's a good game,' murmured Mr Barlow, still more softly, glancing stealthily towards the aunt.

'It is like . . . you do resemble . . . gods!'

'Oh, *well*,' laughed he, and looked about him. Everybody hurried to escape the chill of dusk; the court was being rapidly deserted. 'Would you care to take a little stroll?' he suggested. She evidently failed to understand his idiomatic English. 'I mean, a walk.' She ducked to see if any wakefulness still gleamed beneath the eyelids of the aunt, while he, with arched eyebrows, peered over the *Popolo* to see what the uncle was doing. He nodded to reassure her, and she giggled. 'A *leetle* walk!' she stipulated. 'Oh, as little as anything,' agreed the delighted Mr Barlow. 'The sun's just setting; come as far as the edge of the lake.'

They watched the sunset together, standing on a little jetty. Beneath their feet the water lapped and gurgled. When they turned to go in Mr Barlow sighed. He did not take her back the shortest way.

That night his wife was more impossible than ever. He was as nice as anything to her, at the beginning, asked her twice if she had had a pleasant day, and said, 'Oh, come,' encouragingly, when she responded that she hadn't. Everything was always wrong with Mrs Barlow's days; she made a point of this, it was her little triumph. But she was such a tired woman now, these little triumphs made her feel no better. Tonight she would not talk and would not eat; the waiters, humane men, waxed openly solicitous, and this annoyed her husband. Their table was beside an open window; beyond, the dark-blue velvet night hung like a curtain; one felt the sleeping presence of the lake, and on the water somebody with a guitar began to sing. It was a night of breathless heart-beats and of beating pulses, a night for love. A night to kiss a satin skin as warm as great grape-clusters hanging in the sun. No one round him, Mr Barlow knew, as much as glimpsed the possibilities of such a night. Married couples, family parties – even the honeymoon couples looked bloodless; besides, once the woman was one man's wife one ceased, as it were, to be a Gentleman and became a Player. The Contessina's table was in view, if one leant a little sideways to avoid a pillar, but the Contessina was making an excellent dinner, and had no time left to look about her. Scents crept in from the bushes in the garden, met the smell of dinner, did battle with it and retreated; but Mr Barlow had them, and his nostrils twitched. Now that the chill of dusk had passed, the night was very warm and grew to the accustomed eye still more astonishingly blue.

Mrs Barlow waved away the *canneton sauté*, then

recalled the waiter, and after much deliberation and hovering of the fork and spoon, selected half a dozen peas. These she floated in a pool of gravy and looked down upon despairingly, while her husband looked despairingly across at her. For the last half-hour they had hardly spoken, and the unmarried girls at the next table, a merry party, pressed each other's feet and discreetly giggled. They had all so often told each other marriage was like that. Mr Barlow was good-looking; the shape of his head was pleasant, and his sleeked-back hair defined it. His forehead, jaw, and ears were squared perfection, and his sulky mouth was beautifully cut. Mrs Barlow raised three peas to her lips, then recoiled from them.

'I shan't be able to digest *these*,' she said, and looked across at him with the solemn eyes of some one standing on the brink.

'Then why eat them?' said Mr Barlow. 'Oh, but I *must* eat,' said she; then her chest twitched with a miserable hiccup, as it came over her suddenly that any other woman's husband would have been saying this to *her*. 'Oh yes, of course,' agreed Mr Barlow, and he hummed very softly and tried to look away from her. The electric light poured down upon his wife; even her pink dress looked *triste* and faded, though it was new and expensive, and far too beautiful for the occasion. As for her fair hair – Mr

Barlow always had preferred dark women, and he had realized long ago that it is never wise to make exceptions to one's rules of life.

After dinner the older people gathered on the verandah, while the girls went off together two by two. They would come up out of the dark like moths, glitter under the lights in their pale dresses, then vanish again. Harrison and a Mrs Pym announced that they were going to look for glow-worms, and a whole bevy of girls went after them. The Contessina sat with her relations in a little isolated group at the glassed-in end of the verandah. When Barlow, searching very diligently round them for a newspaper he had forgotten, jerked his head interrogatively towards the lake, she turned away and simply did not see. So he went down to the edge of the lake alone, swung his legs over the parapet, and sat listening to the water sucking at the stones beneath him. He lighted cigarette after cigarette, and allowed each to slip from between his relaxed fingers into the water. Each sizzled, then was silent. It was a pity one couldn't put oneself out like that. The Bellagio lights twinkled very near him, on a level with his eyes; the lake was, after all, so narrow. He longed to row somebody over in a boat, and climb with her into the inviolable dark beneath the trees of Serballoni Hill.

Harrison and Mrs Pym were coming up behind him; he could recognize their voices, talking very low.

'Lovely night,' he said, without turning. 'Oh, lovely,' said Harrison, with a jump. 'Lovely day tomorrow!' he continued. 'Look here'; he turned his head over the other shoulder, to where he knew Mrs Pym was standing. 'I want to take that little Italian kid out tomorrow over to San Giacomo. She's an awfully nice little kid; I promised and she's awfully keen. I said I'd take her over in a boat.'

'The little kid?' said Mrs Pym, grinning in the dark. 'They'd never allow her.'

'Yes, but look here, you work it. Oh, be a sport, woman! You talk their lingo, it'll be your show, you're taking her along, and Harrison and I just come along to row you.'

'Ah, yes,' said Mrs Pym evenly.

The Contessina's aunt found Mrs Pym quite charming. They discovered that they had several friends in common, in Milan and other parts of Italy. She said that it would be delightful for Serafinetta to go for an excursion with the English lady; she loved English ladies, and had had an American governess for three years. At four o'clock on Sunday afternoon, the Contessina was therefore delivered over by her aunt into the hands of Mrs Pym, who explained that English friends of her own had volunteered to row them. It was difficult to hire boatmen on a Sunday afternoon.

Mrs Pym was a fair, burnt-out young woman of twenty-five, who spoke in a deep hoarse drawl, wore pale-grey flannels for boating, and had beautiful feet. She never looked hot. Harrison faintly amused her – she had been Barlow's partner too often at tennis – though nobody, of course, was amusing beyond a certain point. She had reached this point earlier than usual with her husband. The Contessina was allowed to steer; she tugged the wrong rope systematically, looking about her, glinting all over with contentment and mirth. She was fascinated by the swing and dip of the sleek oars over the water. Around them, the blue sky and the blue water blazed; a quivering light struck up into their faces and beat against the underneath of the awning. Once a steamer passed them, slanting over to Bellagio; the boat was sucked into her wake and rocked madly, round her oily shadows slid and spread and darted. The Contessina clutched the sides of the boat and screamed with fear and joy.

The bay of San Giacomo was still golden in the late afternoon, as they grounded their boat on the little strip of beach under the teahouse. Above went up the great sheer sweep of the hill; tree-trunks crowded endlessly, impenetrably, up into the sky. Cars along the road to Milan shrieked like birds, high, high among those unseen branches. Stepping from the boat, the ladies stood looking up into the queer ribbed dusk of the tree-trunks, while the others carried up the oars to the tea-house and put them away for safety. The place was very still, the coast of the lake seemed for miles entirely deserted. Barlow returned and loomed above the Contessina speechlessly. She said, 'Let us go among the trees.'

The others fell away from them. Her ridiculous little feet were useless to her; the high heels flung her whole weight forward on to the blunt little toes, and these scrabbled unavailingly upon the baked, bald earth of the hill. Sometimes she missed her footing altogether, and her whole weight would swing from Barlow's arm. When he had dragged her up about ten feet, she said she would like to come down again, pulled him after her, and they slid the whole way. They skirted the hill and walked for some distance along the edge of the lake, in the opposite direction to that which the others had taken. When they came to a bank of cushiony grass she sat down, and he sat down beside her, tilting his panama over his eyes.

'This is very nice,' said Mr Barlow, looking at the Contessina. She had on a dress of heliotrope organdie, with a fichu folded across the bosom with that best discretion for the display of pretty curves. Her skin was very dark against the heliotrope, as fresh as a young petal, as brown as old, old ivory. Her white Tuscan hat enhanced this peculiar deliciousness, and the little loops of hair corrugated against the curves of her cheeks looked almost blue. Her puffed sleeves were very short, and there was a dimple on each elbow: 'This is very nice, you know,' repeated Mr Barlow, stooping to kiss one of the dimples.

'Oh, yes,' agreed the Contessina, looking down at the elbow.

'You know,' said Mr Barlow, 'you're just the sort of little girl I like; just the sort of little pal I've always wanted—'

'Leetle *what?*'

'Pal – little friend, you know. Amie.'

'Oh, yes. Do you like Italian girls?'

'Don't know about *girls*,' said Barlow, stressing the plural. She supposed, with a sigh, that like everybody else he preferred them married.

'No,' said Mr Barlow, looking at her tenderly, 'not married. No, not *married*, you know.'

'I think,' said she, 'that Englishmen are beautiful. They are like gods.'

'By Jove!' said the intoxicated Mr Barlow. Then he added, with a sigh: 'Some day, perhaps, you'll marry an Englishman.'

'Oh, no. I will marry an Italian gentleman, and then we will go and live in England.'

'But it would be too late then.'

'Oh, yes,' said the Contessina, looking thoughtfully at Mr Barlow. She smoothed the folds of her fichu, and spread the light flounces of her dress about her over the grass.

'Meanwhile,' said he, 'this is wonderful.'

'Oh, yes,' agreed the Contessina, 'it is like Heaven.'

They both paused and looked down at the lake. The Contessina was a little too much of the child that sits with its mouth open, confidently waiting for lollipops. Each lollipop being assimilated, she would thank him prettily, look up with candid greed, and wait for another. And this necessity for direct, unidiomatic English embarrassed Mr Barlow, master of innuendo and *double entendres*; this was more than throwing lollipops, it was spiking buns to an insatiable little eager bear at the end of a stick. But he couldn't resist her; he slid across the last intervening inches of grass and put his arm round the Contessina's waist. Anyone standing at an upper window of their hotel with a pair of field-glasses could have watched them from across the lake, but Mr Barlow decided to risk it. His arm tightened – 'Oh, please!' she said perfunctorily – and he kissed the

Contessina a great many times. She turned her head from side to side, and once he caught her full on the mouth. 'Is that still like Heaven?' he whispered ardently, cupping her chin in his unoccupied hand. 'Oh, yes,' she said politely, just perceptibly wriggling her head.

There was another silence; this time he felt it wonderfully sympathetic. Then the Contessina, whose waist he still encircled, asked him how he liked his wife. Mr Barlow told her; he explained that life was sometimes very difficult.

'Oh, yes,' said the Contessina. 'I wonder how she does like you?'

'Oh, well . . .'

'How many children have you?'

'None,' said Mr Barlow indignantly.

'Oh, that is a pity,' she sighed, looking down into the lake.

'A pity?' said he, picking up a little hand whose fingers curled in his like a baby's. He looked down at it hungrily, while she too watched from under her lashes her hand and the approach of his lips; then he kissed it twice and crushed it up against him. 'It is a pity you have no son,' she sighed. 'He would be like a god.'

'Oh, he would, would he?' said Barlow, indisposed to abdicate.

'Yes,' she said regretfully. 'Who takes your wife in a boat? Does your wife like Italian men?'

'Really, I don't know. Wouldn't it be more interesting to talk about ourselves for a little? Do you know, if I had had a little girl like you to go through life with, I think everything would have been different. A dainty little thing, you know, a little, a little humming-bird.'

'But if I had gone through your life I should be fat,' said the Contessina.

She was adorable. 'You lovely little thing!' he cried, 'you *are* a lovely little thing!'

'You are very very kind,' she said, nestling against his arm like a kitten. 'When I came here I thought it would be so *triste* because there was nobody young but the ladies, but now I shall not have been dull.'

'You'll have something nice to remember. Now I'm going to give you some more to remember.' She uncoiled like a spring and was on to her feet in a flash. 'Oh, no,' she cried, jumping about with delight, and clapping her hands at him as though he were a puppy. 'That is enough to remember, that is enough!'

'Is it, indeed!' quoth Mr Barlow, turning pink with pleasurable excitement. He grabbed at her diaphanous skirts that swirled about her like a ballet dancer's. There was an angry sound of tearing muslin. 'Yah!' shrieked the Contessina, and Mr Barlow recoiled momentarily in dismay. He fell back from sitting posture on to his hands and crouched looking up at her; then, realizing the disadvantages of this position, drew in his long legs and sprang to his feet. The Contessina, breathless even beyond the point of shrieking, swept her mauve skirts round her and went tottering along the beach towards the promontory. She staggered with laughter, her whole body curved upon itself, bowed beneath her weight of mirth.

'Ha!' cried Mr Barlow, making after her with long strides. The air whistled between his teeth, he grinned; this was better than tennis. She was now within the compass of his extended arms, and he leaned forward to enclose her, a happy and confident gurgle rising in his throat. The Contessina ducked with a yelp of delight, sprang ahead surprisingly and missed her footing. She spun round, wavered, beat the air for a second, then came down, *smack*, on to her outstretched palms. Mr Barlow stopped short. 'God!' he whispered, and clapped his hand to his mouth.

The Contessina did not remain prone. Before her cavalier had recovered himself, she was sitting back on her heels to stare at her little bleeding and earthy palms that reared up into her gaze indignantly. Her pose might have been called 'Astonishment.' Then, while he yet beheld, the ivory of the face and neck now visible to him darkened, her open mouth, eclipsing her face, became a cavern into whose menacing profundity Mr Barlow's horrified eyes looked down. A shriek like a needle-point, rounding to a sustained boo-hoo, rent across the silence of San Giacomo. As in response, a stone from miles above dislodged itself and came hurtling down through the trees into the lake. This increased the panic of Mr Barlow, who made a frightened sound and looked about him furtively. She clamoured on without pause, shrieking and sobbing.

'Little darling—' he tendered, dropping on his knees beside her.

'A-ah,' shrilled the Contessina. '*Va via.* I hate you. Go!'

'But look here, listen—'

'Aie, go; you are wicked. You have been wicked with me; it is not so you should behave with a young girl. A-ah!'

She was such a child. Mr Barlow, in a rush of paternal emotion, gathered her against him. '*There*,' he murmured, 'there – there – there!'

But the Contessina positively roared, and disengaging her fists assailed his breast and shoulders with a rain of blows. One of these caught him on the chin, and he released her sharply. Above the intimidating cavern of her mouth, between the smears and crumples of her face, two slits of eyes blazed out upon him icily. Those eyes were pale with contempt. Mr Barlow was appalled by them.

'Yah!' resumed the Contessina. 'Old stupid! Wicked old man!'

'You *are* a little devil,' said Mr Barlow wonderingly, getting up.

The Contessina rose also, with remarkable agility. The front of her dress was soiled irreparably cut right through at the knee and stained with blood. 'You have killed my dress,' she yammered, grimacing down at the torn flounces miserably. 'If it had been the most old and the most ugly I would not have spoilt it for *you*. You are not young, and you are not funny, and you have a hot face, and you do not behave well with a young girl. It is not right. There is no *young* man, an English or an Italian, who would behave so, it is *old* men who are stupid and devils. Let me go to the boat!'

'Oh, all right,' said he very coldly. 'Go on. *I* don't mind where you go. You are a silly little thing to spoil your dress like that, your aunt will be angry.' He wondered, as he spoke, whether she would involve him in a duel with the Italian uncle. With bowed head and heaving shoulders, she preceded him along the beach, sobbing and sniffing. 'Such a hullabaloo!' said Mr Barlow indignantly. 'I never take out a little girl if she doesn't know how to behave.' He followed at a distance.

Mrs Pym and Harrison appeared from round the opposite promontory. Mrs Pym looked vaguely at the Contessina. 'But dear *child*—' she said, in faint expostulation, raising her eyebrows. 'Oh, I *say*!' said Harrison, 'Oh, I say, that's too bad. I say, *Barlow*!'

Barlow explained that she had slipped and fallen while engaged in throwing stones into the lake. Harrison did not hear; he was comforting the Contessina, murmuring things into her ear and patting her little heaving shoulders. The petal-curves of the big Tuscan hat drooped towards him.

'Oh, please,' she gasped, 'if you would be so kind . . . I would like to go back . . . Oh, please . . . Oh, please!'

Barlow, his neck burning scarlet, strode to the tea-house to reclaim the oars, and strode back in disdainful silence. The Contessina could no longer see him; it was as though he had slipped out of her vision down a crack, and the crack had closed above him for ever.

Going home, Harrison changed places with Barlow, and sat *vis-à-vis* to the Contessina. She blinked her tears away, the dimples came out tremulously, her lashes were still wet and the lower lashes clung to her cheek adorably. The sun was going down, the lake was of liquid flame with great cold blue shadows like swords stabbing across it. The hills were blue and sharp, the air crystal. The sleek oars swung and dipped to their reflections rhythmically, and Harrison's sleek head beneath the eyes of the Contessina bowed to the rhythm. The level sunshine crept along the air and brimmed with gold the little dints of mirth and pleasure in the Contessina's cheeks, and drew a curve of gold along the brim of her hat.

'You row like a god,' the Contessina said to Harrison. 'Do you like Italian girls?'

WILLA CATHER

The Enchanted Bluff

We had our swim before sundown, and while we were cooking our supper the oblique rays of light made a dazzling glare on the white sand about us. The translucent red ball itself sank behind the brown stretches of corn field as we sat down to eat, and the warm layer of air that had rested over the water and our clean sand-bar grew fresher and smelled of the rank ironweed and sunflowers growing on the flatter shore. The river was brown and sluggish, like any other of the half-dozen streams that water the Nebraska corn lands. On one shore was an irregular line of bald clay bluffs where a few scrub-oaks with thick trunks and flat, twisted tops threw light shadows on the long grass. The western shore was low and level, with corn fields that stretched to the sky-line, and all along the water's edge were little sandy coves and beaches where slim cottonwoods and willow saplings flickered.

The turbulence of the river in springtime discouraged milling, and, beyond keeping the old red bridge in repair, the busy farmers did not concern themselves with the stream; so the Sandtown boys were left in undisputed possession. In the autumn we hunted quail through the miles of stubble and fodder land along the flat shore, and, after the winter skating season was over and the ice had gone out, the spring freshets and flooded bottoms gave us our great excitement of the year. The channel was never the same for two successive seasons. Every spring the swollen stream undermined a bluff to the east, or bit out a few acres of corn field to the west and whirled the soil away to deposit it in spumy mud banks somewhere else. When the water fell low in midsummer, new sand-bars were thus exposed to dry and whiten in the August sun. Sometimes these were banked so firmly that the fury of the next freshet failed to unseat them; the little willow seedlings emerged triumphantly from the yellow froth, broke into spring leaf, shot up into summer growth, and with their mesh of roots bound together the moist sand beneath them against the batterings of another April. Here and there a cottonwood soon glittered among them, quivering in the low current of air that, even on breathless days when the dust hung like smoke above the wagon road, trembled along the face of the water.

It was on such an island, in the third summer of

its yellow green, that we built our watch-fire; not in the thicket of dancing willow wands, but on the level terrace of fine sand which had been added that spring; a little new bit of world, beautifully ridged with ripple marks, and strewn with the tiny skeletons of turtles and fish, all as white and dry as if they had been expertly cured. We had been careful not to mar the freshness of the place, although we often swam to it on summer evenings and lay on the sand to rest.

This was our last watch-fire of the year, and there were reasons why I should remember it better than any of the others. Next week the other boys were to file back to their old places in the Sandtown High School, but I was to go up to the Divide to teach my first country school in the Norwegian district. I was already homesick at the thought of quitting the boys with whom I had always played; of leaving the river, and going up into a windy plain that was all windmills and corn fields and big pastures; where there was nothing wilful or unmanageable in the landscape, no new islands, and no chance of unfamiliar birds—such as often followed the watercourses.

Other boys came and went and used the river for fishing or skating, but we six were sworn to the spirit of the stream, and we were friends mainly because of the river. There were the two Hassler boys, Fritz and Otto, sons of the little German tailor. They were the youngest of us; ragged boys of ten and twelve, with sunburned hair, weather-stained faces, and pale blue eyes. Otto, the elder, was the best mathematician in school, and clever at his books, but he always dropped out in the spring term as if the river could not get on without him. He and Fritz caught the fat, horned catfish and sold them about the town, and they lived so much in the water that they were as brown and sandy as the river itself.

There was Percy Pound, a fat, freckled boy with chubby cheeks, who took half a dozen boys' story-papers and was always being kept in for reading detective stories behind his desk. There was Tip Smith, destined by his freckles and red hair to be the buffoon in all our games, though he walked like a timid little old man and had a funny, cracked laugh. Tip worked hard in his father's grocery store every afternoon, and swept it out before school in the morning. Even his recreations were laborious. He collected cigarette cards and tin tobacco-tags indefatigably, and would sit for hours humped up over a snarling little scroll-saw which he kept in his attic. His dearest possessions were some little pill-bottles that purported to contain grains of wheat from the Holy Land, water from the Jordan and the Dead Sea, and earth from the Mount of Olives. His father had bought these dull things from a Baptist missionary who peddled them, and Tip seemed to derive great satisfaction from their remote origin.

The tall boy was Arthur Adams. He had fine hazel eyes that were almost too reflective and sympathetic for a boy, and such a pleasant voice that we all loved to hear him read aloud. Even when he had to read poetry aloud at school, no one ever thought of laughing. To be sure, he was not at school very much of the time. He was seventeen and should have finished the High School the year before, but he was always off somewhere with his gun. Arthur's mother was dead, and his father, who was feverishly absorbed in promoting schemes, wanted to send the boy away to school and get him off his hands; but Arthur always begged off for another year and promised to study. I remember him as a tall, brown boy with an intelligent face, always lounging among a lot of us little fellows, laughing at us oftener than with us, but such a soft, satisfied laugh that we felt rather flattered when we provoked it. In after-years people said that Arthur had been given to evil ways even as a lad, and it is true that we often saw him with the gambler's sons and with old Spanish Fanny's boy, but if he learned anything ugly in their company he never betrayed it to us. We would have followed Arthur anywhere, and I am bound to say that he led us into no worse places than the cat-tail marshes and the stubble fields. These, then, were the boys who camped with me that summer night upon the sand-bar.

After we finished our supper we beat the willow thicket for driftwood. By the time we had collected enough, night had fallen, and the pungent, weedy smell from the shore increased with the coolness. We threw ourselves down about the fire and made another futile effort to show Percy Pound the Little Dipper. We had tried it often before, but he could never be got past the big one.

"You see those three big stars just below the handle, with the bright one in the middle?" said Otto Hassler; "that's Orion's belt, and the bright one is the clasp." I crawled behind Otto's shoulder and sighted up his arm to the star that seemed perched upon the tip of his steady forefinger. The Hassler boys did seine-fishing at night, and they knew a good many stars.

Percy gave up the Little Dipper and lay back on the sand, his hands clasped under his head. "I can see the North Star," he announced, contentedly, pointing toward it with his big toe. "Anyone might get lost and need to know that."

We all looked up at it.

"How do you suppose Columbus felt when his compass didn't point north any more?" Tip asked.

Otto shook his head. "My father says that there was another North Star once, and that maybe this one won't last always. I wonder what would happen to us down here if anything went wrong with it?"

Arthur chuckled. "I wouldn't worry, Ott. Nothing's apt to happen to it in your time. Look at the Milky Way! There must be lots of good dead Indians."

We lay back and looked, meditating, at the dark cover of the world. The gurgle of the water had become heavier. We had often noticed a mutinous, complaining note in it at night, quite different from its cheerful daytime chuckle, and seeming like the voice of a much deeper and more powerful stream. Our water had always these two moods: the one of sunny complaisance, the other of inconsolable, passionate regret.

"Queer how the stars are all in sort of diagrams," remarked Otto. "You could do most any proposition in geometry with 'em. They always look as if they meant something. Some folks say everybody's fortune is all written out in the stars, don't they?"

"They believe so in the old country," Fritz affirmed.

But Arthur only laughed at him. "You're thinking of Napoleon, Fritzey. He had a star that went out when he began to lose battles. I guess the stars don't keep any close tally on Sandtown folks."

We were speculating on how many times we could count a hundred before the evening star went down behind the corn fields, when someone cried, "There comes the moon, and it's as big as a cart wheel!"

We all jumped up to greet it as it swam over the bluffs behind us. It came up like a galleon in full sail; an enormous, barbaric thing, red as an angry heathen god.

"When the moon came up red like that, the Aztecs used to sacrifice their prisoners on the temple top," Percy announced.

"Go on, Perce. You got that out of *Golden Days*. Do you believe that, Arthur?" I appealed.

Arthur answered, quite seriously: "Like as not. The moon was one of their gods. When my father was in Mexico City he saw the stone where they used to sacrifice their prisoners."

As we dropped down by the fire again some one asked whether the Mound-Builders were older than the Aztecs. When we once got upon the Mound-Builders we never willingly got away from them, and

THE ENCHANTED BLUFF

we were still conjecturing when we heard a loud splash in the water.

"Must have been a big cat jumping," said Fritz. "They do sometimes. They must see bugs in the dark. Look what a track the moon makes!"

There was a long, silvery streak on the water, and where the current fretted over a big log it boiled up like gold pieces.

"Suppose there ever *was* any gold hid away in this old river?" Fritz asked. He lay like a little brown Indian, close to the fire, his chin on his hand and his bare feet in the air. His brother laughed at him, but Arthur took his suggestion seriously.

"Some of the Spaniards thought there was gold up here somewhere. Seven cities chuck full of gold, they had it, and Coronado and his men came up to hunt it. The Spaniards were all over this country once."

Percy looked interested. "Was that before the Mormons went through?"

We all laughed at this.

"Long enough before. Before the Pilgrim Fathers, Perce. Maybe they came along this very river. They always followed the watercourses."

"I wonder where this river really does begin?" Tip mused. That was an old and a favorite mystery which the map did not clearly explain. On the map the little black line stopped somewhere in western Kansas; but since rivers generally rose in mountains, it was only reasonable to suppose that ours came from the Rockies. Its destination, we knew, was the Missouri, and the Hassler boys always maintained that we could embark at Sandtown in floodtime, follow our noses, and eventually arrive at New Orleans. Now they took up their old argument. "If us boys had grit enough to try it, it wouldn't take no time to get to Kansas City and St. Joe."

We began to talk about the places we wanted to go to. The Hassler boys wanted to see the stockyards in Kansas City, and Percy wanted to see a big store in Chicago. Arthur was interlocutor and did not betray himself.

"Now it's your turn, Tip."

Tip rolled over on his elbow and poked the fire, and his eyes looked shyly out of his queer, tight little face. "My place is awful far away. My Uncle Bill told me about it."

Tip's Uncle Bill was a wanderer, bitten with mining fever, who had drifted into Sandtown with a broken arm, and when it was well had drifted out again.

"Where is it?"

"Aw, it's down in New Mexico somewheres.

There aren't no railroads or anything. You have to go on mules, and you run out of water before you get there and have to drink canned tomatoes."

"Well, go on, kid. What's it like when you do get there?"

Tip sat up and excitedly began his story.

"There's a big red rock there that goes right up out of the sand for about nine hundred feet. The country's flat all around it, and this here rock goes up all by itself, like a monument. They call it the Enchanted Bluff down there, because no white man has ever been on top of it. The sides are smooth rock, and straight up, like a wall. The Indians say that hundreds of years ago, before the Spaniards came, there was a village away up there in the air. The tribe that lived there had some sort of steps, made out of wood and bark, hung down over the face of the bluff, and the braves went down to hunt and carried water up in big jars swung on their backs. They kept a big supply of water and dried meat up there, and never went down except to hunt. They were a peaceful tribe that made cloth and pottery, and they went up there to get out of the wars. You see, they could pick off any war party that tried to get up their little steps. The Indians say they were a handsome people, and they had some sort of queer religion. Uncle Bill thinks they were Cliff-Dwellers who had got into trouble and left home. They weren't fighters, anyhow.

"One time the braves were down hunting and an awful storm came up—a kind of waterspout—and when they got back to their rock they found their little staircase had been all broken to pieces, and only a few steps were left hanging away up in the air. While they were camped at the foot of the rock, wondering what to do, a war party from the north came along and massacred 'em to a man, with all the old folks and women looking on from the rock. Then the war party went on south and left the village to get down the best way they could. Of course they never got down. They starved to death up there, and when the war party came back on their way north, they could hear the children crying from the edge of the bluff where they had crawled out, but they didn't see a sign of a grown Indian, and nobody has ever been up there since."

We exclaimed at this dolorous legend and sat up.

"There couldn't have been many people up there," Percy demurred. "How big is the top, Tip?"

"Oh, pretty big. Big enough so that the rock doesn't look nearly as tall as it is. The top's bigger than the base. The bluff is sort of worn away for several hundred feet up. That's one reason it's so hard to climb."

I asked how the Indians got up, in the first place.

"Nobody knows how they got up or when. A hunting party came along once and saw that there was a town up there, and that was all."

Otto rubbed his chin and looked thoughtful. "Of course there must be some way to get up there. Couldn't people get a rope over someway and pull a ladder up?"

Tip's little eyes were shining with excitement. "I know a way. Me and Uncle Bill talked it all over. There's a kind of rocket that would take a rope over—life-savers use 'em—and then you could hoist a rope-ladder and peg it down at the bottom and make it tight with guy-ropes on the other side. I'm going to climb that there bluff, and I've got it all planned out."

Fritz asked what he expected to find when he got up there.

"Bones, maybe, or the ruins of their town, or pottery, or some of their idols. There might be 'most anything up there. Anyhow, I want to see."

"Sure nobody else has been up there, Tip?" Arthur asked.

"Dead sure. Hardly anybody ever goes down there. Some hunters tried to cut steps in the rock once, but they didn't get higher than a man can reach. The Bluff's all red granite, and Uncle Bill thinks it's a boulder the glaciers left. It's a queer place, anyhow. Nothing but cactus and desert for hundreds of miles, and yet right under the Bluff there's good water and plenty of grass. That's why the bison used to go down there."

Suddenly we heard a scream above our fire, and jumped up to see a dark, slim bird floating southward far above us—a whooping-crane, we knew by her cry and her long neck. We ran to the edge of the island, hoping we might see her alight, but she wavered southward along the rivercourse until we lost her. The Hassler boys declared that by the look of the heavens it must be after midnight, so we threw more wood on our fire, put on our jackets, and curled down in the warm sand. Several of us pretended to doze, but I fancy we were really thinking about Tip's Bluff and the extinct people. Over in the wood the ring-doves were calling mournfully to one another, and once we heard a dog bark, far away. "Somebody getting into old Tommy's melon patch," Fritz murmured sleepily, but nobody answered him. By and by Percy spoke out of the shadows.

"Say, Tip, when you go down there will you take me with you?"

"Maybe."

"Suppose one of us beats you down there, Tip?"

THE ENCHANTED BLUFF

"Whoever gets to the Bluff first has got to promise to tell the rest of us exactly what he finds," remarked one of the Hassler boys, and to this we all readily assented.

Somewhat reassured, I dropped off to sleep. I must have dreamed about a race for the Bluff, for I awoke in a kind of fear that other people were getting ahead of me and that I was losing my chance. I sat up in my damp clothes and looked at the other boys, who lay tumbled in uneasy attitudes about the dead fire. It was still dark, but the sky was blue with the last wonderful azure of night. The stars glistened like crystal globes, and trembled as if they shone through a depth of clear water. Even as I watched, they began to pale and the sky brightened. Day came suddenly, almost instantaneously. I turned for another look at the blue night, and it was gone. Everywhere the birds began to call, and all manner of little insects began to chirp and hop about in the willows. A breeze sprang up from the west and brought the heavy smell of ripened corn. The boys rolled over and shook themselves. We stripped and plunged into the river just as the sun came up over the windy bluffs.

When I came home to Sandtown at Christmas time, we skated out to our island and talked over the whole project of the Enchanted Bluff, renewing our resolution to find it.

Although that was twenty years ago, none of us have ever climbed the Enchanted Bluff. Percy Pound is a stockbroker in Kansas City and will go nowhere that his red touring-car cannot carry him. Otto Hassler went on the railroad and lost his foot braking; after which he and Fritz succeeded their father as the town tailors.

Arthur sat about the sleepy little town all his life—he died before he was twenty-five. The last time I saw him, when I was home on one of my college vacations, he was sitting in a steamer-chair under a cottonwood tree in the little yard behind one of the two Sandtown saloons. He was very untidy and his hand was not steady, but when he rose, unabashed, to greet me, his eyes were as clear and warm as ever. When I had talked with him for an hour and heard him laugh again, I wondered how it was that when Nature had taken such pains with a man, from his hands to the arch of his long foot, she had ever lost him in Sandtown. He joked about Tip Smith's Bluff, and declared he was going down there just as soon as the weather got cooler; he thought the Grand Canyon might be worth while, too.

I was perfectly sure when I left him that he would never get beyond the high plank fence and the comfortable shade of the cottonwood. And, indeed, it was under that very tree that he died one summer morning.

Tip Smith still talks about going to New Mexico. He married a slatternly, unthrifty country girl, has been much tied to a perambulator, and has grown stooped and gray from irregular meals and broken sleep. But the worst of his difficulties are now over, and he has, as he says, come into easy water. When I was last in Sandtown I walked home with him late one moonlight night, after he had balanced his cash and shut up his store. We took the long way around and sat down on the schoolhouse steps, and between us we quite revived the romance of the lone red rock and the extinct people. Tip insists that he still means to go down there, but he thinks now he will wait until his boy Bert is old enough to go with him. Bert has been let into the story, and thinks of nothing but the Enchanted Bluff.

Arthur Conan Doyle

The Adventure of the Devil's Foot

In recording from time to time some of the curious experiences and interesting recollections which I associate with my long and intimate friendship with Mr. Sherlock Holmes, I have continually been faced by difficulties caused by his own aversion to publicity. To his sombre and cynical spirit all popular applause was always abhorrent, and nothing amused him more at the end of a successful case than to hand over the actual exposure to some orthodox official, and to listen with a mocking smile to the general chorus of misplaced congratulation. It was indeed, this attitude upon the part of my friend, and certainly not any lack of interesting material which has caused me of late years to lay very few of my records before the public. My participation in some of his adventures was always a privilege which entailed discretion and reticence upon me.

It was, then, with considerable surprise that I received a telegram from Holmes last Tuesday—he has never been known to write where a telegram would serve—in the following terms: "Why not tell them of the Cornish horror—strangest case I have handled." I have no idea what backward sweep of memory had brought the matter fresh to his mind, or what freak had caused him to desire that I should recount it; but I hasten, before another cancelling telegram may arrive, to hunt out the notes which give me the exact details of the case, and to lay the narrative before my readers.

It was, then, in the spring of the year 1897 that Holmes's iron constitution showed some symptoms of giving way in the face of constant hard work of a most exacting kind, aggravated, perhaps, by occasional indiscretions of his own. In March of that year Dr. Moore Agar, of Harley Street, whose dramatic introduction to Holmes I may some day recount, gave positive injunctions that the famous private agent would lay aside all his cases and surrender himself to complete rest if he wished to avert an absolute break-down. The state of his health was not a matter in which he himself took the faintest interest, for his mental detachment was absolute, but he was induced at last, on the threat of being permanently disqualified from work, to give himself a complete change of scene and air. Thus it was that in the early spring of that year we found ourselves

THE ADVENTURE OF THE DEVIL'S FOOT

together in a small cottage near Poldhu Bay, at the further extremity of the Cornish peninsula.

It was a singular spot, and one peculiarly well suited to the grim humour of my patient. From the windows of our little white-washed house, which stood high upon a grassy headland, we looked down upon the whole sinister semi-circle of Mounts Bay, that old death trap of sailing vessels, with its fringe of black cliffs and surge-swept reefs on which innumerable seamen have met their end. With a northerly breeze it lies placid and sheltered, inviting the storm-tossed craft to tack into it for rest and protection.

Then comes the sudden swirl round of the wind, the blustering gale from the south-west, the dragging anchor, the lee shore, and the last battle in the creaming breakers. The wise mariner stands far out from that evil place.

On the land side our surroundings were as sombre as on the sea. It was a country of rolling moors, lonely and dun-coloured, with an occasional church tower to mark the site of some old-world village. In every direction upon these moors there were traces of some vanished race which had passed utterly away, and left as its sole record strange monuments of stone, irregular mounds which contained the burned ashes of the dead, and curious earthworks which hinted at prehistoric strife. The glamour and mystery of the place, with its sinister atmosphere of forgotten nations, appealed to the imagination of my friend, and he spent much of his time in long walks and solitary meditations upon the moor. The ancient Cornish language had also arrested his attention, and he had, I remember, conceived the idea that it was akin to the Chaldean, and had been largely derived from the Phœnician traders in tin. He had received a consignment of books upon philology and was settling down to develop this thesis, when suddenly, to my sorrow and to his unfeigned delight, we found ourselves, even in that land of dreams, plunged into a problem at our very doors which was more intense, more engrossing, and infinitely more mysterious than any of those which had driven us from London. Our simple life and peaceful, healthy routine were violently interrupted, and we were precipitated into the midst of a series of events which caused the utmost excitement not only in Cornwall, but throughout the whole West of England. Many of my readers may retain some recollection of what was called at the time "The Cornish Horror," though a most imperfect account of the matter reached the London Press. Now, after thirteen years, I will give the true details of this inconceivable affair to the public.

THE ADVENTURE OF THE DEVIL'S FOOT

I have said that scattered towers marked the villages which dotted this part of Cornwall. The nearest of these was the hamlet of Tredannick Wollas, where the cottages of a couple of hundred inhabitants clustered round an ancient, moss-grown church. The vicar of the parish, Mr. Roundhay, was something of an archæologist, and as such Holmes had made his acquaintance. He was a middle-aged man, portly and affable, with a considerable fund of local lore. At his invitation we had taken tea at the vicarage, and had come to know, also, Mr. Mortimer Tregennis, an independent gentleman, who increased the clergyman's scanty resources by taking rooms in his large, straggling house. The vicar, being a bachelor, was glad to come to such an arrangement, though he had little in common with his lodger, who was a thin, dark, spectacled man, with a stoop which gave the impression of actual, physical deformity. I remember that during our short visit we found the vicar garrulous, but his lodger strangely reticent, a sad-faced, introspective man, sitting with averted eyes, brooding apparently upon his own affairs.

These were the two men who entered abruptly into our little sitting-room on Tuesday, March the 16th, shortly after our breakfast hour, as we were smoking together, preparatory to our daily excursion upon the moors.

"Mr. Holmes," said the vicar, in an agitated voice, "the most extraordinary and tragic affair has occurred during the night. It is the most unheard-of business. We can only regard it as a special Providence that you should chance to be here at the time, for in all England you are the one man we need."

I glared at the intrusive vicar with no very friendly eyes; but Holmes toke his pipe from his lips and sat up in his chair like an old hound who hears the view-halloa. He waved his hand to the sofa, and our palpitating visitor with his agitated companion sat side by side upon it. Mr. Mortimer Tregennis was more self-contained than the clergyman, but the twitching of his thin hands and the brightness of his dark eyes showed that they shared a common emotion.

"Shall I speak or you?" he asked of the vicar.

"Well, as you seem to have made the discovery, whatever it may be, and the vicar to have had it second-hand, perhaps you had better do the speaking," said Holmes.

I glanced at the hastily-clad clergyman, with the formally-dressed lodger seated beside him, and was amused at the surprise which Holmes's simple deduction had brought to their faces.

"Perhaps I had best say a few words first," said the vicar, "and then you can judge if you will listen to the details from Mr. Tregennis, or whether we should not hasten at once to the scene of this mysterious affair. I may explain, then, that our friend here spent last evening in the company of his two brothers, Owen and George, and of his sister Brenda, at their house of Tredannick Wartha, which is near the old stone cross upon the moor. He left them shortly after ten o'clock, playing cards round the dining-room table, in excellent health and spirits. This morning, being an early riser, he walked in that direction before breakfast, and was overtaken by the carriage of Dr. Richards, who explained that he had just been sent for on a most urgent call to Tredannick Wartha. Mr. Mortimer Tregennis naturally went with him. When he arrived at Tredannick Wartha he found an extraordinary state of things. His two brothers and his sister were seated round the table exactly as he had left them, the cards still spread in front of them and the candles burned down to their sockets. The sister lay back stone-dead in her chair, while the two brothers sat on each side of her laughing, shouting, and singing, the senses stricken clean out of them. All three of them, the dead woman and the two demented men, retained upon their faces an expression of the utmost horror—a convulsion of terror which was dreadful to look upon. There was no sign of the presence of anyone in the house, except Mrs. Porter, the old cook and housekeeper, who declared that she had slept deeply and heard no sound during the night. Nothing had been stolen or disarranged, and there is absolutely no explanation of what the horror can be which has frightened a woman to death and two strong men out of their senses. There is the situation, Mr. Holmes, in a nutshell, and if you can help us to clear it up you will have done a great work."

I had hoped that in some way I could coax my companion back into the quiet which had been the object of our journey; but one glance at his intense face and contracted eyebrows told me how vain was now the expectation. He sat for some little time in silence, absorbed in the strange drama which had broken in upon our peace.

"I will look into this matter," he said at last. "On the face of it, it would appear to be a case of a very exceptional nature. Have you been there yourself, Mr. Roundhay?"

"No, Mr. Holmes. Mr. Tregennis brought back the account to the vicarage, and I at once hurried over with him to consult you."

"How far is it to the house where this singular tragedy occurred?"

THE ADVENTURE OF THE DEVIL'S FOOT

"About a mile inland."

"Then we shall walk over together. But, before we start, I must ask you a few questions, Mr. Mortimer Tregennis."

The other had been silent all this time, but I had observed that his more controlled excitement was even greater than the obtrusive emotion of the clergyman. He sat with a pale, drawn face, his anxious gaze fixed upon Holmes, and his thin hands clasped convulsively together. His pale lips quivered as he listened to the dreadful experience which had befallen his family, and his dark eyes seemed to reflect something of the horror of the scene.

"Ask what you like, Mr. Holmes," said he eagerly. "It is a bad thing to speak of, but I will answer you the truth."

"Tell me about last night."

"Well, Mr. Holmes, I supped there, as the vicar has said, and my elder brother George proposed a game of whist afterwards. We sat down about nine o'clock. It was a quarter-past ten when I moved to go. I left them all round the table, as merry as could be."

"Who let you out?"

"Mrs. Porter had gone to bed, so I let myself out. I shut the hall door behind me. The window of the room in which they sat was closed, but the blind was not drawn down. There was no change in door or window this morning, nor any reason to think that any stranger had been to the house. Yet there they sat, driven clean mad with terror, and Grenda lying dead of fright, with her head hanging over the arm of the chair. I'll never get the sight of that room out of my mind so long as I live."

"The facts, as you state them, are certainly most remarkable," said Holmes. "I take it that you have no theory yourself which can in any way account for them?"

"It's devilish, Mr. Holmes; devilish!" cried Mortimer Tregennis. "It is not of this world. Something has come into that room which has dashed the light of reason from their minds. What human contrivance could do that?"

"I fear," said Holmes, "that if the matter is beyond humanity it is certainly beyond me. Yet we must exhaust all natural explanations before we fall back upon such a theory as this. As to yourself, Mr. Tregennis, I take it you were divided in some way from your family, since they lived together and you had rooms apart?"

"That is so, Mr. Holmes, though the matter is past and done with. We were a family of tin-miners at Redruth, but we sold out our venture to a

THE ADVENTURE OF THE DEVIL'S FOOT

company, and so retired with enough to keep us. I won't deny that there was some feeling about the division of the money and it stood between us for a time, but it was all forgiven and forgotten, and we were the best of friends together."

"Looking back at the evening which you spent together, does anything stand out in your memory as throwing any possible light upon the tragedy? Think carefully, Mr. Tregennis, for any clue which can help me."

"There is nothing at all, sir."

"Your people were in their usual spirits?"

"Never better."

"Were they nervous people? Did they ever show any apprehension of coming danger?"

"Nothing of the kind."

"You have nothing to add then, which could assist me?"

Mortimer Tregennis considered earnestly for a moment.

"There is one thing occurs to me," said he at last. "As we sat at the table my back was to the window, and my brother George, he being my partner at cards, was facing it. I saw him once look hard over my shoulder, so I turned round and looked also. The blind was up and the window shut, but I could just make out the bushes on the lawn, and it seemed to me for a moment that I saw something moving among them. I couldn't even say if it were man or animal, but I just thought there was something there. When I asked him what he was looking at, he told me that he had the same feeling. That is all that I can say."

"Did you not investigate?"

"No; the matter passed as unimportant."

"You left them, then, without any premonition of evil?"

"None at all."

"I am not clear how you came to hear the news so early this morning."

"I am an early riser, and generally take a walk before breakfast. This morning I had hardly started when the doctor in his carriage overtook me. He told me that old Mrs. Porter had sent a boy down with an urgent message. I sprang in beside him and we drove on. When we got there we looked into that dreadful room. The candles and the fire must have burned out hours before, and they had been sitting there in the dark until dawn had broken. The doctor said Brenda must have been dead at least six hours. There were no signs of violence. She just lay across the arm of the chair with that look on her face. George and Owen were singing snatches of songs and gibbering like two great apes. Oh, it was awful

THE ADVENTURE OF THE DEVIL'S FOOT

to see! I couldn't stand it, and the doctor was as white as a sheet. Indeed, he fell into a chair in a sort of faint, and we nearly had him on our hands as well."

"Remarkable—most remarkable!" said Holmes, rising and taking his hat. "I think, perhaps, we had better go down to Tredannick Wartha without further delay. I confess that I have seldom known a case which at first sight presented a more singular problem."

Our proceedings of that first morning did little to advance the investigation. It was marked, however, at the outset by an incident which left the most sinister impression upon my mind. The approach to the spot at which the tragedy occurred is down a narrow, winding, country lane. While we made our way along it we heard the rattle of a carriage coming towards us, and stood aside to let it pass. As it drove by us I caught a glimpse through the closed window of a horribly contorted, grinning face glaring out at us. Those staring eyes and gnashing teeth flashed past us like a dreadful vision.

"My brothers!" cried Mortimer Tregennis, white to his lips. "They are taking them to Helston."

We looked with horror after the black carriage, lumbering upon its way. Then we turned our steps towards this ill-omened house in which they had met their strange fate.

It was a large and bright dwelling, rather a villa than a cottage, with a considerable garden which was already, in that Cornish air, well filled with spring flowers. Towards this garden the window of the sitting-room fronted, and from it, according to Mortimer Tregennis, must have come that thing of evil which had by sheer horror in a single instant blasted their minds. Holmes walked slowly and thoughtfully among the flower-plots and along the path before we entered the porch. So absorbed was he in his thoughts, I remember, that he stumbled over the watering-pot, upset its contents, and deluged both our feet and the garden path. Inside the house we were met by the elderly Cornish housekeeper, Mrs. Porter, who, with the aid of a young girl, looked after the wants of the family. She readily answered all Holmes's questions. She had heard nothing in the night. Her employers had all been in excellent spirits lately, and she had never known them more cheerful and prosperous. She had fainted with horror upon entering the room in the morning and seeing that dreadful company round the table. She had, when she recovered, thrown open the window to let the morning air in, and had run down to the lane, whence she sent a farm-lad for the doctor. The lady was on her bed upstairs, if we cared to see her. It took four strong men to get the brothers into the asylum carriage. She would not herself stay in the house another day, and was starting that very afternoon to rejoin her family at St. Ives.

We ascended the stairs and viewed the body. Miss Brenda Tregennis had been a very beautiful girl, though now verging upon middle age. Her dark, clear-cut face was handsome, even in death, but there still lingered upon it something of that convulsion of horror which had been her last human emotion. From her bedroom we descended to the sitting-room where this strange tragedy had actually occurred. The charred ashes of the overnight fire lay in the grate. On the table were the four guttered and burned-out candles, with the cards scattered over its surface. The chairs had been moved back against the walls, but all else was as it had been the night before. Holmes paced with light, swift steps about the room; he sat in the various chairs, drawing them up and reconstructing their positions. He tested how much of the garden was visible; he examined the floor, the ceiling, and the fireplace; but never once did I see that sudden brightening of his eyes and tightening of his lips which would have told me that he saw some gleam of light in this utter darkness.

"Why a fire?" he asked once. "Had they always a fire in this small room on a spring evening?"

Mortimer Tregennis explained that the night was cold and damp. For that reason, after his arrival, the fire was lit. "What are you going to do now, Mr. Holmes?" he asked.

My friend smiled and laid his hand upon my arm. "I think, Watson, that I shall resume that course of tobacco-poisoning which you have so often and so justly condemned," said he. "With your permission, gentlemen, we will now return to our cottage, for I am not aware that any new factor is likely to come to our notice here. I will turn the facts over in my mind, Mr. Tregennis, and should anything occur to me I will certainly communicate with you and the vicar. In the meantime I wish you both good morning."

It was not until long after we were back in Poldhu Cottage that Holmes broke his complete and absorbed silence. He sat coiled in his arm-chair, his haggard and ascetic face hardly visible amid the blue swirl of his tobacco smoke, his black brows drawn down, his forehead contracted, his eyes vacant and far away. Finally, he laid down his pipe and sprang to his feet.

"It won't do, Watson!" said he, with a laugh. "Let us walk along the cliffs together and search for flint

THE ADVENTURE OF THE DEVIL'S FOOT

arrows. We are more likely to find them than clues to this problem. To let the brain work without sufficient material is like racing an engine. It racks itself to pieces. The sea air, sunshine, and patience, Watson—all else will come.

"Now, let us calmly define our position, Watson," he continued, as we skirted the cliffs together. "Let us get a firm grip of the very little which we *do* know, so that when fresh facts arise we may be ready to fit them into their places. I take it, in the first place, that neither of us is prepared to admit diabolical intrusions into the affairs of men. Let us begin by ruling that entirely out of our minds. Very good. There remain three persons who have been grievously stricken by some conscious or unconscious human agency. That is firm ground. Now, when did this occur? Evidently, assuming his narrative to be true, it was immediately after Mr. Mortimer Tregennis had left the room. That is a very important point. The presumption is that it was within a few minutes afterwards. The cards still lay upon the table. It was already past their usual hour for bed. Yet they had not changed their position or pushed back their chairs. I repeat, then, that the occurrence was immediately after his departure, and not later than eleven o'clock last night.

"Our next obvious step is to check, so far as

we can, the movements of Mortimer Tregennis after he left the room. In this there is no difficulty, and they seem to be above suspicion. Knowing my methods as you do, you were, of course, conscious of the somewhat clumsy water-pot expedient by which I obtained a clearer impress of his foot than might otherwise have been possible. The wet, sandy path took it admirably. Last night was also wet, you will remember, and it was not difficult—having obtained a sample print—to pick out his track among others and to follow his movements. He appears to have walked away swiftly in the direction of the vicarage.

"If, then, Mortimer Tregennis disappeared from the scene, and yet some outside person affected the card-players, how can we reconstruct that person, and how was such an impression of horror conveyed? Mrs. Porter may be eliminated. She is evidently harmless. Is there any evidence that someone crept up to the garden window and in some manner produced so terrific an effect that he drove those who saw it out of their senses? The only suggestion in this direction comes from Mortimer Tregennis himself, who says that his brother spoke about some movement in the garden. That is certainly remarkable, as the night was rainy, cloudy, and dark. Anyone who had the design to alarm these people would be compelled to place his very face against the glass before he could be seen. There is a three-foot flower-border outside this window, but no indication of a footmark. It is difficult to imagine, then, how an outsider could have made so terrible an impression upon the company, nor have we found any possible motive for so strange and elaborate an attempt. You perceive our difficulties, Watson?"

"They are only too clear," I answered, with conviction.

"And yet, with a little more material, we may prove that they are not insurmountable," said Holmes. "I fancy that among your extensive archives, Watson, you may find some which were nearly as obscure. Meanwhile, we shall put the case aside until more accurate data are available, and devote the rest of our morning to the pursuit of neolithic man."

I may have commented upon my friend's power of mental detachment, but never have I wondered at it more than upon that spring morning in Cornwall when for two hours he discoursed upon celts, arrowheads, and shards, as lightly as if no sinister mystery was waiting for his solution. It was not until we had returned in the afternoon to our cottage that we found a visitor awaiting us, who soon brought our minds back to the matter in hand. Neither of us needed to be told who that visitor was. The huge body, the craggy and deeply-seamed face with the fierce eyes and hawk-like nose, the grizzled hair which nearly brushed our cottage ceiling, the beard—golden at the fringes and white near the lips, save for the nicotine stain from his perpetual cigar—all these were as well known in London as in Africa, and could only be associated with the tremendous personality of Dr. Leon Sterndale, the great lion-hunter and explorer.

We had heard of his presence in the district, and had once or twice caught sight of his tall figure upon the moorland paths. He made no advances to us, however, nor would we have dreamed of doing so to him, as it was well known that it was his love of seclusion which caused him to spend the greater part of the intervals between his journeys in a small bungalow buried in the lonely wood of Beauchamp Arriance. Here, amid his books and his maps, he lived an absolutely lonely life, attending to his own simple wants, and paying little apparent heed to the affairs of his neighbours. It was a surprise to me, therefore, to hear him asking Holmes in an eager voice, whether he had made any advance in his reconstruction of this mysterious episode. "The county police are utterly at fault," said he; "but perhaps your wider experience has suggested some

THE ADVENTURE OF THE DEVIL'S FOOT

conceivable explanation. My only claim to being taken into your confidence is that during my many residences here I have come to know this family of Tregennis very well—indeed, upon my Cornish mother's side I could call them cousins—and their strange fate has naturally been a great shock to me. I may tell you that I had got as far as Plymouth upon my way to Africa, but the news reached me this morning, and I came straight back again to help in the inquiry."

Holmes raised his eyebrows.

"Did you lose your boat through it?"

"I will take the next."

"Dear me! that is friendship indeed."

"I tell you they were relatives."

"Quite so—cousins of your mother. Was your baggage aboard the ship?"

"Some of it, but the main part at the hotel."

"I see. But surely this event could not have found its way into the Plymouth morning papers?"

"No, sir; I had a telegram."

"Might I ask from whom?"

A shadow passed over the gaunt face of the explorer.

"You are very inquisitive, Mr. Holmes."

"It is my business."

With an effort, Dr. Sterndale recovered his ruffled composure.

"I have no objection to telling you," he said. "It was Mr. Roundhay, the vicar, who sent me the telegram which recalled me."

"Thank you," said Holmes. "I may say in answer to your original question, that I have not cleared my mind entirely on the subject of this case, but that I have every hope of reaching some conclusion. It would be premature to say more."

"Perhaps you would not mind telling me if your suspicions point in any particular direction?"

"No, I can hardly answer that."

"Then I have wasted my time, and need not prolong my visit." The famous doctor strode out of our cottage in considerable ill-humour, and within five minutes Holmes had followed him. I saw him no more until the evening, when he returned with a slow step and haggard face which assured me that he had made no great progress with his investigation. He glanced at a telegram which awaited him, and threw it into the grate.

"From the Plymouth hotel, Watson," he said. "I learned the name of it from the vicar, and I wired to make certain that Dr. Leon Sterndale's account was true. It appears that he did indeed spend last night there, and that he has actually allowed some of his

THE ADVENTURE OF THE DEVIL'S FOOT

baggage to go on to Africa, while he returned to be present at this investigation. What do you make of that, Watson?"

"He is deeply interested."

"Deeply interested—yes. There is a thread here which we have not yet grasped, and which might lead us through the tangle. Cheer up, Watson, for I am very sure that our material has not yet all come to hand. When it does, we may soon leave our difficulties behind us."

Little did I think how soon the words of Holmes would be realised, or how strange and sinister would be that new development which opened up an entirely fresh line of investigation. I was shaving at my window in the morning when I heard the rattle of hoofs, and, looking up, saw a dogcart coming at a gallop down the road. It pulled up at our door, and our friend the vicar sprang from it and rushed up our garden path. Holmes was already dressed, and we hastened down to meet him.

Our visitor was so excited that he could hardly articulate, but at last in gasps and bursts his tragic story came out of him.

"We are devil-ridden, Mr. Holmes! My poor parish is devil-ridden!" he cried. "Satan himself is loose in it! We are given over into his hands!" He danced about in his agitation, a ludicrous object if it were not for his ashy face and startled eyes. Finally he shot out his terrible news.

"Mr. Mortimer Tregennis died during the night, and with exactly the same symptoms as the rest of his family."

Holmes sprang to his feet, all energy in an instant.

"Can you fit us both into your dogcart?"

"Yes, I can."

"Then, Watson, we will postpone our breakfast. Mr. Roundhay, we are entirely at your disposal. Hurry—hurry, before things get disarranged."

The lodger occupied two rooms at the vicarage, which were in an angle by themselves, the one above the other. Below was a large sitting-room; above, his bedroom. They looked out upon a croquet lawn which came up to the windows. We had arrived before the doctor or the police, so that everything was absolutely undisturbed. Let me describe exactly the scene as we saw it upon that misty March morning. It has left an impression which can never be effaced from my mind.

The atmosphere of the room was of a horrible and depressing stuffiness. The servant who had first entered had thrown up the window, or it would have been even more intolerable. This might partly be due to the fact that a lamp stood flaring and smoking on the centre table. Beside it sat the dead man, leaning back in his chair, his thin beard projecting, his spectacles pushed up on to his forehead, and his lean, dark face turned towards the window and twisted into the same distortion of terror which had marked the features of his dead sister. His limbs were convulsed and his fingers contorted as though he had died in a very paroxysm of fear. He was fully clothed, though there were signs that his dressing had been done in a hurry. We had already learned that his bed had been slept in, and that the tragic end had come to him in the early morning.

One realised the red-hot energy which underlay Holmes's phlegmatic exterior when one saw the sudden change which came over him from the moment that he entered the fatal apartment. In an instant he was tense and alert, his eyes shining, his face set, his limbs quivering with eager activity. He was out on the lawn, in through the window, round the room, and up into the bedroom, for all the world like a dashing foxhound drawing a cover. In the bedroom he made a rapid cast around, and ended by throwing open the window, which appeared to give him some fresh cause for excitement, for he leaned out of it with loud ejaculations of interest and delight. Then he rushed down the stair, out through the open window, threw himself upon his face on the lawn, sprang up and into the room once more, all with the energy of the hunter who is at the very heels of his quarry. The lamp, which was an ordinary standard, he examined with minute care, making certain measurements upon its bowl. He carefully scrutinised with his lens the talc shield which covered the top of the chimney, and scraped off some ashes which adhered to its upper surface, putting some of them into an envelope, which he placed in his pocket-book. Finally, just as the doctor and the official police put in an appearance, he beckoned to the vicar and we all three went out upon the lawn.

"I am glad to say that my investigation has not been entirely barren," he remarked. "I cannot remain to discuss the matter with the police, but I should be exceedingly obliged, Mr. Roundhay, if you would give the inspector my compliments and direct his attention to the bedroom window and to the sitting-room lamp. Each is suggestive, and together they are almost conclusive. If the police would desire further information I shall be happy to see any of them at the cottage. And now, Watson, I think that, perhaps, we shall be better employed elsewhere."

It may be that the police resented the intrusion of an amateur, or that they imagined themselves to be upon some hopeful line of investigation; but it is certain that we heard nothing from them for the next two days. During this time Holmes spent some of his time smoking and dreaming in the cottage; but a greater portion in country walks which he undertook alone, returning after many hours without remark as to where he had been. One experiment served to show me the line of his investigation. He had bought a lamp which was the duplicate of the one which had burned in the room of Mortimer Tregennis on the morning of the tragedy. This he filled with the same oil as that used at the vicarage, and he carefully timed the period which it would take to be exhausted. Another experiment which he made was of a more unpleasant nature, and one which I am not likely ever to forget.

"You will remember, Watson," he remarked one afternoon, "that there is a single common point of resemblance in the varying reports which have reached us. This concerns the effect of the atmosphere of the room in each case upon those who had first entered it. You will recollect that Mortimer Tregennis, in describing the episode of his last visit to his brother's house, remarked that the doctor on entering the room fell into a chair? You had forgotten? Well, I can answer for it that it was so. Now, you will remember also that Mrs. Porter, the housekeeper, told us that she herself fainted upon entering the room and had afterwards opened the window. In the second case—that of Mortimer Tregennis himself—you cannot have forgotten the horrible stuffiness of the room when we arrived, though the servant had thrown open the window. That servant, I found upon inquiry, was so ill that she had gone to her bed. You will admit, Watson, that these facts are very suggestive. In each case there is evidence of a poisonous atmosphere. In each case, also, there is combustion going on in the room—in the one case a fire, in the other a lamp. The fire was needed, but the lamp was lit—as a comparison of the oil consumed will show—long after it was broad daylight. Why? Surely because there is some connection between three things—the burning, the stuffy atmosphere, and, finally, the madness or death of those unfortunate people. That is clear, is it not?"

"It would appear so."

"At least we may accept it as a working hypothesis. We will suppose, then, that something was burned in each case which produced an atmosphere causing strange toxic effects. Very good. In the first instance—that of the Tregennis family—this substance was placed in the fire. Now the window was shut, but the fire would naturally carry fumes to some extent up the chimney. Hence one would expect the effects of the poison to be less than in the second case, where there was less escape for the vapour. The result seems to indicate that it was so, since in the first case only the woman, who had presumably the more sensitive organism, was killed, the others exhibiting that temporary or permanent lunacy which is evidently the first effect of the drug. In the second case the result was complete. The facts, therefore, seem to bear out the theory of a poison which worked by combustion.

"With this train of reasoning in my head I naturally looked about in Mortimer Tregennis's room to find some remains of this substance. The obvious place to look was the talc shield or smoke-guard of the lamp. There, sure enough, I perceived a number of flaky ashes, and round the edges a fringe of brownish powder, which had not yet been consumed. Half of this I took, as you saw, and I placed it in an envelope."

"Why half, Holmes?"

"It is not for me, my dear Watson, to stand in the way of the official police force. I leave them all the evidence which I found. The poison still remained upon the talc, had they the wit to find it. Now, Watson, we will light our lamp; we will, however, take the precaution to open our window to avoid the premature decease of two deserving members of society, and you will seat yourself near that open window in an arm-chair, unless, like a sensible man, you determine to have nothing to do with the affair. Oh, you will see it out, will you? I thought I knew my Watson. This chair I will place opposite yours, so that we may be the same distance from the poison, and face to face. The door we will leave ajar. Each is now in a position to watch the other and to bring the experiment to an end should the symptoms seem alarming. Is that all clear? Well, then, I take our powder—or what remains of it—from the envelope, and I lay it above the burning lamp. So! Now, Watson, let us sit down and await developments."

They were not long in coming. I had hardly settled in my chair before I was conscious of a thick, musky odour, subtle and nauseous. At the very first whiff of it my brain and my imagination were beyond all control. A thick, black cloud swirled before my eyes, and my mind told me that in this cloud, unseen as yet, but about to spring out upon my appalled senses, lurked all that was vaguely horrible, all that was monstrous and inconceivably wicked in the universe. Vague shapes swirled and swam amid the dark cloudbank, each a menace and a warning of something coming, the advent of some unspeakable dweller upon the threshold, whose very shadow would blast my soul. A freezing horror took possession of me. I felt that my hair was rising, that my eyes were protruding, that my mouth was opened, and my tongue like leather. The turmoil within my brain was such that something must surely snap. I tried to scream, and was vaguely aware of some hoarse croak which was my own voice, but distant and detached from myself. At the same moment, in some effort of escape, I broke through that cloud of despair, and had a glimpse of Holmes's face, white, rigid, and drawn with horror—the very look which I had seen upon the features of the dead. It was that vision which gave me an instant of sanity and of strength. I dashed from my chair, threw my arms round Holmes, and together we lurched through the door, and an instant afterwards had thrown ourselves down upon the grass plot and were lying side by side, conscious only of the glorious sunshine which was bursting its way through the hellish cloud of terror which had girt us in. Slowly it rose from our souls like the mists from a landscape, until peace and reason had returned, and we were sitting upon the grass, wiping our clammy foreheads, and looking with apprehension at each other to mark the last traces of that terrific experience which we had undergone.

"Upon my word, Watson!" said Holmes at last,

with an unsteady voice, "I owe you both my thanks and an apology. It was an unjustifiable experiment even for oneself, and doubly so for a friend. I am really very sorry."

"You know," I answered, with some emotion, for I had never seen so much of Holmes's heart before, "that it is my greatest joy and privilege to help you."

He relapsed at once into the half-humorous, half-cynical vein which was his habitual attitude to those about him. "It would be superfluous to drive us mad, my dear Watson," said he. "A candid observer would certainly declare that we were so already before we embarked upon so wild an experiment. I confess that I never imagined that the effect could be so sudden and so severe." He dashed into the cottage, and reappearing with the burning lamp held at full arm's length, he threw it among a bank of brambles. "We must give the room a little time to clear. I take it, Watson, that you have no longer a shadow of a doubt as to how these tragedies were produced?"

"None whatever."

"But the cause remains as obscure as before. Come into the arbour here and let us discuss it together. That villainous stuff seems still to linger round my throat. I think we must admit that all the evidence points to this man, Mortimer Tregennis, having been the criminal in the first tragedy, though he was the victim in the second one. We must remember, in the first place, that there is some story of a family quarrel, followed by a reconciliation. How bitter that quarrel may have been, or how hollow the reconciliation we cannot tell. When I think of Mortimer Tregennis, with the foxy face and the small shrewd, beady eyes, behind the spectacles, he is not a man whom I should judge to be of a particularly forgiving disposition. Well, in the next place, you will remember that this idea of someone moving in the garden, which took our attention for a moment from the real cause of the tragedy, emanated from him. He had a motive in misleading us. Finally, if he did not throw this substance into the fire at the moment of leaving the room, who did do so? The affair happened immediately after his departure. Had anyone else come in, the family would certainly have risen from the table. Besides, in peaceful Cornwall, visitors do not arrive after ten o'clock at night. We may take it, then, that all the evidence points to Mortimer Tregennis as the culprit."

"Then his own death was suicide!"

"Well, Watson, it is on the face of it a not impossible supposition. The man who had the guilt upon his soul of having brought such a fate upon his own family might well be driven by remorse to inflict it upon himself. There are, however, some cogent reasons against it. Fortunately, there is one man in England who knows all about it, and I have made arrangements by which we shall hear the facts this afternoon from his own lips. Ah! he is a little before his time. Perhaps you would kindly step this way, Dr. Leon Sterndale. We have been conducting a chemical experiment indoors which has left our little room hardly fit for the reception of so distinguished a visitor."

I had heard the click of the garden gate, and now the majestic figure of the great African explorer appeared upon the path. He turned in some surprise towards the rustic arbour in which we sat.

"You sent for me, Mr. Holmes. I had your note about an hour ago, and I have come, though I really do not know why I should obey your summons."

"Perhaps we can clear the point up before we separate," said Holmes. "Meanwhile, I am much obliged to you for your courteous acquiescence. You will excuse this informal reception in the open air, but my friend Watson and I have nearly furnished an additional chapter to what the papers call the Cornish Horror, and we prefer a clear atmosphere for the present. Perhaps, since the matters which we have to discuss will affect you personally in a very intimate

THE ADVENTURE OF THE DEVIL'S FOOT

fashion, it is as well that we should talk where there can be no eavesdropping."

The explorer took his cigar from his lips and gazed sternly at my companion.

"I am at a loss to know, sir," he said, "what you can have to speak about which affects me personally in a very intimate fashion."

"The killing of Mortimer Tregennis," said Holmes.

For a moment I wished that I were armed. Sterndale's fierce face turned to a dusky red, his eyes glared, and the knotted, passionate veins started out in his forehead, while he sprang forward with clenched hands towards my companion. Then he stopped, and with a violent effort he resumed a cold, rigid calmness, which was, perhaps, more suggestive of danger than his hot-headed out-burst.

"I have lived so long among savages and beyond the law," said he, "that I have got into the way of being a law to myself. You would do well, Mr. Holmes, not to forget it, for I have no desire to do you an injury."

"Nor have I any desire to do you an injury, Dr. Sterndale. Surely the clearest proof of it is that, knowing what I know, I have sent for you and not for the police."

Sterndale sat down with a gasp, overawed for,

perhaps, the first time in his adventurous life. There was a calm assurance of power in Holmes's manner which could not be withstood. Our visitor stammered for a moment, his great hands opening and shutting in his agitation.

"What do you mean?" he asked, at last. "If this is bluff upon your part, Mr. Holmes, you have chosen a bad man for your experiment. Let us have no more beating about the bush. What *do* you mean?"

"I will tell you," said Holmes, "and the reason why I tell you is that I hope frankness may beget frankness. What my next step may be will depend entirely upon the nature of your own defence."

"My defence?"

"Yes, sir."

"My defence against what?"

"Against the charge of killing Mortimer Tregennis."

Sterndale mopped his forehead with his handkerchief. "Upon my word, you are getting on," said he. "Do all your successes depend upon this prodigious power of bluff?"

"The bluff," said Holmes, sternly, "is upon your side, Dr. Leon Sterndale, and not upon mine. As a proof I will tell you some of the facts upon which my conclusions are based. Of your return from Plymouth, allowing much of your property to go on to Africa, I will say nothing save that it first informed me that you were one of the factors which had to be taken into account in reconstructing this drama—"

"I came back—"

"I have heard your reasons and regard them as unconvincing and inadequate. We will pass that. You came down here to ask me whom I suspected. I refused to answer you. You then went to the vicarage, waited outside it for some time, and finally returned to your cottage."

"How do you know that?"

"I followed you."

"I saw no one."

"That is what you may expect to see when I follow you. You spent a restless night at your cottage, and you formed certain plans, which in the early morning you proceeded to put into execution. Leaving your door just as day was breaking, you filled your pocket with some reddish gravel that was lying heaped beside your gate."

Sterndale gave a violent start and looked at Holmes in amazement.

"You then walked swiftly for the mile which separated you from the vicarage. You were wearing, I may remark, the same pair of ribbed tennis shoes which are at the present moment upon your feet. At the vicarage you passed through the orchard and the side hedge, coming out under the window of the lodger Tregennis. It was now daylight, but the household was not yet stirring. You drew some of the gravel from your pocket, and you threw it up at the window above you."

Sterndale sprang to his feet.

"I believe that you are the devil himself!" he cried.

Holmes smiled at the compliment. "It took two, or possibly three, handfuls before the lodger came to the window. You beckoned him to come down. He dressed hurriedly and descended to his sitting-room. You entered by the window. There was an interview—a short one—during which you walked up and down the room. Then you passed out and closed the window, standing on the lawn outside smoking a cigar and watching what occurred. Finally, after the death of Tregennis, you withdrew as you had come. Now, Dr. Sterndale, how do you justify such conduct, and what were the motives for your actions? If you prevaricate or trifle with me, I give you my assurance that the matter will pass out of my hands for ever."

Our visitor's face had turned ashen grey as he listened to the words of his accuser. Now he sat for some time in thought with his face sunk in his hands. Then with a sudden impulsive gesture he plucked a photograph from his breast-pocket and threw it on the rustic table before us.

"That is why I have done it," said he.

It showed the bust and face of a very beautiful woman. Holmes stooped over it.

"Brenda Tregennis," said he.

"Yes, Brenda Tregennis," repeated our visitor. "For years I have loved her. For years she has loved me. There is the secret of that Cornish seclusion which people have marvelled at. It has brought me close to the one thing on earth that was dear to me. I could not marry her, for I have a wife who has left me for years and yet whom, by the deplorable laws of England, I could not divorce. For years Brenda waited. For years I waited. And this is what we have waited for." A terrible sob shook his great frame, and he clutched his throat under his brindled beard. Then with an effort he mastered himself and spoke on.

"The vicar knew. He was in our confidence. He would tell you that she was an angel upon earth. That was why he telegraphed to me and I returned. What was my baggage or Africa to me when I learned that such a fate had come upon my darling? There you have the missing clue to my action, Mr. Holmes."

"Proceed," said my friend.

Dr. Sterndale drew from his pocket a paper packet and laid it upon the table. On the outside was written, "*Radix pedis diaboli*" with a red poison label beneath it. He pushed it towards me. "I understand that you are a doctor, sir. Have you ever heard of this preparation?"

"Devil's-foot root! No, I have never heard of it."

"It is no reflection upon your professional knowledge," said he, "for I believe that, save for one sample in a laboratory at Buda, there is no other specimen in Europe. It has not yet found its way either into the pharmacopœia or into the literature of toxicology. The root is shaped like a foot, half human, half goatlike; hence the fanciful name given by a botanical missionary. It is used as an ordeal poison by the medicine-men in certain districts of West Africa, and is kept as a secret among them. This particular specimen I obtained under very extraordinary circumstances in the Ubanghi country." He opened the paper as he spoke, and disclosed a heap of reddish-brown, snuff-like powder.

"Well, sir?" asked Holmes sternly.

"I am about to tell you, Mr. Holmes, all that actually occurred, for you already know so much that it is clearly to my interest that you should know all. I have already explained the relationship in which I stood to the Tregennis family. For the sake of the sister I was friendly with the brothers. There was a family quarrel about money which estranged this man Mortimer, but it was supposed to be made up, and I afterwards met him as I did the others. He was a sly, subtle, scheming man, and several things arose which gave me a suspicion of him, but I had no cause for any positive quarrel.

"One day, only a couple of weeks ago, he came down to my cottage and I showed him some of my African curiosities. Among other things I exhibited this powder, and I told him of its strange properties, how it stimulates those brain centres which control the emotion of fear, and how either madness or death is the fate of the unhappy native who is subjected to the ordeal by the priest of his tribe. I told him also how powerless European science would be to detect it. How he took it I cannot say, for I never left the room, but there is no doubt that it was then, while I was opening cabinets and stooping to boxes, that he managed to abstract some of the devil's-foot root. I well remember how he plied me with questions as to the amount and the time that was needed for its effect, but I little dreamed that he could have a personal reason for asking.

"I thought no more of the matter until the vicar's telegram reached me at Plymouth. This villain had thought that I would be at sea before the news could reach me, and that I should be lost for years in Africa. But I returned at once. Of course, I could not listen to the details without feeling assured that my poison had been used. I came round to see you on the chance that some other explanation had suggested itself to you. But there could be none. I was convinced that Mortimer Tregennis was the murderer; that for the sake of money, and with the idea, perhaps, that if the other members of his family were all insane he would be the sole guardian of their joint property, he had used the devil's-foot powder upon them, driven two of them out of their senses, and killed his sister Brenda, the one human being whom I have ever loved or who has ever loved me. There was his crime; what was to be his punishment?

"Should I appeal to the law? Where were my proofs? I knew that the facts were true, but could I help to make a jury of countrymen believe so fantastic a story? I might or I might not. But I could not afford to fail. My soul cried out for revenge. I have said to you once before, Mr. Holmes, that I have spent much of my life outside the law, and that I have come at last to be a law to myself. So it was now. I determined that the fate which he had given to others should be shared by himself. Either that or I would do justice upon him with my own hand. In all England there can be no man who sets less value upon his own life than I do at the present moment.

"Now I have told you all. You have yourself supplied the rest. I did, as you say, after a restless night, set off early from my cottage. I foresaw the difficulty of arousing him, so I gathered some gravel from the pile which you have mentioned, and I used it to throw up to his window. He came down and admitted me through the window of the sitting-room. I laid his offence before him. I told him that I had come both as judge and executioner. The wretch sank into a chair paralysed at the sight of my revolver. I lit the lamp, put the powder above it, and stood outside the window, ready to carry out my threat to shoot him should he try to leave the room. In five minutes he died. My God! how he died! But my heart was flint, for he endured nothing which my innocent darling had not felt before him. There is my story, Mr. Holmes. Perhaps, if you loved a woman, you would have done as much yourself. At any rate, I am in your hands. You can take what steps you like. As I have already said, there is no man living who can fear death less than I do."

Holmes sat for some little time in silence.

"What were your plans?" he asked, at last.

"I had intended to bury myself in Central Africa. My work there is but half finished."

"Go and do the other half," said Holmes. "I, at least, am not prepared to prevent you."

Dr. Sterndale raised his giant figure, bowed gravely, and walked from the arbour. Holmes lit his pipe and handed me his pouch.

"Some fumes which are not poisonous would be a welcome change," said he. "I think you must agree, Watson, that it is not a case in which we are called upon to interfere. Our investigation has been independent, and our action shall be so also. You would not denounce the man?"

"Certainly not," I answered.

"I have never loved, Watson, but if I did and if the woman I loved had met such an end, I might act even as our lawless lion-hunter has done. Who knows? Well, Watson, I will not offend your intelligence by explaining what is obvious. The gravel upon the window-sill was, of course, the starting-point of my research. It was unlike anything in the vicarage garden. Only when my attention had been drawn to Dr. Sterndale and his cottage did I find its counterpart. The lamp shining in broad daylight and the remains of powder upon the shield were successive links in a fairly obvious chain. And now, my dear Watson, I think we may dismiss the matter from our mind, and go back with a clear conscience to the study of those Chaldean roots which are surely to be traced in the Cornish branch of the great Celtic speech."

Edward Thomas

The Flower-Gatherer

'Herself a fairer flower.' – MILTON

So strong was the young beauty of the year, it might have seemed at its height were it not that each day it grew stronger. The new day excelled the one that was past, only to be outshone by the next. Day after day the sun poured out a great light and heat and joy over the earth and the delicately clouded sky. The south wind flowed in a river straight from the sun itself, and divided the fresh leaves with never-ceasing noise of amorous and joyful motion. So mighty was the sun that the miles of pale new foliage shimmered mistily like snow, yet each leaf was cool and moist with youth, and the voices of the birds creeping and fluttering among the branches were as the souls of that coolness and moistness and youth. If one moment the myriad forms of life and happiness intoxicated the delighted senses, at another a glimpse of the broad mild land stretched out below, and of the sun ruling it in the blue above, gave also a calm and a celestial dignity and simplicity to the whole. One after another the pools, the rivers and rivulets, the windows or glass roofs of the vale, caught the sun and sparkled as if Vega and Gemma and Arcturus and Sirius and Aldebaran and Algol had fallen among the meadows and woods.

On some days the sense of oneness, of wide power and splendour uniting earth and sky, of infinite simplicity, triumphed. On others the spirit was content to bathe and half lose itself in numbers, exuberance, complexity, in the odours and colours and forms, one by one, in the rich rising flood of the grass, in the hurrying to and fro of preparation that was nevertheless not over much troubled about the end.

The children seemed to be trying to gather all the flowers. It was their way of striving to grasp the infinite. They were scattered over the hillside, where the pale sward was made an airy or liquid substance by the innumerable cowslips nodding upon its surface, as upon a lake, that held their small shadows each quite clear. All day they gathered flowers, and threw them away, and gathered more, and still there were no less. The earth continued to murmur with blissful ease, as if, like the wandering humble bee, it were drowsed with the warmth and the abundance.

THE FLOWER-GATHERER

One child separated herself from the rest, moving down instead of across or up the hill. Often she went on her knees among the flowers, with bent eyes that saw only the hundreds close at hand. But from time to time she raised her head, her delicately browned and yet more rosy face, her gleamy hair, that was as pale as barley on her temples but elsewhere golden brown as wheat, her round and calm yet lively eyes, her restless happy lips – and looked steadily for a moment at the whole of earth and sky, and grew solemn, only to return to the other pleasure of the hundred cowslips just at her feet, the crystal and emerald wings among them, the pearly snails, the daisies and the chips of chalk like daisies. Tighter grew her hand round the swelling bunch. She slipped; the flowers fell and not all were picked up again; and so there was yet room for bluebells when she reached the wood below. In the moister fields still lower there were kingcups of gold and cuckoo flowers pink and white, looking as if they had fluttered down from the sky; and for these also a place had to be found. The stitchworts of a hedge side lured and piloted her to the hollow hardly larger than a great hall, where a brook ran straight, for once in its life.

By the slow stream forget-me-nots made a continuous haze on either bank. She was now quite alone, under the old cherry tree of the forsaken garden at the water's edge. Six or eight huge crooked branches rising out of the rocky trunk bore up a dome that was all flowers. They were in rounded clusters as of bubbling snow, and close as honeycomb. The lovely freckled white smelt bitter and sweet at once. The flowers hummed with bees, and between the clusters were streaks and wedges of the blue. The child looked up suddenly at this glorious roof, and her smile of surprise passed into what would have been indifference, because the blossoms were inaccessible, if she had not caught sight of the forget-me-nots when the flight of a cuckoo that had been calling out of the cherry-tree carried her eyes away to where he skimmed the water. He did not fly far, nor cease to call while he was flying, or when he was seated on one of the alders by the brook. She looked at him as she was plucking the forget-me-nots. This narrow hollow was his room, she thought. Yet it was full of other songs. There were blackbirds hidden in the hazels, or clearly defined against the may flower or the bronzed flowering oaks. Thrushes talked and called out to her a hundred times: 'Did she do it? Did she do it? Did she? Did she? She did, she did!' and she laughed. A swallow flew over his image in the water as if about to dive in after it, and then rose up and curved away. Smaller

THE FLOWER-GATHERER

unfamiliar birds sang rillets and minute cascades of hurrying song. The gold-crest repeated a tune like the unwinding of a tiny sweetly-creaking winch, like the well-winch at home. But the lazy cuckoo was lord of all.

Now she had filled both hands, and each time she grasped a new stalk some of the old fell out. So presently she laid them down in the grass to rearrange them. But she now noticed the tall sedges of the brook and wanted some. She looked round to see if anyone could see her doing this forbidden thing, and then went to the edge and stretched out her hand: they were too far. The water was gliding under her, flashing like brandished steel, and yet as clear as air over the green stars of its bed. Everything had always been kind to her, and this water was one of the kindest, so playful and bright, so pure that sometimes they came far to fetch some of it in a pail for the house. She leaned out, and even moved one foot as if to step towards the green sedge. She lost her footing and fell, not quite reaching the blades as she splashed. She was scolded for getting wet, but never much, and she used to laugh as they were dressing her in fresh clothes; and to-day it was so warm . . . It was an adventure. But her hair was all wet; she did not like that: and the water, though so pure, was not pleasant in mouth, nostrils, eyes, and ears, nor could she get rid of it. Her hands touched the green stars; she could see them; but the sky was gone. She was surprised, indignant, anxious to be out. Why this cruelty? It was not a game to go on like this. She was angry . . . terrified . . . numbed. She could see nothing but water, she heard, smelt, breathed, tasted, touched water everywhere. Who could have done it? Something is cruel! . . . Why? . . . She could not bear it. No! No! Where were her flowers? Where was her mother?

She rose up a little, and saw the sun, and the cuckoo on the branch through the waves, and heard the man calling to his horses in the next field. Then solitude: all pleasure gone, love, light, warmth, movement was nothing, was over there, was past, or never had been, would never be again. It was better now. Sleep, sleep. But in the sleep, songs, visions of the house, forms and faces moving to and fro, and herself going in and out amongst them, far away, long ago, over there, in that other place. She was hurrying faster and faster, running too fast for her legs, carried away off them into the air, but swaying and rising easily and more easily now. She sighed as she seemed to float higher and lighter into soft darkness, into utter darkness, into nothing at all, where there was never anything or will be anything. The mud settled down. The stream flowed clear and sweet. The sun had not so much to do but that he could wilt the flowers lying on the bank. Life went on exuberant, joyous, august, looking neither to the right nor to the left. The cuckoo called. The birds' songs became so drowsy that they were not missed when they ceased, and only its own echo replied to the cuckoo. The child's white forehead was just above the water, and a fly perched on it and preened his diamond wings. A quarter of a mile away the dinner bell at home was swung merrily again and again by a strong arm that enjoyed the task.

A. A. Milne

A Summer Cold

When I am not feeling very well I go to Beatrice for sympathy and advice. Anyhow, I get the advice.

'I think,' I said carelessly, wishing to break it to her as gently as possible, 'I think I have hay-fever.'

'Nonsense,' said Beatrice.

That annoyed me. Why shouldn't I have hay-fever if I wanted to?

'If you're going to begrudge me every little thing,' I began.

'You haven't even got a cold.'

As luck would have it, a sneeze chose that moment for its arrival.

'There!' I said triumphantly.

'Why, my dear boy, if you had hay-fever you'd be sneezing all day.'

'That was only a sample. There are lots more where that came from.'

'Don't be so silly. Fancy starting hay-fever in September.'

'I'm not starting it. I am, I earnestly hope, just

finishing it. If you want to know, I've had a cold all the summer.'

'Well, I haven't noticed it.'

'That's because I'm such a good actor. I've been playing the part of a man who hasn't had a cold all the summer. My performance is considered to be most life-like.'

Beatrice disdained to answer, and by and by I sneezed again.

'You certainly have a cold,' she said, putting down her work.

'Come, this is something.'

'You must be careful. How did you catch it?'

'I didn't catch it. It caught me.'

'Last week-end?'

'No, last May.'

Beatrice picked up her work again impatiently. I sneezed a third time.

'Is this more the sort of thing you want?' I said.

'What I say is that you couldn't have had hay-fever all the summer without people knowing.'

'But, my dear Beatrice, people do know. In this quiet little suburb you are rather out of the way of the busy world. Rumours of war, depressions on the Stock Exchange, my hay-fever—these things pass you by. But the clubs are full of it. I assure you that, all over the country, England's stately homes have been plunged into mourning by the news of my sufferings, historic piles have bowed their heads and wept.'

'I suppose you mean that in every house you've been to this summer you've told them that you had it, and they've been foolish enough to believe you.'

'That's putting it a little crudely. What happens is—'

'Well, all I can say is, you know a very silly lot of people.'

'What happens is that when the mahogany has been cleared of its polished silver and choice napery, and wine of a rare old vintage is circulating from hand to hand—'

'If they wanted to take any notice of you at all, they could have given you a bread-poultice and sent you to bed.'

'Then, as we impatiently bite the ends off our priceless Havanas—'

'They might know that you couldn't possibly have hay-fever.'

I sat up suddenly and spoke to Beatrice.

'Why on earth *shouldn't* I have hay-fever?' I demanded. 'Have you any idea what hay-fever is? I suppose you think I ought to be running about wildly trying to eat hay—or yapping and showing an unaccountable aversion from dried grass? I take it that there are grades of hay-fever, as there are of everything else. I have it at present in a mild form. Instead of being thankful that it is no worse, you—'

'My dear boy, hay-fever is a thing people have all their lives, and it comes on every summer. You've never even pretended to have it before this year.'

'Yes, but you must start *some* time. I'm a little backward, perhaps. Just because there are a few infant prodigies about, don't despise me. In a year or two I shall be as regular as the rest of them.' And I sneezed again.

Beatrice got up with an air of decision and left the room. For a moment I thought she was angry and had gone for a policeman, but as the minutes went by and she didn't return I began to fear that she might have left the house for good. I was wondering how I should break the news to her husband when, to my relief, she came in again.

'You may be right,' she said, putting down a small package and unpinning her hat. 'Try this. The chemist says it's the best hay-fever cure there is.'

'It's in a lot of languages,' I said as I took the wrapper off. 'I suppose German hay is the same as any other sort of hay? Oh, here it is in English. I say, this is a what-d'you-call-it cure.'

'So the man said.'

'Homœopathic. It's made from the pollen that

causes hay-fever. Yes. Ah, yes.' I coughed slightly, and looked at Beatrice out of the corner of my eye. 'I suppose', I said carelessly, 'if anybody took this who *hadn't* got hay-fever, the results might be rather—I mean that he might then find that he—in fact—er—*had* got it.'

'Sure to,' said Beatrice.

'Yes. That makes us a little thoughtful; we don't want to overdo this thing.' I went on reading the instructions. 'You know, it's rather odd about my hay-fever—it's generally worse in town than in the country.'

'But then you started so late, dear. You haven't really got into the swing of it yet.'

'Yes, but still—you know, I have my doubts about the gentleman who invented this. We don't see eye to eye in this matter. Beatrice, you may be right—perhaps I haven't got hay-fever.'

'Oh, don't give up.'

'But all the same, I know I've got something. It's a funny thing about my being worse in town than in the country. That looks rather as if—By Jove, I know what it is—I've got just the opposite of hay-fever.'

'What is the opposite of hay?'

'Why, bricks and things.'

I gave a last sneeze and began to wrap up the cure.

'Take this pollen stuff back', I said to Beatrice, 'and ask the man if he's got anything homœopathic made from paving-stones. Because, you know, that's what I really want.'

'You *have* got a cold,' said Beatrice.

Thomas Hardy

An Imaginative Woman

When William Marchmill had finished his inquiries for lodgings at a well-known watering-place in Upper Wessex, he returned to the hotel to find his wife. She, with the children, had rambled along the shore, and Marchmill followed in the direction indicated by the military-looking hall-porter.

'By Jove, how far you've gone! I am quite out of breath,' Marchmill said, rather impatiently, when he came up with his wife, who was reading as she walked, the three children being considerably further ahead with the nurse.

Mrs. Marchmill started out of the reverie into which the book had thrown her. 'Yes,' she said, 'you've been such a long time. I was tired of staying in that dreary hotel. But I am sorry if you have wanted me, Will?'

'Well, I have had trouble to suit myself. When you see the airy and comfortable rooms heard of, you find they are stuffy and uncomfortable. Will you come and see if what I've fixed on will do? There is not much room, I am afraid; but I can light on nothing better. The town is rather full.'

The pair left the children and nurse to continue their ramble, and went back together.

In age well-balanced, in personal appearance fairly matched, and in domestic requirements conformable, in temper this couple differed, though even here they did not often clash, he being equable, if not lymphatic, and she decidedly nervous and sanguine. It was to their tastes and fancies, those smallest, greatest particulars, that no common denominator could be applied. Marchmill considered his wife's likes and inclinations somewhat silly; she considered his sordid and material. The husband's business was that of a gunmaker in a thriving city northwards, and his soul was in that business always; the lady was best characterized by that superannuated phrase of elegance 'a votary of the muse.' An impressionable, palpitating creature was Ella, shrinking humanely from detailed knowledge of her husband's trade whenever she reflected that everything he manufactured had for its purpose the destruction of life. She could only recover her equanimity by assuring herself that some, at least, of his weapons were sooner or later used for the extermination of horrid vermin and animals almost as cruel to their inferiors in species as human beings were to theirs.

She had never antecedently regarded this occupation of his as any objection to having him for a husband. Indeed, the necessity of getting life-leased at all cost, a cardinal virtue which all good mothers teach, kept her from thinking of it at all till she had closed with William, had passed the honeymoon, and reached the reflecting stage. Then, like a person who has stumbled upon some object in the dark, she wondered what she had got; mentally walked round it, estimated it; whether it were rare or common; contained gold, silver, or lead; were a clog or a pedestal, everything to her or nothing.

She came to some vague conclusions, and since then had kept her heart alive by pitying her proprietor's obtuseness and want of refinement, pitying herself, and letting off her delicate and ethereal emotions in imaginative occupations, day-dreams, and night-sighs, which perhaps would not much have disturbed William if he had known of them.

Her figure was small, elegant, and slight in build, tripping, or rather bounding, in movement. She was dark-eyed, and had that marvellously bright and liquid sparkle in each pupil which characterizes persons of Ella's cast of soul, and is too often a cause of heartache to the possessor's male friends, ultimately sometimes to herself. Her husband was a tall, long-featured man, with a brown beard; he had a pondering regard; and was, it must be added, usually kind and tolerant to her. He spoke in squarely shaped sentences, and was supremely satisfied with a condition of sublunary things which made weapons a necessity.

Husband and wife walked till they had reached the house they were in search of, which stood in a terrace facing the sea, and was fronted by a small garden of wind-proof and salt-proof evergreens, stone steps leading up to the porch. It had its number in the row, but, being rather larger than the rest, was in addition sedulously distinguished as Coburg House by its landlady, though everybody else called it 'Thirteen, New Parade.' The spot was bright and lively now; but in winter it became necessary to place sandbags against the door, and to stuff up the keyhole against the wind and rain, which had worn the paint so thin that the priming and knotting showed through.

The householder, who had been watching for the gentleman's return, met them in the passage, and showed the rooms. She informed them that she was a professional man's widow, left in needy circumstances by the rather sudden death of her husband,

and she spoke anxiously of the conveniences of the establishment.

Mrs. Marchmill said that she liked the situation and the house; but, it being small, there would not be accommodation enough, unless she could have all the rooms.

The landlady mused with an air of disappointment. She wanted the visitors to be her tenants very badly, she said, with obvious honesty. But unfortunately two of the rooms were occupied permanently by a bachelor gentleman. He did not pay season prices, it was true; but as he kept on his apartments all the year round, and was an extremely nice and interesting young man, who gave no trouble, she did not like to turn him out for a month's 'let,' even at a high figure. 'Perhaps, however,' she added, 'he might offer to go for a time.'

They would not hear of this, and went back to the hotel, intending to proceed to the agent's to inquire further. Hardly had they sat down to tea when the landlady called. Her gentleman, she said, had been so obliging as to offer to give up his rooms for three or four weeks rather than drive the new-comers away.

'It is very kind, but we won't inconvenience him in that way,' said the Marchmills.

'O, it won't inconvenience him, I assure you!'

said the landlady eloquently. 'You see, he's a different sort of young man from most—dreamy, solitary, rather melancholy—and he cares more to be here when the south-westerly gales are beating against the door, and the sea washes over the Parade, and there's not a soul in the place, than he does now in the season. He'd just as soon be where, in fact, he's going temporarily, to a little cottage on the Island opposite, for a change.' She hoped therefore that they would come.

The Marchmill family accordingly took possession of the house next day, and it seemed to suit them very well. After luncheon Mr. Marchmill strolled out towards the pier, and Mrs. Marchmill, having despatched the children to their outdoor amusements on the sands, settled herself in more completely, examining this and that article, and testing the reflecting powers of the mirror in the wardrobe door.

In the small back sitting-room, which had been the young bachelor's, she found furniture of a more personal nature than in the rest. Shabby books, of correct rather than rare editions, were piled up in a queerly reserved manner in corners, as if the previous occupant had not conceived the possibility that any incoming person of the season's bringing could care to look inside them. The landlady hovered on the threshold to rectify anything that Mrs. Marchmill might not find to her satisfaction.

'I'll make this my own little room,' said the latter, 'because the books are here. By the way, the person who has left seems to have a good many. He won't mind my reading some of them, Mrs. Hooper, I hope?'

'O dear no, ma'am. Yes, he has a good many. You see, he is in the literary line himself somewhat. He is a poet—yes, really a poet—and he has a little income of his own, which is enough to write verses on, but not enough for cutting a figure, even if he cared to.'

'A poet! O, I did not know that.'

Mrs. Marchmill opened one of the books, and saw the owner's name written on the title-page. 'Dear me!' she continued; 'I know his name very well—Robert Trewe—of course I do; and his writings! And it is *his* rooms we have taken, and *him* we have turned out of his home?'

Ella Marchmill, sitting down alone a few minutes later, thought with interested surprise of Robert Trewe. Her own latter history will best explain that interest. Herself the only daughter of a struggling man of letters, she had during the last year or two taken to writing poems, in an endeavour to find a congenial channel in which to let flow her painfully embayed emotions, whose former limpidity and sparkle seemed departing in the stagnation caused by the routine of a practical household and the gloom of bearing children to a commonplace father. These poems, subscribed with a masculine pseudonym, had appeared in various obscure magazines, and in two cases in rather prominent ones. In the second of the latter the page which bore her effusion at the bottom, in smallish print, bore at the top, in large print, a few verses on the same subject by this very man, Robert Trewe. Both of them had, in fact, been struck by a tragic incident reported in the daily papers, and had used it simultaneously as an inspiration, the editor remarking in a note upon the coincidence, and that the excellence of both poems prompted him to give them together.

After that event Ella, otherwise 'John Ivy,' had watched with much attention the appearance anywhere in print of verse bearing the signature of Robert Trewe, who, with a man's unsusceptibility on the question of sex, had never once thought of passing himself off as a woman. To be sure, Mrs. Marchmill had satisfied herself with a sort of reason for doing the contrary in her case; that nobody might believe in her inspiration if they found that the sentiments came from a pushing tradesman's wife, from the mother of three children by a matter-of-fact small-arms manufacturer.

Trewe's verse contrasted with that of the rank and file of recent minor poets in being impassioned rather than ingenious, luxuriant rather than finished. Neither *symboliste* nor *décadent*, he was a pessimist in so far as that character applies to a man who looks at the worst contingencies as well as the best in the human condition. Being little attracted by excellences of form and rhythm apart from content, he sometimes, when feeling outran his artistic speed, perpetrated sonnets in the loosely rhymed Elizabethan fashion, which every right-minded reviewer said he ought not to have done.

With sad and hopeless envy, Ella often and often scanned the rival poet's work, so much stronger as it always was than her own feeble lines. She had imitated him, and her inability to touch his level would send her into fits of despondency. Months passed away thus, till she observed from the publishers' list that Trewe had collected his fugitive pieces into a volume, which was duly issued, and was much or little praised according to chance, and had a sale quite sufficient to pay for the printing.

This step onward had suggested to John Ivy the idea of collecting her pieces also, or at any rate of making up a book of her rhymes by adding many in manuscript to the few that had seen the light, for she had been able to get no great number into print. A ruinous charge was made for costs of publication; a few reviews noticed her poor little volume; but nobody talked of it, nobody bought it, and it fell dead in a fortnight—if it had ever been alive.

The author's thoughts were diverted to another groove just then by the discovery that she was going to have a third child, and the collapse of her poetical venture had perhaps less effect upon her mind than it might have done if she had been domestically unoccupied. Her husband had paid the publisher's bill with the doctor's, and there it all had ended for the time. But, though less than a poet of her century, Ella was more than a mere multiplier of her kind, and latterly she had begun to feel the old afflatus once more. And now by an odd conjunction she found herself in the rooms of Robert Trewe.

She thoughtfully rose from her chair and searched the apartment with the interest of a fellow-tradesman. Yes, the volume of his own verse was among the rest. Though quite familiar with its contents, she read it here as if it spoke aloud to her, then called up Mrs. Hooper, the landlady, for some trivial service, and inquired again about the young man.

'Well, I'm sure you'd be interested in him,

ma'am, if you could see him, only he's so shy that I don't suppose you will.' Mrs. Hooper seemed nothing loth to minister to her tenant's curiosity about her predecessor. 'Lived here long? Yes, nearly two years. He keeps on his rooms even when he's not here: the soft air of this place suits his chest, and he likes to be able to come back at any time. He is mostly writing or reading, and doesn't see many people, though, for the matter of that, he is such a good, kind young fellow that folks would only be too glad to be friendly with him if they knew him. You don't meet kind-hearted people every day.'

'Ah, he's kind-hearted . . . and good.'

'Yes; he'll oblige me in anything if I ask him. "Mr. Trewe," I say to him sometimes, "you are rather out of spirits." "Well, I am, Mrs. Hooper," he'll say, "though I don't know how you should find it out." "Why not take a little change?" I ask. Then in a day or two he'll say that he will take a trip to Paris, or Norway, or somewhere; and I assure you he comes back all the better for it.'

'Ah, indeed! His is a sensitive nature, no doubt.'

'Yes. Still he's odd in some things. Once when he had finished a poem of his composition late at night he walked up and down the room rehearsing it; and the floors being so thin—jerry-built houses, you know, though I say it myself—he kept me awake up above him till I wished him further . . . But we get on very well.'

This was but the beginning of a series of conversations about the rising poet as the days went on. On one of these occasions Mrs. Hooper drew Ella's attention to what she had not noticed before: minute scribblings in pencil on the wall-paper behind the curtains at the head of the bed.

'O! let me look,' said Mrs. Marchmill, unable to conceal a rush of tender curiosity as she bent her pretty face close to the wall.

'These,' said Mrs. Hooper, with the manner of a woman who knew things, 'are the very beginnings and first thoughts of his verses. He has tried to rub most of them out, but you can read them still. My belief is that he wakes up in the night, you know, with some rhyme in his head, and jots it down there on the wall lest he should forget it by the morning. Some of these very lines you see here I have seen afterwards in print in the magazines. Some are newer; indeed, I have not seen that one before. It must have been done only a few days ago.'

'O! yes! . . .'

Ella Marchmill flushed without knowing why, and suddenly wished her companion would go away, now that the information was imparted. An indescribable consciousness of personal interest rather than literary made her anxious to read the inscription alone; and she accordingly waited till she could do so, with a sense that a great store of emotion would be enjoyed in the act.

Perhaps because the sea was choppy outside the Island, Ella's husband found it much pleasanter to go sailing and steaming about without his wife, who was a bad sailor, than with her. He did not disdain to go thus alone on board the steamboats of the cheap-trippers, where there was dancing by moonlight, and where the couples would come suddenly down with a lurch into each other's arms; for, as he blandly told her, the company was too mixed for him to take her amid such scenes. Thus, while this thriving manufacturer got a great deal of change and sea-air out of his sojourn here, the life, external at least, of Ella was monotonous enough, and mainly consisted in passing a certain number of hours each day in bathing and walking up and down a stretch of shore. But the poetic impulse having again waxed strong, she was possessed by an inner flame which left her hardly conscious of what was proceeding around her.

She had read till she knew by heart Trewe's last little volume of verses, and spent a great deal of time in vainly attempting to rival some of them, till, in her failure, she burst into tears. The personal element in the magnetic attraction exercised by this circumambient, unapproachable master of hers was so much stronger than the intellectual and abstract that she could not understand it. To be sure, she was surrounded noon and night by his customary environment, which literally whispered of him to her at every moment; but he was a man she had never seen, and that all that moved her was the instinct to specialize a waiting emotion on the first fit thing that came to hand did not, of course, suggest itself to Ella.

In the natural way of passion under the too practical conditions which civilization has devised for its fruition, her husband's love for her had not survived, except in the form of fitful friendship, any more than, or even so much as, her own for him; and, being a woman of very living ardours, that required sustenance of some sort, they were beginning to feed on this chancing material, which was, indeed, of a quality far better than chance usually offers.

One day the children had been playing hide-and-seek in a closet, whence, in their excitement, they pulled out some clothing. Mrs. Hooper explained that it belonged to Mr. Trewe, and hung it up in the closet again. Possessed of her fantasy, Ella went later in the afternoon, when nobody was in that part of the house, opened the closet, unhitched one of the articles, a mackintosh, and put it on, with the waterproof cap belonging to it.

'The mantle of Elijah!' she said. 'Would it might inspire me to rival him, glorious genius that he is!'

Her eyes always grew wet when she thought like that, and she turned to look at herself in the glass. *His* heart had beat inside that coat, and *his* brain had worked under that hat at levels of thought she would never reach. The consciousness of her weakness beside him made her feel quite sick. Before she had got the things off her the door opened, and her husband entered the room.

'What the devil—'

She blushed, and removed them.

'I found them in the closet here,' she said, 'and put them on in a freak. What have I else to do? You are always away!'

'Always away? Well . . .

That evening she had a further talk with the landlady, who might herself have nourished a half-tender regard for the poet, so ready was she to discourse ardently about him.

'You are interested in Mr. Trewe, I know, ma'am,' she said; 'and he has just sent to say that he is going to call to-morrow afternoon to look up some books of his that he wants, if I'll be in, and he may select them from your room?'

'O yes!'

'You could very well meet Mr. Trewe then, if you'd like to be in the way!'

She promised with secret delight, and went to bed musing of him.

Next morning her husband observed: 'I've been thinking of what you said, Ell: that I have gone about a good deal and left you without much to amuse you. Perhaps it's true. To-day, as there's not much sea, I'll take you with me on board the yacht.'

For the first time in her experience of such an offer Ella was not glad. But she accepted it for the moment. The time for setting out drew near, and she went to get ready. She stood reflecting. The longing to see the poet she was now distinctly in love with overpowered all other considerations.

'I don't want to go,' she said to herself. 'I can't bear to be away! And I won't go.'

She told her husband that she had changed her mind about wishing to sail. He was indifferent, and went his way.

For the rest of the day the house was quiet, the children having gone out upon the sands. The blinds waved in the sunshine to the soft, steady stroke of the sea beyond the wall; and the notes of the Green Silesian band, a troop of foreign gentlemen hired for the season, had drawn almost all the residents and promenaders away from the vicinity of Coburg House. A knock was audible at the door.

Mrs. Marchmill did not hear any servant go to answer it, and she became impatient. The books were in the room where she sat; but nobody came up. She rang the bell.

'There is some person waiting at the door,' she said.

'O no, ma'am! He's gone long ago. I answered it.'

Mrs. Hooper came in herself.

'So disappointing!' she said. 'Mr. Trewe not coming after all!'

'But I heard him knock, I fancy!'

'No; that was somebody inquiring for lodgings who came to the wrong house. I forgot to tell you that Mr. Trewe sent a note just before lunch to say I needn't get any tea for him, as he should not require the books, and wouldn't come to select them.'

Ella was miserable, and for a long time could not even re-read his mournful ballad on 'Severed Lives,' so aching was her erratic little heart, and so tearful her eyes. When the children came in with wet stockings, and ran up to her to tell her of their adventures, she could not feel that she cared about them half as much as usual.

*

'Mrs. Hooper, have you a photograph of—the gentleman who lived here?' She was getting to be curiously shy in mentioning his name.

'Why, yes. It's in the ornamental frame on the mantelpiece in your own bedroom, ma'am.'

'No; the Royal Duke and Duchess are in that.'

'Yes, so they are; but he's behind them. He belongs rightly to that frame, which I bought on purpose; but as he went away he said: "Cover me up from those strangers that are coming, for God's sake. I don't want them staring at me, and I am sure they won't want me staring at them." So I slipped in the Duke and Duchess temporarily in front of him, as they had no frame, and Royalties are more suitable for letting furnished than a private young man. If you take 'em out you'll see him under. Lord, ma'am, he wouldn't mind if he knew it! He didn't think the next tenant would be such an attractive lady as you, or he wouldn't have thought of hiding himself, perhaps.'

'Is he handsome?' she asked timidly.

'*I* call him so. Some, perhaps, wouldn't.'

'Should I?' she asked, with eagerness.

'I think you would, though some would say he's more striking than handsome; a large-eyed thoughtful fellow, you know, with a very electric flash in his eye when he looks round quickly, such as you'd expect a poet to be who doesn't get his living by it.'

'How old is he?'

'Several years older than yourself, ma'am; about thirty-one or two, I think.'

Ella was, as a matter of fact, a few months over thirty herself; but she did not look nearly so much. Though so immature in nature, she was entering on that tract of life in which emotional women begin to suspect that last love may be stronger than first love; and she would soon, alas, enter on the still more melancholy tract when at least the vainer ones of her sex shrink from receiving a male visitor otherwise than with their backs to the window or the blinds half down. She reflected on Mrs. Hooper's remark, and said no more about age.

Just then a telegram was brought up. It came from her husband, who had gone down the Channel as far as Budmouth with his friends in the yacht, and would not be able to get back till next day.

After her light dinner Ella idled about the shore with the children till dusk, thinking of the yet uncovered photograph in her room, with a serene sense of something ecstatic to come. For, with the subtle luxuriousness of fancy in which this young woman was an adept, on learning that her husband was to be absent that night she had refrained from incontinently rushing upstairs and opening the picture-frame, preferring to reserve the inspection till she could be alone, and a more romantic tinge be imparted to the occasion by silence, candles, solemn sea and stars outside, than was afforded by the garish afternoon sunlight.

The children had been sent to bed, and Ella soon followed, though it was not yet ten o'clock. To gratify her passionate curiosity she now made her preparations, first getting rid of superfluous garments and putting on her dressing-gown, then arranging a chair in front of the table and reading several pages of Trewe's tenderest utterances. Then she fetched the portrait-frame to the light, opened the back, took out the likeness, and set it up before her.

It was a striking countenance to look upon. The poet wore a luxuriant black moustache and imperial, and a slouched hat which shaded the forehead. The large dark eyes, described by the landlady, showed an unlimited capacity for misery; they looked out from beneath well-shaped brows as if they were reading the universe in the microcosm of the confronter's face, and were not altogether overjoyed at what the spectacle portended.

Ella murmured in her lowest, richest, tenderest

tone: 'And it's *you* who've so cruelly eclipsed me these many times!'

As she gazed long at the portrait she fell into thought, till her eyes filled with tears, and she touched the cardboard with her lips. Then she laughed with a nervous lightness, and wiped her eyes.

She thought how wicked she was, a woman having a husband and three children, to let her mind stray to a stranger in this unconscionable manner. No, he was not a stranger! She knew his thoughts and feelings as well as she knew her own; they were, in fact, the selfsame thoughts and feelings as hers, which her husband distinctly lacked; perhaps luckily for himself, considering that he had to provide for family expenses.

'He's nearer my real self, he's more intimate with the real me than Will is, after all, even though I've never seen him,' she said.

She laid his book and picture on the table at the bedside, and when she was reclining on the pillow she re-read those of Robert Trewe's verses which she had marked from time to time as most touching and true. Putting these aside, she set up the photograph on its edge upon the coverlet, and contemplated it as she lay. Then she scanned again by the light of the candle the half-obliterated pencillings on the wallpaper beside her head. There they were—phrases, couplets, *bouts-rimés*, beginnings and middles of lines, ideas in the rough, like Shelley's scraps, and the least of them so intense, so sweet, so palpitating, that it seemed as if his very breath, warm and loving, fanned her cheeks from those walls, walls that had surrounded his head times and times as they surrounded her own now. He must often have put up his hand so—with the pencil in it. Yes, the writing was sideways, as it would be if executed by one who extended his arm thus.

These inscribed shapes of the poet's world,

'Forms more real than living man,
   Nurslings of immortality,'

were, no doubt, the thoughts and spirit-strivings which had come to him in the dead of night, when he could let himself go and have no fear of the frost of criticism. No doubt they had often been written up hastily by the light of the moon, the rays of the lamp, in the blue-grey dawn, in full daylight perhaps never. And now her hair was dragging where his arm had lain when he secured the fugitive fancies; she was sleeping on a poet's lips, immersed in the very essence of him, permeated by his spirit as by an ether.

While she was dreaming the minutes away thus, a footstep came upon the stairs, and in a moment she heard her husband's heavy step on the landing immediately without.

'Ell, where are you?'

What possessed her she could not have described, but, with an instinctive objection to let her husband know what she had been doing, she slipped the photograph under the pillow just as he flung open the door, with the air of a man who had dined not badly.

'O, I beg pardon,' said William Marchmill. 'Have you a headache? I am afraid I have disturbed you.'

'No, I've not got a headache,' said she. 'How is it you've come?'

'Well, we found we could get back in very good time after all, and I didn't want to make another day of it, because of going somewhere else to-morrow.'

'Shall I come down again?'

'O no. I'm as tired as a dog. I've had a good feed, and I shall turn in straight off. I want to get out at six o'clock to-morrow if I can . . . I shan't disturb you by my getting up; it will be long before you are awake.' And he came forward into the room.

While her eyes followed his movements, Ella softly pushed the photograph further out of sight.

'Sure you're not ill?' he asked, bending over her.

'No, only wicked!'

'Never mind that.' And he stooped and kissed her.

Next morning Marchmill was called at six o'clock; and in waking and yawning she heard him muttering to himself: 'What the deuce is this that's been crackling under me so?' Imagining her asleep he searched round him and withdrew something. Through her half-opened eyes she perceived it to be Mr. Trewe.

'Well, I'm damned!' her husband exclaimed.

'What, dear?' said she.

'O, you are awake? Ha! ha!'

'What *do* you mean?'

'Some bloke's photograph—a friend of our landlady's, I suppose. I wonder how it came here; whisked off the table by accident perhaps when they were making the bed.'

'I was looking at it yesterday, and it must have dropped in then.'

'O, he's a friend of yours? Bless his picturesque heart!'

Ella's loyalty to the object of her admiration could not endure to hear him ridiculed. 'He's a clever man!' she said, with a tremor in her gentle voice which she herself felt to be absurdly uncalled for. 'He is a rising poet—the gentleman who occupied two of these rooms before we came, though I've never seen him.'

'How do you know, if you've never seen him?'

'Mrs. Hooper told me when she showed me the photograph.'

'O; well, I must up and be off. I shall be home rather early. 'Sorry I can't take you to-day, dear. Mind the children don't go getting drowned.'

That day Mrs. Marchmill inquired if Mr. Trewe were likely to call at any other time.

'Yes,' said Mrs. Hooper. 'He's coming this day week to stay with a friend near here till you leave. He'll be sure to call.'

Marchmill did return quite early in the afternoon; and, opening some letters which had arrived in his absence, declared suddenly that he and his family would have to leave a week earlier than they had expected to do—in short, in three days.

'Surely we can stay a week longer?' she pleaded. 'I like it here.'

'I don't. It is getting rather slow.'

'Then you might leave me and the children!'

'How perverse you are, Ell! What's the use? And have to come to fetch you! No: we'll all return together; and we'll make out our time in North Wales or Brighton a little later on. Besides, you've three days longer yet.'

It seemed to be her doom not to meet the man for whose rival talent she had a despairing admiration, and to whose person she was now absolutely attached. Yet she determined to make a last effort; and having gathered from her landlady that Trewe was living in a lonely spot not far from the fashionable town on the Island opposite, she crossed over in the packet from the neighbouring pier the following afternoon.

What a useless journey it was! Ella knew but vaguely where the house stood, and when she fancied she had found it, and ventured to inquire of a pedestrian if he lived there, the answer returned by the man was that he did not know. And if he did live there, how could she call upon him? Some women might have the assurance to do it, but she had not. How crazy he would think her. She might have asked him to call upon her, perhaps; but she had not the courage for that, either. She lingered mournfully about the picturesque seaside eminence till it was time to return to the town and enter the steamer for recrossing, reaching home for dinner without having been greatly missed.

At the last moment, unexpectedly enough, her husband said that he should have no objection to letting her and the children stay on till the end of the week, since she wished to do so, if she felt herself able to get home without him. She concealed the pleasure this extension of time gave her; and Marchmill went off the next morning alone.

But the week passed, and Trewe did not call.

On Saturday morning the remaining members of the Marchmill family departed from the place which had been productive of so much fervour in her. The dreary, dreary train; the sun shining in moted beams upon the hot cushions; the dusty permanent way; the mean rows of wire—these things were her accompaniment: while out of the window the deep blue sea-levels disappeared from her gaze, and with them her poet's home. Heavy-hearted, she tried to read, and wept instead.

Mr. Marchmill was in a thriving way of business, and he and his family lived in a large new house, which stood in rather extensive grounds a few miles outside the city wherein he carried on his trade. Ella's life was lonely here, as the suburban life is apt to be, particularly at certain seasons; and she had ample time to indulge her taste for lyric and elegiac composition. She had hardly got back when she encountered a piece by Robert Trewe in the new number of her favourite magazine, which must have been written almost immediately before her visit to Solentsea, for it contained the very couplet she had seen pencilled on the wallpaper by the bed, and Mrs. Hooper had declared to be recent. Ella could resist no longer, but seizing a pen impulsively, wrote to him as a brother-poet, using the name of John Ivy, congratulating him in her letter on his triumphant executions in metre and rhythm of thoughts that moved his soul, as compared with her own brow-beaten efforts in the same pathetic trade.

To this address there came a response in a few days, little as she had dared to hope for it—a civil and brief note, in which the young poet stated that, though he was not well acquainted with Mr. Ivy's verse, he recalled the name as being one he had seen attached to some very promising pieces; that he was glad to gain Mr. Ivy's acquaintance by letter, and should certainly look with much interest for his productions in the future.

There must have been something juvenile or timid in her own epistle, as one ostensibly coming from a man, she declared to herself; for Trewe quite adopted the tone of an elder and superior in this reply. But what did it matter? He had replied; he had written to her with his own hand from that very room she knew so well, for he was now back again in his quarters.

The correspondence thus begun was continued for two months or more, Ella Marchmill sending him from time to time some that she considered to be the best of her pieces, which he very kindly accepted, though he did not say he sedulously read them, nor did he send her any of his own in return. Ella would have been more hurt at this than she was if she had not known that Trewe laboured under the impression that she was one of his own sex.

Yet the situation was unsatisfactory. A flattering little voice told her that, were he only to see her, matters would be otherwise. No doubt she would have helped on this by making a frank confession of womanhood, to begin with, if something had not happened, to her delight, to render it unnecessary. A friend of her husband's, the editor of the most important newspaper in the city and county, who was dining with them one day, observed during their conversation about the poet that his (the editor's) brother the landscape-painter was a friend of Mr. Trewe's, and that the two men were at that very moment in Wales together.

Ella was slightly acquainted with the editor's brother. The next morning down she sat and wrote, inviting him to stay at her house for a short time on his way back, and requesting him to bring with him, if practicable, his companion Mr. Trewe, whose acquaintance she was anxious to make. The answer arrived after some few days. Her correspondent and his friend Trewe would have much satisfaction in accepting her invitation on their way southward, which would be on such and such a day in the following week.

Ella was blithe and buoyant. Her scheme had succeeded; her beloved though as yet unseen one was coming. "Behold, he standeth behind our wall; he looked forth at the windows, showing himself through the lattice," she thought ecstatically. "And, lo, the winter is past, the rain is over and gone, the flowers appear on the earth, the time of the singing of birds is come, and the voice of the turtle is heard in our land."

But it was necessary to consider the details of lodging and feeding him. This she did most solicitously, and awaited the pregnant day and hour.

It was about five in the afternoon when she heard a ring at the door and the editor's brother's voice in the hall. Poetess as she was, or as she thought herself, she had not been too sublime that day to dress with infinite trouble in a fashionable robe of rich material, having a faint resemblance to the *chiton* of the Greeks, a style just then in vogue among ladies of an artistic and romantic turn, which had been obtained by Ella of her Bond Street dressmaker when she was last in London. Her visitor entered the drawing-room. She looked towards his rear; nobody else came through the door. Where, in the name of the God of Love, was Robert Trewe?

'O, I'm sorry,' said the painter, after their introductory words had been spoken. 'Trewe is a curious fellow, you know, Mrs. Marchmill. He said he'd come; then he said he couldn't. He's rather dusty. We've been doing a few miles with knapsacks, you know; and he wanted to get on home.'

'He—he's not coming?'

'He's not; and he asked me to make his apologies.'

'When did you p-p-part from him?' she asked, her nether lip starting off quivering so much that it was like a *tremolo*-stop opened in her speech. She longed to run away from this dreadful bore and cry her eyes out.

'Just now, in the turnpike road yonder there.'

'What! he has actually gone past my gates?'

'Yes. When we got to them—handsome gates they are, too, the finest bit of modern wrought-iron work I have seen—when we came to them we stopped, talking there a little while, and then he wished me good-bye and went on. The truth is, he's a little bit depressed just now, and doesn't want to see anybody. He's a very good fellow, and a warm friend, but a little uncertain and gloomy sometimes; he thinks too much of things. His poetry is rather too erotic and passionate, you know, for some tastes; and he has just come in for a terrible slating from the— *Review* that was published yesterday; he saw a copy of it at the station by accident. Perhaps you've read it?'

'No.'

'So much the better. O, it is not worth thinking of; just one of those articles written to order, to please the narrow-minded set of subscribers upon whom the circulation depends. But he's upset by it. He says it is the misrepresentation that hurts him so; that, though he can stand a fair attack, he can't stand lies that he's powerless to refute and stop from spreading. That's just Trewe's weak point. He lives so much by himself that these things affect him much more than they would if he were in the bustle of fashionable or commercial life. So he wouldn't come here, making the excuse that it all looked so new and monied—if you'll pardon—'

'But—he must have known—there was sympathy here! Has he never said anything about getting letters from this address?'

'Yes, yes, he has, from John Ivy—perhaps a relative of yours, he thought, visiting here at the time?'

'Did he—like Ivy, did he say?'

'Well, I don't know that he took any great interest in Ivy.'

'Or in his poems?'

'Or in his poems—so far as I know, that is.'

Robert Trewe took no interest in her house, in her poems, or in their writer. As soon as she could get away she went into the nursery and tried to let off her emotion by unnecessarily kissing the children, till she had a sudden sense of disgust at being reminded how plain-looking they were, like their father.

The obtuse and single-minded landscape-painter never once perceived from her conversation that it was only Trewe she wanted, and not himself. He made the best of his visit, seeming to enjoy the society of Ella's husband, who also took a great fancy to him, and showed him everywhere about the neighbourhood, neither of them noticing Ella's mood.

The painter had been gone only a day or two when, while sitting upstairs alone one morning, she glanced over the London paper just arrived, and read the following paragraph:—

'SUICIDE OF A POET

'Mr. Robert Trewe, who has been favourably known for some years as one of our rising lyrists, committed suicide at his lodgings at Solentsea on Saturday evening last by shooting himself in the right temple with a revolver. Readers hardly need to be reminded that Mr. Trewe has recently attracted the attention of a much wider public than had hitherto known him, by his new volume of verse, mostly of an impassioned kind, entitled "Lyrics to a Woman Unknown," which has been already favourably noticed in these pages for the extraordinary gamut of feeling it traverses, and which has been made the subject of a severe, if not ferocious, criticism in the—*Review*. It is supposed, though not certainly known, that the article may have partially conduced to the sad act, as a copy of the review in question was found on his writing-table; and he has been observed to be in a somewhat depressed state of mind since the critique appeared.'

Then came the report of the inquest, at which the following letter was read, it having been addressed to a friend at a distance:—

'DEAR—, Before these lines reach your hands I shall be delivered from the inconveniences of seeing, hearing, and knowing more of the things around me. I will not trouble you by giving my reasons for the step I have taken, though I can assure you they were sound and logical. Perhaps had I been blessed with a mother, or a sister, or a female friend of another sort tenderly devoted to me, I might have thought it worth while to continue my present existence. I have long dreamt of such an unattainable creature, as you know; and she, this undiscoverable, elusive one, inspired my last volume; the imaginary woman alone, for, in spite of what has been said in some quarters, there is no real woman behind the title. She has continued to the last unrevealed, unmet, unwon. I think it desirable to mention this in order that no blame may attach to any real woman as having been the cause of my decease by cruel or cavalier treatment of me. Tell my landlady that I am sorry to have caused her this unpleasantness; but my occupancy of the rooms will soon be forgotten. There are ample funds in my name at the bank to pay all expenses.

R. TREWE.'

Ella sat for a while as if stunned, then rushed into the adjoining chamber and flung herself upon her face on the bed.

Her grief and distraction shook her to pieces; and she lay in this frenzy of sorrow for more than an hour. Broken words came every now and then from her quivering lips: 'O, if he had only known of me—known of me—me! . . . O, if I had only once met him—only once; and put my hand upon his hot forehead—kissed him—let him know how I loved him—that I would have suffered shame and scorn, would have lived and died, for him! Perhaps it would have saved his dear life! . . . But no—it was not allowed! God is a jealous God; and that happiness was not for him and me!'

All possibilities were over; the meeting was stultified. Yet it was almost visible to her in her fantasy even now, though it could never be substantiated—

> 'The hour which might have been,
> yet might not be,
> Which man's and woman's heart
> conceived and bore,
> Yet whereof life was barren.'

She wrote to the landlady at Solentsea in the third person, in as subdued a style as she could command, enclosing a postal order for a sovereign, and informing Mrs. Hooper that Mrs. Marchmill had seen in the papers the sad account of the poet's death, and having been, as Mrs. Hooper was aware, much interested in Mr. Trewe during her stay at Coburg House, she would be obliged if Mrs. Hooper could obtain a small portion of his hair before his coffin was closed down, and send it her as a memorial of him, as also the photograph that was in the frame.

By the return-post a letter arrived containing what had been requested. Ella wept over the portrait and secured it in her private drawer; the lock of hair she tied with white ribbon and put in her bosom, whence she drew it and kissed it every now and then in some unobserved nook.

'What's the matter?' said her husband, looking up from his newspaper on one of these occasions. 'Crying over something? A lock of hair? Whose is it?'

'He's dead!' she murmured.

'Who?'

'I don't want to tell you, Will, just now, unless you insist!' she said, a sob hanging heavy in her voice.

'O, all right.'

'Do you mind my refusing? I will tell you some day.'

'It doesn't matter in the least, of course.'

He walked away whistling a few bars of no tune in particular; and when he had got down to his factory in the city the subject came into Marchmill's head again.

He, too, was aware that a suicide had taken place recently at the house they had occupied at Solentsea. Having seen the volume of poems in his wife's hand of late, and heard fragments of the landlady's conversation about Trewe when they were her tenants, he all at once said to himself, 'Why of course it's he! . . . How the devil did she get to know him? What sly animals women are!'

Then he placidly dismissed the matter, and went on with his daily affairs. By this time Ella at home had come to a determination. Mrs. Hooper, in sending the hair and photograph, had informed her of the day of the funeral; and as the morning and noon wore on an overpowering wish to know where they were laying him took possession of the sympathetic woman. Caring very little now what her husband or any one else might think of her eccentricities, she wrote Marchmill a brief note, stating that she was called away for the afternoon and evening, but would return on the following morning. This she left on his desk, and having given the same information to the servants, went out of the house on foot.

When Mr. Marchmill reached home early in the afternoon the servants looked anxious. The nurse took him privately aside, and hinted that her mistress's sadness during the past few days had been such that she feared she had gone out to drown herself. Marchmill reflected. Upon the whole he thought that she had not done that. Without saying whither he was bound he also started off, telling them not to sit up for him. He drove to the railway-station, and took a ticket for Solentsea.

It was dark when he reached the place, though he had come by a fast train, and he knew that if his wife had preceded him thither it could only have been by a slower train, arriving not a great while before his own. The season at Solentsea was now past: the parade was gloomy, and the flys were few and cheap. He asked the way to the Cemetery, and soon reached it. The gate was locked, but the keeper let him in, declaring, however, that there was nobody within the precincts. Although it was not late, the autumnal darkness had now become intense; and he found some difficulty in keeping to the serpentine path which led to the quarter where, as the man had told him, the one or two interments for the day had taken place. He stepped upon the grass, and, stumbling over some pegs, stooped now and then to discern if possible a figure against the sky. He could see none; but lighting on a spot where the soil was trodden, beheld a crouching object beside a newly made grave. She heard him, and sprang up.

'Ell, how silly this is!' he said indignantly. 'Running away from home—I never heard such a thing! Of course I am not jealous of this unfortunate man; but it is too ridiculous that you, a married woman with three children and a fourth coming, should go losing your head like this over a dead lover! . . . Do you know you were locked in? You might not have been able to get out all night.'

She did not answer.

'I hope it didn't go far between you and him, for your own sake.'

'Don't insult me, Will.'

'Mind, I won't have any more of this sort of thing; do you hear?'

'Very well,' she said.

He drew her arm within his own, and conducted her out of the Cemetery. It was impossible to get back that night; and not wishing to be recognized in their present sorry condition, he took her to a miserable little coffee-house close to the station, whence they departed early in the morning, travelling almost without speaking, under the sense that it was one of those dreary situations occurring in married life which words could not mend, and reaching their own door at noon.

The months passed, and neither of the twain ever ventured to start a conversation upon this episode. Ella seemed to be only too frequently in a sad and listless mood, which might almost have been called pining. The time was approaching when she would have to undergo the stress of childbirth for a fourth time, and that apparently did not tend to raise her spirits.

'I don't think I shall get over it this time!' she said one day.

'Pooh! what childish foreboding! Why shouldn't it be as well now as ever?'

She shook her head. 'I feel almost sure I am going to die; and I should be glad, if it were not for Nelly, and Frank, and Tiny.'

'And me!'

'You'll soon find somebody to fill my place,' she murmured, with a sad smile. 'And you'll have a perfect right to; I assure you of that.'

'Ell, you are not thinking still about that—poetical friend of yours?'

She neither admitted nor denied the charge. 'I am not going to get over my illness this time,' she reiterated. 'Something tells me I shan't.'

This view of things was rather a bad beginning, as it usually is; and, in fact, six weeks later, in the month of May, she was lying in her room, pulseless and bloodless, with hardly strength enough left to follow up one feeble breath with another, the infant for whose unnecessary life she was slowly parting with her own being fat and well. Just before her death she spoke to Marchmill softly:—

'Will, I want to confess to you the entire circumstances of that—about you know what—that time we visited Solentsea. I can't tell what possessed me—how I could forget you so, my husband! But I had got into a morbid state: I thought you had been unkind; that you had neglected me; that you weren't up to my intellectual level, while he was, and far above it. I wanted a fuller appreciator, perhaps, rather than another lover—'

She could get no further then for very exhaustion; and she went off in sudden collapse a few hours later, without having said anything more to her husband on the subject of her love for the poet. William Marchmill, in truth, like most husbands of several years' standing, was little disturbed by retrospective jealousies, and had not shown the least anxiety to press her for confessions concerning a man dead and gone beyond any power of inconveniencing him more.

But when she had been buried a couple of years it chanced one day that, in turning over some forgotten papers that he wished to destroy before his second wife entered the house, he lighted on a lock of hair in an envelope, with the photograph of the deceased poet, a date being written on the back in his late wife's hand. It was that of the time they spent at Solentsea.

Marchmill looked long and musingly at the hair and portrait, for something struck him. Fetching the little boy who had been the death of his mother, now a noisy toddler, he took him on his knee, held the lock of hair against the child's head, and set up the photograph on the table behind, so that he could closely compare the features each countenance presented. There were undoubtedly strong traces of resemblance; the dreamy and peculiar expression of the poet's face sat, as the transmitted idea, upon the child's, and the hair was of the same hue.

'I'm damned if I didn't think so!' murmured Marchmill. 'Then she *did* play me false with that fellow at the lodgings! Let me see: the dates—the second week in August . . . the third week in May . . . Yes . . . yes . . . Get away, you poor little brat! You are nothing to me!'

Selma Lagerlöf

The Musician

No one in Ullerud could say anything of fiddler Lars Larsson but that he was both meek and modest in his later years. But he had not always been thus, it seems. In his youth he had been so overbearing and boastful that people were in despair about him. It is said that he was changed and made over in a single night, and this is the way it happened.

Lars Larsson went out for a stroll late one Saturday night, with his fiddle under his arm. He was excessively gay and jovial, for he had just come from a party where his playing had tempted both young and old to dance. He walked along, thinking that while his bow was in motion no one had been able to sit still. There had been such a whirl in the cabin that once or twice he fancied the chairs and tables were dancing too! "I verily believe they have never before had a musician like me in these parts," he remarked to himself. "But I had a mighty rough time of it before I became such a clever chap!" he continued. "When I was a child, it was no fun for me when my parents put me to tending cows and sheep and when I forgot everything else to sit and twang my fiddle. And just fancy! they wouldn't so much as give me a real violin. I had nothing to play on but an old wooden box over which I had stretched some strings. In the daytime, when I could be alone in the woods, I fared rather well; but it was none too cheerful to come home in the evening when the cattle had strayed from me! Then I heard often enough, from both father and mother, that I was a good-for-nothing and never would amount to anything."

In that part of the forest where Lars Larsson was strolling a little river was trying to find its way. The ground was stony and hilly, and the stream had great difficulty in getting ahead, winding this way and that way, rolling over little falls and rapids – and yet it appeared to get nowhere. The path where the fiddler walked, on the other hand, tried to go as straight ahead as possible. Therefore it was continually meeting the sinuous stream, and each time it would dart across it by using a little bridge. The musician also had to cross the stream repeatedly, and he was glad of it. He thought it was as though he had found company in the forest.

Where he was tramping it was light summer-night. The sun had not yet come up, but its being away made no difference, for it was as light as day all the same.

Still the light was not quite what it is in the daytime. Everything had a different color. The sky was perfectly white, the trees and the growths on the ground were grayish, but everything was as distinctly visible as in the daytime, and when Lars Larsson paused on any of the numerous bridges and looked down into the stream, he could distinguish every ripple on the water.

"When I see a stream like this in the wilderness," he thought, "I am reminded of my own life. As persistent as this stream have I been in forcing my way past all that has obstructed my path. Father has been my rock ahead, and mother tried to hold me back and bury me between moss-tufts, but I stole past both of them and got out in the world. Hay-ho, hi, hi! I think mother is still sitting at home and weeping for me. But what do I care! She might have known that I should amount to something some day, instead of trying to oppose me!"

Impatiently he tore some leaves from a branch and threw them into the river.

"Look! thus have I torn myself loose from everything at home," he said, as he watched the leaves borne away by the water. "I am wondering if mother knows that I'm the best musician in Vermland?" he remarked as he went farther.

He walked on rapidly until he came across the stream again. Then he stopped and looked into the water.

Here the river went along in a struggling rapid, creating a terrible racket. As it was night, one heard from the stream sounds quite different from those of the daytime, and the musician was perfectly astonished when he stood still and listened. There was no bird song in the trees and no music in the pines and no rustling in the leaves. No wagon wheels creaked in the road and no cow-bells tinkled in the wood. One heard only the rapid; but because all the other things were hushed, it could be heard so much better than during the day. It sounded as though everything thinkable and unthinkable was rioting and clamoring in the depths of the stream. First, it sounded as if some one were sitting down there and grinding grain between stones, and then it sounded as though goblets were clinking in a drinking-bout; and again there was a murmuring, as when the congregation had left the church and were standing on the church knoll after the service, talking earnestly together.

"I suppose this, too, is a kind of music," thought the fiddler, "although I can't find anything much in it! I think the air that I composed the other day was much more worth listening to."

But the longer Lars Larsson listened to the music of the rapid, the better he thought it sounded.

"I believe you are improving," he said to the rapid. "It must have dawned upon you that the best musician in Vermland is listening to you!"

The instant he had made this remark, he fancied he heard a couple of clear metallic sounds, as when some one picks a violin string to hear if it is in tune.

"But see, hark! The Water-Sprite himself has arrived. I can hear how he begins to thrum on the violin. Let us hear now if you can play better than I!" said Lars Larsson, laughing. "But I can't stand here all night waiting for you to begin," he called to the water. "Now I must be going; but I promise you that I will also stop at the next bridge and listen, to hear if you can cope with me."

He went farther and, as the stream in its winding course ran into the wood, he began thinking once more of his home.

"I wonder how the little brooklet that runs by our house is getting on? I should like to see it again. I ought to go home once in a while, to see if mother is suffering want and hardship since father's death. But busy as I am, it is almost impossible. As busy as

I am just now, I say, I can't look after anything but the fiddle. There is hardly an evening in the week that I am at liberty."

In a little while he met the stream again, and his thoughts were turned to something else. At this crossing the river did not come rushing on in a noisy rapid, but glided ahead rather quietly. It lay perfectly black and shiny under the night-gray forest trees, and carried with it one and another patch of snow-white scum from the rapids above.

When the musician came down upon the bridge and heard no sound from the stream but a soft swish now and then, he began to laugh.

"I might have known that the Water-Sprite wouldn't care to come to the meeting," he shouted. "To be sure, I have always heard that he is considered an excellent performer, but one who lies still forever in a brook and never hears anything new can't know very much! He perceives, no doubt, that here stands one who knows more about music than he, therefore he doesn't care to let me hear him."

Then he went farther and lost sight of the river again. He came into a part of the forest which he had always thought dismal and bleak to wander through. There the ground was covered with big stone heaps, and gnarled pine stumps lay uprooted among them. If there was anything magical or fearsome in the forest, one would naturally think that it concealed itself here.

When the musician came in among the wild stone blocks, a shudder passed through him, and he began to wonder if it had not been unwise of him to boast in the presence of the Water-Sprite. He fancied the large pine roots began to gesticulate, as if they were threatening him. "Beware, you who think yourself cleverer than the Water-Sprite!" it seemed as if they wanted to say.

Lars Larsson felt how his heart contracted with dread. A heavy weight bore down upon his chest, so that he could scarcely breathe, and his hands became ice-cold. Then he stopped in the middle of the wood and tried to talk sense to himself.

"Why, there's no musician in the waterfall!" said he. "Such things are only superstition and nonsense! It's of no consequence what I have said or haven't said to him."

As he spoke, he looked around him, as if for some confirmation of the truth of what he said. Had it been daytime, every tiny leaf would have winked at him that there was nothing dangerous in the wood; but now, at night, the leaves on the trees were closed and silent and looked as though they were hiding all sorts of dangerous secrets.

Lars Larsson grew more and more alarmed. That

which caused him the greatest fear was having to cross the stream once more before it and the road parted company and went in different directions. He wondered what the Water-Sprite would do to him when he walked across the last bridge – if he might perhaps stretch a big black hand out of the water and drag him down into the depths.

He had worked himself into such a state of fright that he thought of turning back. But then he would meet the stream again. And if he were to turn out of the road and go into the wood, he would also meet it, the way it kept bending and winding itself!

He felt so nervous that he didn't know what to do. He was snared and captured and bound by that stream, and saw no possibility of escape.

Finally he saw before him the last bridge crossing. Directly opposite him, on the other side of the stream, stood an old mill, which must have been abandoned these many years. The big mill-wheel hung motionless over the water. The sluice-gate lay mouldering on the land; the mill-race was moss-grown, and its sides were lined with common fern and beard-moss.

"If all had been as formerly and there were people here," thought the musician, "I should be safe now from all danger."

But, at all events, he felt reassured in seeing a

building constructed by human hands, and, as he crossed the stream, he was scarcely frightened at all. Nor did anything dreadful happen to him. The Water-Sprite seemed to have no quarrel with him. He was simply amazed to think he had worked himself into a panic over nothing whatever.

He felt very happy and secure, and became even happier when the mill door opened and a young girl came out to him. She looked like an ordinary peasant girl. She had a cotton kerchief on her head and wore a short skirt and full jacket, but her feet were bare.

She walked up to the musician and said to him without further ceremony, "If you will play for me, I'll dance for you."

"Why, certainly," said the fiddler, who was in fine spirits now that he was rid of his fear. "That I can do, of course. I have never in my life refused to play for a pretty girl who wants to dance."

He took his place on a stone near the edge of the mill-pond, raised the violin to his chin, and began to play.

The girl took a few steps in rhythm with the music; then she stopped. "What kind of a polka are you playing?" said she. "There is no vim in it."

The fiddler changed his tune; he tried one with more life in it.

The girl was just as dissatisfied. "I can't dance to such a draggy polka," said she.

Then Lars Larsson struck up the wildest air he knew. "If you are not satisfied with this one," he said, "you will have to call hither a better musician than I am."

The instant he said this, he felt that a hand caught his arm at the elbow and began to guide the bow and increase the tempo. Then from the violin there poured forth a strain the like of which he had never before heard. It moved in such a quick tempo he thought that a rolling wheel couldn't have kept up with it.

"Now, that's what I call a polka!" said the girl, and began to swing round.

But the musician did not glance at her. He was so astonished at the air he was playing that he stood with closed eyes, to hear better. When he opened them after a moment, the girl was gone. But he did not wonder much at this. He continued to play on, long and well, only because he had never before heard such violin playing.

"It must be time now to finish with this," he thought finally, and wanted to lay down the bow. But the bow kept up its motion; he couldn't make it stop. It travelled back and forth over the strings and jerked the hand and arm with it; and the hand that held the neck of the violin and fingered the strings could not free itself, either.

The cold sweat stood out on Lars Larsson's brow, and he was frightened now in earnest.

"How will this end? Shall I sit here and play till doomsday?" he asked himself in despair.

The bow ran on and on, and magically called forth one tune after another. Always it was something new, and it was so beautiful that the poor fiddler must have known how little his own skill was worth. And it was this that tortured him worse than the fatigue.

"He who plays upon my violin understands the art. But never in all my born days have I been anything but a bungler. Now for the first time I'm learning how music should sound."

For a few seconds he became so transported by the music that he forgot his evil fate; then he felt how his arm ached from weariness and he was seized anew with despair.

"This violin I cannot lay down until I have played myself to death. I can understand that the Water-Sprite won't be satisfied with less."

He began to weep over himself, but all the while he kept on playing.

"It would have been better for me had I stayed at

home in the little cabin with mother. What is all the glory worth if it is to end in this way?"

He sat there hour after hour. Morning came on, the sun rose, and the birds sang all around him; but he played and he played, without intermission.

As it was a Sunday that dawned, he had to sit there by the old mill all alone. No human beings tramped in this part of the forest. They went to church down in the dale, and to the villages along the big highway.

Forenoon came along, and the sun stepped higher and higher in the sky. The birds grew silent, and the wind began to murmur in the long pine needles.

Lars Larsson did not let the summer day's heat deter him. He played and played. At last evening was ushered in, the sun sank, but his bow needed no rest, and his arm continued to move.

"It is absolutely certain that this will be the death of me!" said he. "And it is a righteous punishment for all my conceit."

Far along in the evening a human being came wandering through the wood. It was a poor old woman with bent back and white hair, and a countenance that was furrowed by many sorrows.

"It seems strange," thought the player, "but I think I recognize that old woman. Can it be possible that it is my mother? Can it be possible that mother has grown so old and gray?"

He called aloud and stopped her. "Mother, mother, come here to me!" he cried.

She paused, as if unwillingly. "I hear now with my own ears that you are the best musician in Vermland," said she. "I can well understand that you do not care any more for a poor old woman like me!"

"Mother, mother, don't pass me by!" cried Lars Larsson. "I'm no great performer – only a poor wretch. Come here that I may speak with you!"

Then the mother came nearer and saw how he sat and played. His face was as pale as death, his hair dripped sweat, and blood oozed out from under the roots of his nails.

"Mother, I have fallen into misfortune because of my vanity, and now I must play myself to death. But tell me, before this happens, if you can forgive me, who left you alone and poor in your old age!"

His mother was seized with a great compassion for the son, and all the anger she had felt toward him was as if blown away. "Why, surely I forgive you!" said she. And as she saw his anguish and bewilderment and wanted him to understand that she meant what she said, she repeated it in the name of God.

"In the name of God our Redeemer, I forgive you!"

And when she said this, the bow stopped, the violin fell to the ground, and the musician arose saved and redeemed. For the enchantment was broken, because his old mother had felt such compassion for his distress that she had spoken God's name over him.

Guy De Maupassant

The Fishing Hole

CUTS AND WOUNDS WHICH CAUSED DEATH. That was the heading of the charge which brought Leopold Renard, upholsterer, before the Assize Court.

Round him were the principal witnesses, Madame Flamèche, widow of the victim, and Louis Ladureau, cabinetmaker, and Jean Durdent, plumber.

Near the criminal was his wife, dressed in black, a little ugly woman, who looked like a monkey dressed as a lady.

This is how Renard (Leopold) recounted the drama:

"Good heavens, it is a misfortune of which I was the first victim all the time, and with which my will has nothing to do. The facts are their own commentary, Monsieur le Président. I am an honest man, a hard working man, an upholsterer in the same street for the last sixteen years, known, liked, respected and esteemed by all, as my neighbors have testified, even the porter who is not *folâtre* every day. I am fond of work, I am fond of saving, I like honest men, and respectable pleasures. That is what has ruined me, so much the worse for me; but as my will had nothing to do with it, I continue to respect myself.

"Every Sunday for the last five years, my wife and I have been to spend the day at Passy. We get fresh air, without counting that we are fond of fishing. Oh! we are as fond of it as we are of small onions. Mélie inspired me with that passion, the jade, and she is more enthusiastic than I am, the scold, seeing that all the mischief in this business is her fault, as you will see immediately.

"I am strong and mild-tempered, without a pennyworth of malice in me. But she! oh! la! la! she looks like nothing, she is short and thin; very well, she does more mischief than a weasel. I do not deny that she has some good qualities; she has some, and very important ones for a man in business. But her character! Just ask about it in the neighborhood, and even the porter's wife, who has just sent me about my business . . . she will tell you something about it.

"Every day she used to find fault with my mild temper: 'I would not put up with this! I would not put up with that.' If I had listened to her, Monsieur le Prèsident, I should have had at least three bouts of fisticuffs a month . . ."

THE FISHING HOLE

Madame Renard interrupted him: "And for good reasons too; they laugh best who laugh last."

He turned towards her frankly: "Oh! very well, I can charge you, since you were the cause of it."

Then, facing the President again he said:

"I will continue. We used to go to Passy every Saturday evening, so as to be able to begin fishing at daybreak the next morning. It is a habit which has become a second nature with us, as the saying is. Three years ago this summer I discovered a place, oh! such a spot! Oh! there! in the shade, eight feet of water at least and perhaps ten, a hole with *retour* under the bank, a regular nest for fish and a paradise for the fisherman. I might look upon that hole as my property, Monsieur le Prèsident, as I was its Christopher Columbus. Everybody in the neighborhood knew it, without making any opposition. They used to say: 'That is Renard's place;' and nobody would have gone to it, not even Monsieur Plumsay, who is well known, be it said without any offense, for boning other peoples' places.

"Well, I returned to my place of which I felt certain, just as if I had owned it. I had scarcely got there on Saturday, when I got into *Delila*, with my wife. *Delila* is my Norwegian boat, which I had built by Fourmaise, and which is light and safe. Well, as I said, we got into the boat and we were going to bait, and for baiting, there is nobody to be compared with me, and they all know it. You want to know with what I bait? I cannot answer that question; it has nothing to do with the accident; I cannot answer, that is my secret. There are more than three hundred people who have asked me; I have been offered glasses of brandy and liquors, fried fish, matelotes, to make me tell! But just go and try whether the chub will come. Ah! they have patted my stomach to get at my secret, my recipe . . . Only my wife knows . . . and she will not tell it, any more than I shall! . . . Is not that so Mélie?"

The President of the Court interrupted him.

"Just get to the facts as soon as you can," and the accused continued: "I am getting to them; I am getting to them. Well, on Saturday July 8, we left by the twenty-five past five train, and before dinner we went to ground-bait as usual. The weather promised to keep fine, and I said to Mélie: 'All right for tomorrow!' And she replied: 'It looks like it.' We never talk more than that together.

"And then we returned to dinner. I was happy and thirsty, and that was the cause of everything. I said to Mélie: 'Look here Mélie, it is fine weather, so suppose I drink a bottle of *Casque à mèche*.' That is a little white wine which we have christened so, because if you drink too much of it it prevents you from sleeping and takes the place of a nightcap. Do you understand me?

"She replied: 'You can do as you please, but you will be ill again, and I will not be able to get up tomorrow.' That was true, sensible and prudent, clear-sighted, I must confess. Nevertheless, I could not withstand it, and I drank my bottle. It all comes from that.

"Well, I could not sleep. By Jove! It kept me awake till two o'clock in the morning, and then I went to sleep so soundly that I should not have heard the angel shouting at the last Judgment.

"In short, my wife woke me at six o'clock, and I jumped out of bed, hastily put on my trousers and jersey, washed my face and jumped on board *Delila*. But it was too late, for when I arrived at my hole it was already taken! Such a thing had never happened to me in three years, and it made me feel as if I were being robbed under my own eyes. I said to myself, 'Confound it all! confound it!' And then my wife began to nag at me. 'Eh! What about your *Casque à mèche*! Get along, you drunkard! Are you satisfied, you great fool?' I could say nothing, because it was all quite true, and so I landed all the same near the spot and tried to profit by what was left. Perhaps after all the fellow might catch nothing, and go away.

"He was a little thin man, in white linen coat and waistcoat, and with a large straw hat, and his wife, a fat woman who was doing embroidery, was behind him.

"When she saw us take up our position close to their place, she murmured: 'I suppose there are no other places on the river!' And my wife, who was furious, replied: 'People who know how to behave, make inquiries about the habits of the neighborhood before occupying reserved spots.'

"As I did not want a fuss, I said to her: 'Hold your tongue, Mélie. Let them go on, let them go on; we shall see.'

"Well, we had fastened *Delila* under the willow trees, and had landed and were fishing side by side, Mélie and I, close to the two others; but here, Monsieur, I must enter into details.

"We had only been there about five minutes when our male neighbor's float began to go down two or three times, and then he pulled out a chub as thick as my thigh, rather less, perhaps, but nearly as big! My heart beat, and the perspiration stood on my forehead, and Mélie said to me: 'Well, you sot, did you see that?'

"Just then, Monsieur Bru, the grocer of Poissy, who is fond of gudgeon fishing, passed in a boat, and called out to me; 'So somebody has taken your usual place, Monsieur Renard?' And I replied: 'Yes, Monsieur Bru, there are some people in this world who do not know the usages of common politeness.'

"The little man in linen pretended not to hear, nor his fat lump of a wife, either."

Here the President interrupted him a second time: "Take care, you are insulting the widow, Madame Flamèche, who is present."

Renard made his excuses: "I beg your pardon, I beg pardon, my anger carried me away. Well, not a quarter of an hour had passed when the little man caught another chub and another almost immediately, and another five minutes later.

"The tears were in my eyes, and then I knew that Madame Renard was boiling with rage, for she kept on nagging at me: 'Oh! how horrid! Don't you see that he is robbing you of your fish? Do you think that you will catch anything? Not even a frog, nothing whatever. Why my hands are burning, just to think of it.'

"But I said to myself: 'Let us wait until twelve o'clock. Then this poaching fellow will go to lunch, and I shall get my place again.' As for me, Monsieur le Président, I lunch on the spot every Sunday; we bring our provisions in *Delila*. But there! At twelve o'clock, the wretch produced a fowl out of a newspaper, and while he was eating, actually he caught another chub!

"Mélie and I had a morsel also, just a thumb-piece, a mere nothing, for our heart was not in it.

"Then I took up my newspaper, to aid my digestion. Every Sunday I read the *Gil Blas* in the shade like that, by the side of the water. It is Columbine's day, you know, Columbine who writes the articles in the *Gil Blas*. I generally put Madame Renard into a passion by pretending to know this Columbine. It is not true, for I do not know her, and have never seen her, but that does not matter; she writes very well, and then she says things straight out for a woman. She suits me, and there are not many of her sort.

"Well, I began to tease my wife, but she got angry immediately, and very angry, and so I held my tongue, and at that moment our two witnesses who are present here, Monsieur Ladureau and Monsieur Durdent, appeared on the other side of the river. We knew each other by sight. The little man began to fish again, and he caught so many that I trembled with vexation, and his wife said: 'It is an uncommonly good spot, and we will come here always Désiré.' As for me, a cold shiver ran down my back, and Madame Renard kept repeating: 'You are not a man; you have the blood of a chicken in your veins'; and suddenly I said to her: 'Look here, I would rather go away, or I shall only be doing something foolish.'

"And she whispered to me as if she had put a red-hot iron under my nose: 'You are not a man. Now you are going to run away, and surrender your place! Off you go, Bazaine!'

"Well, I felt that, but yet I did not move, while the other fellow pulled out a bream, oh! I never saw such a large one before, never! And then my wife began to talk aloud, as if she were thinking, and you can see her trickery. She said: 'That is what one might call stolen fish, seeing that we baited the place ourselves. At any rate, they ought to give us back the money we have spent on bait.'

"Then the fat woman in the cotton dress said in turn: 'Do you mean to call us thieves, Madame?' And they began to explain, and then they came to words. Oh! Lord! those creatures know some good ones. They shouted so loud, that our two witnesses, who were on the other bank, began to call out by way of a joke: 'Less noise over there; you will prevent your husbands from fishing.'

"The fact is that neither of us moved any more than if we had been two tree-stumps. We remained there, with our noses over the water, as if we had heard nothing, but by Jove, we heard all the same. 'You are a mere liar.—You are nothing better than a streetwalker.—you are only a trollop.—You are a regular strumpet.' And so on, and so on; a sailor could not have said more.

"Suddenly I heard a noise behind me, and turned round. It was the other one, the fat woman, who had fallen onto my wife with her parasol. *Whack! whack!* Mélie got two of them, but she was furious, and she hits hard when she is in a rage, so she caught the fat woman by the hair and then, *thump, thump*, and slaps in the face rained down like ripe plums. I should have let them go on; women among themselves; men among themselves; it does not do to mix the blows, but the little man in the linen jacket jumped up like a devil and was going to rush at my wife. Ah! no, no, not that my friend! I caught the gentleman with the end of my fist, and *crash, crash*, one on the nose, the other in the stomach. He threw up his arms and legs and fell on his back into the river, just into the hole.

"I should have fished him out most certainly, Monsieur le Président, if I had had the time. But unfortunately the fat woman got the better of it, and she was drubbing Mélie terribly. I know that I ought not to have assisted her while the man was drinking his fill, but I never thought that he would drown, and said to myself: 'Bah, it will cool him.'

"I therefore ran up to the women to separate

them, and all I received was scratches and bites. Good Lord, what creatures! Well, it took me five minutes, and perhaps ten to separate those two viragoes, and when I turned round, there was nothing more to be seen, and the water was as smooth as a lake, while the others yonder kept shouting: 'Fish him out!' and though it was all very well to say that, I cannot swim and still less dive!

"At last the man from the dam came, and two gentlemen with boat hooks, but it had taken over a quarter of an hour. He was found at the bottom of the hole in eight feet of water, as I have said, but he had got it, the poor little man in his linen suit! There are the facts, such as I have sworn to. I am innocent, on my honor."

The witnesses having deposed to the same effect, the accused was acquitted.

Algernon Blackwood

The Olive

He laughed involuntarily as the olive rolled towards his chair across the shiny parquet floor of the hotel dining-room.

His table in the cavernous *salle-à-manger* was apart: he sat alone, a solitary guest; the table from which the olive fell and rolled towards him was some distance away. The angle, however, made him an unlikely objective. Yet the lob-sided, juicy thing, after hesitating once or twice *en route* as it plopped along, came to rest finally against his feet.

It settled with an inviting, almost an aggressive, air. And he stooped and picked it up, putting it rather self-consciously, because of the girl from whose table it had come, on the white tablecloth beside his plate.

Then, looking up, he caught her eye, and saw that she, too, was laughing, though not a bit self-consciously. As she helped herself to the *hors d'œuvres* a false move had sent it flying. She watched him pick the olive up and set it beside his plate. Her eyes then suddenly looked away again—at her mother—questioningly.

The incident was closed. But the little oblong, succulent olive lay beside his plate, so that his fingers played with it. He fingered it automatically from time to time until his lonely meal was finished.

When no one was looking he slipped it into his pocket, as though, having taken the trouble to pick it up, this was the very least he could do with it. Heaven alone knows why, but he then took it upstairs with him, setting it on the marble mantelpiece among his field glasses, tobacco tins, inkbottles, pipes, and candlestick. At any rate, he kept it—the moist, shiny, lob-sided, juicy little oblong olive. The hotel lounge wearied him; he came to his room after dinner to smoke at his ease, his coat off and his feet on a chair; to read another chapter of Freud, to write a letter or two he didn't in the least want to write, and then to go to bed at ten o'clock. But this evening the olive kept rolling between him and the thing he read; it rolled between the paragraphs, between the lines; the olive was more vital than the interest of these eternal "complexes" and "suppressed desires."

The truth was that he kept seeing the eyes of the laughing girl beyond the bouncing olive. She had smiled at him in such a natural, spontaneous, friendly way before her mother's glance had checked her—a smile, he felt, that might lead to acquaintance on the morrow.

He wondered! A thrill of possible adventure ran through him.

She was a merry-looking sort of girl, with a happy, half-roguish face that seemed on the look-out for somebody to play with. Her mother, like most of the people in the big hotel, was an invalid; the girl, a dutiful and patient daughter. They had arrived that very day apparently.

A laugh is a revealing thing, he thought as he fell asleep, to dream of a lob-sided olive rolling consciously towards him, and of a girl's eyes that watched its awkward movements, then looked up into his own and laughed. In his dream the olive had been deliberately and cleverly dispatched upon its uncertain journey. It was a message.

He did not know, of course, that the mother, chiding her daughter's awkwardness, had muttered:

"There you are again, child! True to your name, you never see an olive without doing something queer and odd with it!"

A youngish man, whose knowledge of chemistry, including invisible inks and such-like mysteries, had proved so valuable to the Censor's Department that for five years he had overworked without a holiday, the Italian Riviera had attracted him, and he had come out for a two months' rest. It was his first visit. Sun, mimosa, blue seas and brilliant skies had tempted him; exchange made a pound worth forty, fifty, sixty, and seventy shillings. He found the place lovely, but somewhat untenanted.

He stayed on, however, caught by the sunshine and the good exchange, also without the physical energy to discover a better, livelier place. He went for walks among the olive groves, he sat beside the sea and palms, he visited shops and bought things he did not want because the exchange made them seem cheap; he paid immense "extras" in his weekly bill, then chuckled as he reduced them to shillings and found that a few pence covered them; he lay with a book for hours among the olive groves.

The olive groves! His daily life could not escape the olive groves; to olive groves, sooner or later, his walks, his expeditions, his meanderings by the sea, his shopping—all led him to these ubiquitous olive groves.

If he bought a picture postcard to send home, there was sure to be an olive grove in one corner of it. The whole place was smothered with olive groves, the people owed their incomes and existence to these irrepressible trees. The villages among the hills swam roof-deep in them. They swarmed even in the hotel gardens.

The guide-books praised them as persistently as the residents brought them, sooner or later, into every conversation. They grew lyrical over them:

"And how do you like our olive trees? Ah, you think them pretty. At first, most people are disappointed. They grow on one."

"They do," he agreed.

"I'm glad you appreciate them. I find them the embodiment of grace. And when the wind lifts the underleaves across a whole mountain slope—why, it's wonderful, isn't it? One realises the meaning of 'olive-green.'"

"One does." He sighed. "But, all the same, I should like to get one to eat—an olive, I mean."

"Ah, to eat, yes. That's not so easy. You see, the crop is . . ."

"Exactly," he interrupted impatiently, weary of the habitual and evasive explanations. "But I should like to taste the *fruit*. I should like to enjoy one."

For, after a stay of six weeks, he had never once seen an olive on the table, in the shops, nor even on the street barrows at the market-place. He had never tasted one. No one sold olives, though olive trees were a drug in the place; no one bought them, no one asked for them; it seemed that no one wanted them. The trees, when he looked closely, were thick with a dark little berry that seemed more like a sour sloe than the succulent, delicious spicy fruit associated with its name.

Men climbed the trunks, everywhere shaking the laden branches and hitting them with long bamboo poles to knock the fruit off, while women and children, squatting on their haunches, spent laborious hours filling baskets underneath, then loading mules and donkeys with their daily "catch." But an olive to eat was unobtainable. He had never cared for olives, but now he craved with all his soul to feel his teeth in one.

"Ach! But it is the Spanish olive that you *eat*," explained the head waiter, a German "from Basel." "These are for oil only." After which he disliked the olive more than ever—until that night when he saw the first eatable specimen rolling across the shiny parquet floor, propelled towards him by the careless hand of a pretty girl, who then looked up into his eyes and smiled.

He was convinced that Eve, similarly, had rolled the apple towards Adam across the emerald sward of the first garden in the world. The dull, accumulated resentment he had come to feel, subconsciously perhaps, against an elusive fruit, was changed in the

THE OLIVE

twinkling of an eye, into a source of joy, a symbol of romance.

He slept usually like the dead. It must have been something very real that made him open his eyes and sit up in bed alertly. There was a noise against his door. He listened. The room was still quite dark. It was early morning. The noise was not repeated.

"Who's there?" he asked in a sleepy whisper. "What is it?"

The noise came again. Someone was scratching on the door. No, it was somebody tapping.

"What d'you want?" he demanded in a louder voice. "Come in," he added, wondering sleepily whether he was presentable. Either the hotel was on fire or the porter was waking the wrong person for some sunrise expedition.

Nothing happened. Wide awake now, he turned the switch on, but no light flooded the room. The electricians, he remembered with a curse, were out on strike. He fumbled for the matches, and as he did so a voice in the corridor became distinctly audible. It was just outside his door.

"Aren't you ready?" he heard. "You sleep for ever."

And the voice, although, never having heard it before, he could not have recognised it, belonged, he knew suddenly, to the girl who had let the olive fall. In an instant he was out of bed. He lit a candle.

"I'm coming," he called softly, as he slipped rapidly into some clothes. "I'm sorry I've kept you. I shan't be a minute."

"Be quick then!" he heard, while the candle flame slowly grew, and he found his garments. Less than three minutes later he opened the door and, candle in hand, peered into the dark passage.

"Blow it out!" came a peremptory whisper. He obeyed, but not quick enough. A pair of red lips emerged from the shadows. There was a puff, and the candle was extinguished. "I've got my reputation to consider. We mustn't be seen, of course!"

The face vanished in the darkness, but he had recognised it—the shining skin, the bright glancing eyes. The sweet breath touched his cheek. The candlestick was taken from him by a swift, deft movement. He heard it knock the wainscoting as it was set down. He went out into a pitch-black corridor, where a soft hand seized his own and led him—by a back door, it seemed—out into the open air of the hill-side immediately behind the hotel.

He saw the stars. The morning was cool and fragrant, the sharp air waked him, and the last vestiges of sleep went flying. He had been drowsy and confused, had obeyed the summons without thinking. He now realised suddenly that he was engaged in an act of madness.

The girl, dressed in some flimsy material thrown loosely about her head and body, stood a few feet away, looking, he thought, like some figure called out of dreams and slumber of a forgotten world, out of legend almost. He saw her evening shoes peep out; he divined an evening dress beneath the gauzy covering. The light wind blew it close against her figure. He thought of a nymph.

"I say—but haven't you been to bed?" he asked stupidly.

He had meant to expostulate, to apologise for his foolish rashness, to scold and say they must go back at once. Instead, this sentence came. He guessed she had been sitting up all night. He stood still a second, staring in mute admiration, his eyes full of bewildered question.

"Watching the stars," she met his thought with a happy laugh. "Orion has touched the horizon. I came for you at once. We've got just four hours!" The voice, the smile, the eyes, the reference to Orion, swept him off his feet. Something in him broke loose and flew wildly, recklessly to the stars.

"Let us be off!" he cried, "before the Bear tilts

down. Already Alcyone begins to fade. I'm ready. Come!"

She laughed. The wind blew the gauze aside to show two ivory-white limbs. She caught his hand again, and they scampered together up the steep hillside towards the woods. Soon the big hotel, the villas, the white houses of the little town where natives and visitors still lay soundly sleeping, were out of sight. The farther sky came down to meet them. The stars were paling, but no sign of actual dawn was yet visible. The freshness stung their cheeks.

Slowly, the heavens grew lighter, the east turned rose, the outline of the trees defined themselves, there was a stirring of the silvery-green leaves. They were among olive groves—but the spirits of the trees were dancing. Far below them, a pool of deep colour, they saw the ancient sea. They saw the tiny specks of distant fishing-boats. The sailors were singing to the dawn, and birds among the mimosa of the hanging gardens answered them.

Pausing a moment at length beneath a gaunt old tree, whose struggle to leave the clinging earth had tortured its great writhing arms and trunk, they took their breath, gazing at one another with eyes full of happy dreams.

"You understood so quickly," said the girl, "my

little message. I knew by your eyes and ears you would." And she first tweaked his ears with two slender fingers mischievously, then laid her soft palm with a momentary light pressure on both eyes.

"You're half-and-half, at any rate," she went on, looking him up and down for a swift instant of appraisement, "if you're not altogether." The laughter showed her white, even little teeth.

"You know how to play, and that's something," she added. Then, as if to herself, "You'll be altogether before I've done with you."

"Shall I?" he stammered, afraid to look at her.

Puzzled, some spirit of compromise still lingering in him, he knew not what she meant; he knew only that the current of life flowed increasingly through his veins, but that her eyes confused him.

"I'm longing for it," he added. "How wonderfully you did it! They roll so awkwardly—"

"Oh, that!" She peered at him through a wisp of hair. "You've kept it, I hope."

"Rather. It's on my mantelpiece—"

"You're sure you haven't eaten it?" and she made a delicious mimicry with her red lips, so that he saw the tip of a small pointed tongue.

"I shall keep it," he swore, "as long as these arms have life in them," and he seized her just as she was crouching to escape, and covered her with kisses.

"I knew you longed to play," she panted, when he released her. "Still, it was sweet of you to pick it up before another got it."

"Another!" he exclaimed.

"The gods decide. It's a lob-sided thing, remember. It can't roll straight." She looked oddly mischievous, elusive.

He stared at her.

"If it had rolled elsewhere—and another had picked it up—?" he began.

"I should be with that other now!" And this time she was off and away before he could prevent her, and the sound of her silvery laughter mocked among the olive trees beyond. He was up and after her in a second, following her slim whiteness in and out of the old-world grove, as she flitted lightly, her hair flying in the wind, her figure flashing like a ray of sunlight or the race of foaming water—till at last he caught her and drew her down upon his knees, and kissed her wildly, forgetting who and where and what he was.

"Hark!" she whispered breathlessly, one arm close about his neck. "I hear their footsteps. Listen! It is the pipe!"

"The pipe—!" he repeated, conscious of a tiny but delicious shudder.

For a sudden chill ran through him as she said it. He gazed at her. Her hair fell loose about her cheeks, flushed and rosy with his hot kisses. Her eyes were bright and wild for all their softness. Her face, turned sideways to him as she listened, wore an extraordinary look that for an instant made his blood run cold. He saw the parted lips, the small white teeth, the slim neck of ivory, the young bosom panting from his tempestuous embrace. Of an unearthly loveliness and brightness she seemed to him, yet with this strange, remote expression that touched his soul with sudden terror.

Her face turned slowly.

"Who *are* you?" he whispered. He sprang to his feet without waiting for her answer.

He was young and agile; strong, too, with that quick response of muscle they have who keep their bodies well; but he was no match for her. Her speed and agility outclassed his own with ease. She leaped. Before he had moved one leg forward towards escape, she was clinging with soft, supple arms and limbs about him, so that he could not free himself, and as her weight bore him downwards to the ground, her lips found his own and kissed them into silence. She lay buried again in his embrace, her hair across his eyes, her heart against his heart, and he forgot his question, forgot his little fear, forgot the very world he knew . . .

"They come, they come," she cried gaily. "The Dawn is here. Are you ready?"

"I've been ready for five thousand years," he answered, leaping to his feet beside her.

"Altogether!" came upon a sparkling laugh that was like wind among the olive leaves.

Shaking her last gauzy covering from her, she snatched his hand, and they ran forward together to join the dancing throng now crowding up the slope beneath the trees. Their happy singing filled the sky. Decked with vine and ivy, and trailing silvery green branches, they poured in a flood of radiant life along the mountain side. Slowly they melted away into the blue distance of the breaking dawn, and, as the last figure disappeared, the sun came up slowly out of a purple sea . . .

They came to the place he knew—the deserted earthquake village—and a faint memory stirred in him. He did not actually recall that he had visited it already, had eaten his sandwiches with "hotel friends" beneath its crumbling walls; but there was a dim troubling sense of familiarity—nothing more. The houses still stood, but pigeons lived in them, and weasels, stoats, and snakes had their uncertain homes in ancient bedrooms. Not twenty years ago the peasants thronged its narrow streets, through which the dawn now peered and cool wind breathed among dew-laden brambles.

"I know the house," she cried, "the house where we would live!" and raced, a flying form of air and sunlight, into a tumbled cottage that had no roof, no floor or windows. Wild bees had hung a nest against the broken wall.

He followed her. There was sunlight in the room, and there were flowers. Upon a rude, simple table lay a bowl of cream, with eggs, and honey and butter close against a home-made loaf. They sank into each other's arms upon a couch of fragrant grass and boughs against the window where wild roses bloomed . . . and the bees flew in and out.

It was Bussana, the so-called earthquake village, because a sudden earthquake had fallen on it one summer morning when all the inhabitants were at church. The crashing roof killed sixty, the tumbling walls another hundred, and the rest had left it where it stood.

"The Church," he said, vaguely remembering the story. "They were at prayer—"

The girl laughed carelessly in his ear, setting his blood in a rush and quiver of delicious joy. He felt himself untamed, wild as the wind and animals.

"The true God claimed His own," she whispered. "He came back. Ah, they were not ready—the old priests had seen to that. But He came. They heard His music. Then His tread shook the olive groves, the old ground danced, the hills leapt for joy—"

"They called it earthquake! And the houses crumbled," he laughed as he pressed her closer to his heart.

"And now we've come back!" she cried merrily. "We've come back to worship and be glad!" She nestled into him, while the sun rose higher.

"I hear them—hark!" she cried, and again leapt, dancing, from his side. Again he followed her like wind. Through the broken window they saw the naked fauns and nymphs and satyrs rolling, dancing, shaking their soft hoofs amid the ferns and brambles. Towards the ruptured church they sped with feet of light and air. A roar of happy song and laughter rose.

"Come!" he cried. "We must go too."

Hand in hand they raced to join the tumbling, dancing throng. She was in his arms and on his back and flung across his shoulders, as he ran. They reached the broken building, its whole roof gone sliding years ago, its walls a-tremble still, its shattered shrines alive with nestling birds.

THE OLIVE

"Hush!" she whispered, in a tone of awe, yet pleasure. "*He* is there!" She pointed, her bare arm outstretched, above the bending heads.

There, in the empty space, where once stood sacred Host and cup, He sat, filling the niche sublimely and with awful power. His shaggy form, benign yet terrible, rose through the broken stone. The great eyes shone and smiled. The feet were lost in brambles . . .

"God!" cried a wild, frightened voice, yet with deep worship in it—and the old familiar panic came with portentous swiftness. The great Figure rose.

The birds flew screaming, the animals sought holes, the worshippers, laughing and glad a moment ago, rushed tumbling over one another for the doors.

"He goes again! Who called? Who called like that? His feet shake the ground!"

"It is the earthquake!" screamed a woman's shrill accents in ghastly terror.

"Kiss me—one kiss before we forget again . . .!" sighed a laughing, passionate voice against his ear. "Once more your arms, your heart beating on my lips . . .! You recognised his power. You are now *altogether*! We shall remember!"

But he woke, with the heavy bed-clothes stuffed

against his mouth and the wind of early morning sighing mournfully about the hotel walls.

"Have they left again—those ladies?" he enquired casually of the head waiter, pointing to the table. "They were here last night at dinner."

"Who do you mean?" replied the man stupidly, gazing at the spot indicated with a face quite blank. "Last night—at dinner?" He tried to think.

"An English lady, elderly, with—her daughter—" at which moment precisely the girl came in alone. Lunch was over, the room empty.

There was a second's difficult pause. It seemed ridiculous not to speak. Their eyes met. The girl blushed furiously.

He was very quick for an Englishman. "I was allowing myself to ask after your mother," he began. "I was afraid"—he glanced at the table laid for one—"she was not well, perhaps?"

"Oh, but that's very kind of you, I'm sure." She smiled. He saw the small white even teeth . . .

And before three days had passed, he was so deeply in love that he simply couldn't help himself.

"I believe," he said lamely, "this is yours. You dropped it, you know. Er—may I keep it? It's only an olive."

THE OLIVE

They were, of course, in an olive grove when he asked it, and the sun was setting.

She looked at him, looked him up and down, looked at his ears, his eyes. He felt that in another second her little fingers would slip up and tweak the first or close the second with a soft pressure—

"Tell me," he begged: "did you dream anything—that first night I saw you?"

She took a quick step backwards. "No," she said, as he followed her more quickly still, "I don't think I did. But," she went on breathlessly as he caught her up, "I knew—from the way you picked it up—"

"Knew what?" he demanded, holding her tightly so that she could not get away again.

"That you were already half and half, but would soon be altogether."

And, as he kissed her, he felt her soft fingers tweak his ears.

KATHERINE MANSFIELD

At the Bay

I

Very early morning. The sun was not yet risen, and the whole of Crescent Bay was hidden under a white sea-mist. The big bush-covered hills at the back were smothered. You could not see where they ended and the paddocks and bungalows began. The sandy road was gone and the paddocks and bungalows the other side of it; there were no white dunes covered with reddish grass beyond them; there was nothing to mark which was beach and where was the sea. A heavy dew had fallen. The grass was blue. Big drops hung on the bushes and just did not fall; the silvery, fluffy toi-toi was limp on its long stalks, and all the marigolds and the pinks in the bungalow gardens were bowed to the earth with wetness. Drenched were the cold fuchsias, round pearls of dew lay on the flat nasturtium leaves. It looked as though the sea had beaten up softly in the darkness, as though one immense wave had come rippling, rippling—how far? Perhaps if you had waked up in the middle of the night you might have seen a big fish flicking in at the window and gone again . . .

Ah-Aah! sounded the sleepy sea. And from the bush there came the sound of little streams flowing, quickly, lightly, slipping between the smooth stones, gushing into ferny basins and out again; and there was the splashing of big drops on large leaves, and something else—what was it?—a faint stirring and shaking, the snapping of a twig and then such silence that it seemed some one was listening.

Round the corner of Crescent Bay, between the piled-up masses of broken rock, a flock of sheep came pattering. They were huddled together, a small, tossing, woolly mass, and their thin, stick-like legs trotted along quickly as if the cold and the quiet had frightened them. Behind them an old sheep-dog, his soaking paws covered with sand, ran along with his nose to the ground, but carelessly, as if thinking of something else. And then in the rocky gateway the shepherd himself appeared. He was a lean, upright old man, in a frieze coat that was covered with a web of tiny drops, velvet trousers tied under the knee, and a wide-awake with a folded blue handkerchief round the brim. One hand was crammed into his belt, the other grasped a beautifully smooth yellow stick. And as he walked, taking his time, he kept up a very soft light whistling, an airy, far-away fluting that sounded mournful and tender. The old dog cut an ancient caper or two and then drew up sharp, ashamed of his levity, and walked a few dignified paces by his master's side. The sheep ran forward in little pattering rushes; they began to bleat, and ghostly flocks and herds answered them from under the sea. "Baa! Baaaa!" For a time they seemed to be always on the same piece of ground. There ahead was stretched the sandy road with shallow puddles; the same soaking bushes showed on either side and the same shadowy palings. Then something immense came into view; an enormous shock-haired giant with his arms stretched out. It was the big gum-tree outside Mrs. Stubbs's shop, and as they passed by there was a strong whiff of eucalyptus. And now big spots of light gleamed in the mist. The shepherd stopped whistling; he rubbed his red nose and wet beard on his wet sleeve and, screwing up his eyes, glanced in the direction of the sea. The sun was rising. It was marvellous how quickly the mist thinned, sped away, dissolved from the shallow plain, rolled up from the bush and was gone as if in a hurry to escape; big twists and curls jostled and shouldered each other as the silvery beams broadened. The far-away sky—a bright, pure blue—was reflected in the puddles, and the drops, swimming along the telegraph poles, flashed into points of light. Now the leaping, glittering sea was so bright it made one's eyes ache to look at it. The shepherd drew a pipe, the bowl as small as an acorn, out of his breast pocket, fumbled for a chunk of speckled tobacco, pared off a few shavings and stuffed the bowl. He was a grave, fine-looking old man. As he lit up and the blue smoke wreathed his head, the dog, watching, looked proud of him.

"Baa! Baaa!" The sheep spread out into a fan. They were just clear of the summer colony before the first sleeper turned over and lifted a drowsy head; their cry sounded in the dreams of little children . . . who lifted their arms to drag down, to cuddle the darling little woolly lambs of sleep. Then the first inhabitant appeared; it was the Burnells' cat Florrie, sitting on the gatepost, far too early as usual, looking for their milk-girl. When she saw the old sheep-dog she sprang up quickly, arched her back, drew in her tabby head, and seemed to give a little fastidious shiver. "Ugh! What a coarse, revolting creature!" said Florrie. But the old sheep-dog, not looking up, waggled past, flinging out his legs from side to side. Only one of his ears twitched to prove that he saw, and thought her a silly young female.

The breeze of morning lifted in the bush and the smell of leaves and wet black earth mingled with the sharp smell of the sea. Myriads of birds were singing. A goldfinch flew over the shepherd's head and, perching on the tiptop of a spray, it turned to the sun, ruffling its small breast feathers. And now they had passed the fisherman's hut, passed the charred-looking little *whare* where Leila the milk-girl lived with her old Gran. The sheep strayed over a yellow swamp and Wag, the sheep-dog, padded after, rounded them up and headed them for the steeper, narrower rocky pass that led out of Crescent Bay and towards Daylight Cove. "Baa! Baa!" Faint the cry came as they rocked along the fast-drying road. The shepherd put away his pipe, dropping it into his breast-pocket so that the little bowl hung over. And straightway the soft airy whistling began again. Wag ran out along a ledge of rock after something that smelled, and ran back again disgusted. Then pushing, nudging, hurrying, the sheep rounded the bend and the shepherd followed after out of sight.

II

A few moments later the back door of one of the bungalows opened, and a figure in a broad-striped bathing suit flung down the paddock, cleared the stile, rushed through the tussock grass into the hollow, staggered up the sandy hillock, and raced for dear life over the big porous stones, over the cold, wet pebbles, on to the hard sand that gleamed like oil. Splish-splosh! Splish-splosh! The water bubbled round his legs as Stanley Burnell waded out exulting. First man in as usual! He'd beaten them all again. And he swooped down to souse his head and neck.

"Hail, brother! All hail, Thou Mighty One!" A velvety bass voice came booming over the water.

Great Scott! Damnation take it! Stanley lifted up to see a dark head bobbing far out and an arm lifted. It was Jonathan Trout—there before him! "Glorious morning!" sang the voice.

"Yes, very fine!" said Stanley briefly. Why the dickens didn't the fellow stick to his part of the sea? Why should he come barging over to this exact spot? Stanley gave a kick, a lunge and struck out, swimming overarm. But Jonathan was a match for him. Up he came, his black hair sleek on his forehead, his short beard sleek.

"I had an extraordinary dream last night!" he shouted.

What was the matter with the man? This mania for conversation irritated Stanley beyond words. And it was always the same—always some piffle about a dream he'd had, or some cranky idea he'd got hold of, or some rot he'd been reading. Stanley turned over on his back and kicked with his legs till he was a living waterspout. But even then . . . "I dreamed I was hanging over a terrifically high cliff, shouting to some one below." You would be! thought Stanley. He could stick no more of it. He stopped splashing. "Look here, Trout," he said, "I'm in rather a hurry this morning."

"You're WHAT?" Jonathan was so surprised—or pretended to be—that he sank under the water, then reappeared again blowing.

"All I mean is," said Stanley, "I've no time to—to—to fool about. I want to get this over. I'm in a hurry. I've work to do this morning—see?"

Jonathan was gone before Stanley had finished. "Pass, friend!" said the bass voice gently, and he slid away through the water with scarcely a ripple . . . But curse the fellow! He'd ruined Stanley's bathe. What an unpractical idiot the man was! Stanley struck out to sea again, and then as quickly swam in again, and away he rushed up the beach. He felt cheated.

Jonathan stayed a little longer in the water. He floated, gently moving his hands like fins, and letting the sea rock his long, skinny body. It was curious, but in spite of everything he was fond of Stanley Burnell. True, he had a fiendish desire to tease him sometimes, to poke fun at him, but at bottom he was sorry for the fellow. There was something pathetic in his determination to make a job of everything. You couldn't help feeling he'd be caught out one day, and then what an almighty cropper he'd come! At that moment an immense wave lifted Jonathan, rode past him, and broke along the beach with a joyful sound. What a beauty! And now there came another. That was the way to live—carelessly, recklessly, spending oneself. He got on to his feet and began to wade towards the shore, pressing his toes into the firm, wrinkled sand. To take things easy, not to fight against the ebb and flow of life, but to give way to it—that was what was needed. It was this tension that was all wrong. To live—to live! And the perfect morning, so fresh and fair, basking in the light, as though laughing at its own beauty, seemed to whisper, "Why not?"

But now he was out of the water Jonathan turned blue with cold. He ached all over; it was as though some one was wringing the blood out of him. And stalking up the beach, shivering, all his muscles tight, he too felt his bathe was spoilt. He'd stayed in too long.

III

Beryl was alone in the living-room when Stanley appeared, wearing a blue serge suit, a stiff collar and a spotted tie. He looked almost uncannily clean and brushed; he was going to town for the day. Dropping into his chair, he pulled out his watch and put it beside his plate.

"I've just got twenty-five minutes," he said. "You might go and see if the porridge is ready, Beryl?"

"Mother's just gone for it," said Beryl. She sat down at the table and poured out his tea.

"Thanks!" Stanley took a sip. "Hallo!" he said in an astonished voice, "you've forgotten the sugar."

"Oh, sorry!" But even then Beryl didn't help him; she pushed the basin across. What did this mean? As Stanley helped himself his blue eyes widened; they seemed to quiver. He shot a quick glance at his sister-in-law and leaned back.

"Nothing wrong, is there?" he asked carelessly, fingering his collar.

Beryl's head was bent; she turned her plate in her fingers.

"Nothing," said her light voice. Then she too looked up, and smiled at Stanley. "Why should there be?"

"O-oh! No reason at all as far as I know. I thought you seemed rather—"

At that moment the door opened and the three little girls appeared, each carrying a porridge plate. They were dressed alike in blue jerseys and knickers; their brown legs were bare, and each had her hair plaited and pinned up in what was called a horse's tail. Behind them came Mrs. Fairfield with the tray.

"Carefully, children," she warned. But they were taking the very greatest care. They loved being allowed to carry things. "Have you said good morning to your father?"

"Yes, grandma." They settled themselves on the bench opposite Stanley and Beryl.

"Good morning, Stanley!" Old Mrs. Fairfield gave him his plate.

"Morning, mother! How's the boy?"

"Splendid! He only woke up once last night. What a perfect morning!" The old woman paused, her hand on the loaf of bread, to gaze out of the open door into the garden. The sea sounded. Through the wide-open window streamed the sun on to the yellow varnished walls and bare floor. Everything on the table flashed and glittered. In the middle there was an old salad bowl filled with yellow and red nasturtiums. She smiled, and a look of deep content shone in her eyes.

"You might *cut* me a slice of that bread, mother," said Stanley. "I've only twelve and a half minutes before the coach passes. Has any one given my shoes to the servant girl?"

"Yes, they're ready for you." Mrs. Fairfield was quite unruffled.

AT THE BAY

"Oh, Kezia! Why are you such a messy child!" cried Beryl despairingly.

"Me, Aunt Beryl?" Kezia stared at her. What had she done now? She had only dug a river down the middle of her porridge, filled it, and was eating the banks away. But she did that every single morning, and no one had said a word up till now.

"Why can't you eat your food properly like Isabel and Lottie?" How unfair grown-ups are!

"But Lottie always makes a floating island, don't you, Lottie?"

"I don't," said Isabel smartly. "I just sprinkle mine with sugar and put on the milk and finish it. Only babies play with their food."

Stanley pushed back his chair and got up.

"Would you get me those shoes, mother? And, Beryl, if you've finished, I wish you'd cut down to the gate and stop the coach. Run in to your mother, Isabel, and ask her where my bowler hat's been put. Wait a minute—have you children been playing with my stick?"

"No, father!"

"But I put it here." Stanley began to bluster. "I remember distinctly putting it in this corner. Now, who's had it? There's no time to lose. Look sharp! The stick's got to be found."

Even Alice, the servant-girl, was drawn into the

chase. "You haven't been using it to poke the kitchen fire with by any chance?"

Stanley dashed into the bedroom where Linda was lying. "Most extraordinary thing. I can't keep a single possession to myself. They've made away with my stick, now!"

"Stick, dear? What stick?" Linda's vagueness on these occasions could not be real, Stanley decided. Would nobody sympathize with him?

"Coach! Coach, Stanley!" Beryl's voice cried from the gate.

Stanley waved his arm to Linda. "No time to say good-bye!" he cried. And he meant that as a punishment to her.

He snatched his bowler hat, dashed out of the house, and swung down the garden path. Yes, the coach was there waiting, and Beryl, leaning over the open gate, was laughing up at somebody or other just as if nothing had happened. The heartlessness of women! The way they took it for granted it was your job to slave away for them while they didn't even take the trouble to see that your walking-stick wasn't lost. Kelly trailed his whip across the horses.

"Good-bye, Stanley," called Beryl, sweetly and gaily. It was easy enough to say good-bye! And there she stood, idle, shading her eyes with her hand. The worst of it was Stanley had to shout good-bye too, for the sake of appearances. Then he saw her turn, give a little skip and run back to the house. She was glad to be rid of him!

Yes, she was thankful. Into the living-room she ran and called "He's gone!" Linda cried from her room: "Beryl! Has Stanley gone?" Old Mrs. Fairfield appeared, carrying the boy in his little flannel coatee.

"Gone?"

"Gone!"

Oh, the relief, the difference it made to have the man out of the house. Their very voices were changed as they called to one another; they sounded warm and loving and as if they shared a secret. Beryl went over to the table. "Have another cup of tea, mother. It's still hot." She wanted, somehow, to celebrate the fact that they could do what they liked now. There was no man to disturb them; the whole perfect day was theirs.

"No, thank you, child," said old Mrs. Fairfield, but the way at that moment she tossed the boy up and said "a-goos-a-goos-a-ga!" to him meant that she felt the same. The little girls ran into the paddock like chickens let out of a coop.

Even Alice, the servant-girl, washing up the dishes in the kitchen, caught the infection and used the precious tank water in a perfectly reckless fashion.

"Oh, these men!" said she, and she plunged the teapot into the bowl and held it under the water even after it had stopped bubbling, as if it too was a man and drowning was too good for them.

IV

"Wait for me, Isa-bel! Kezia, wait for me!"

There was poor little Lottie, left behind again, because she found it so fearfully hard to get over the stile by herself. When she stood on the first step her knees began to wobble; she grasped the post. Then you had to put one leg over. But which leg? She never could decide. And when she did finally put one leg over with a sort of stamp of despair—then the feeling was awful. She was half in the paddock still and half in the tussock grass. She clutched the post desperately and lifted up her voice. "Wait for me!"

"No, don't you wait for her, Kezia!" said Isabel. "She's such a little silly. She's always making a fuss. Come on!" And she tugged Kezia's jersey. "You can use my bucket if you come with me," she said kindly. "It's bigger than yours." But Kezia couldn't leave Lottie all by herself. She ran back to her. By this time Lottie was very red in the face and breathing heavily.

"Here, put your other foot over," said Kezia.

"Where?"

Lottie looked down at Kezia as if from a mountain height.

"Here where my hand is." Kezia patted the place.

"Oh, *there* do you mean!" Lottie gave a deep sigh and put the second foot over.

"Now—sort of turn round and sit down and slide," said Kezia.

"But there's nothing to sit down *on*, Kezia," said Lottie.

She managed it at last, and once it was over she shook herself and began to beam.

"I'm getting better at climbing over stiles, aren't I, Kezia?"

Lottie's was a very hopeful nature.

The pink and the blue sunbonnet followed Isabel's bright red sunbonnet up that sliding, slipping hill. At the top they paused to decide where to go and to have a good stare at who was there already. Seen from behind, standing against the skyline, gesticulating largely with their spades, they looked like minute puzzled explorers.

The whole family of Samuel Josephs was there already with their lady-help, who sat on a camp-stool and kept order with a whistle that she wore tied round her neck, and a small cane with which she directed operations. The Samuel Josephs never played by themselves or managed their own game. If they did, it ended in the boys pouring water down the girls' necks or the girls trying to put little black crabs into the boys' pockets. So Mrs. S. J. and the poor lady-help drew up what she called a "brogramme" every morning to keep them "abused and out of bischief." It was all competitions or races or round games. Everything began with a piercing blast of the lady-help's whistle and ended with another. There were even prizes—large, rather dirty paper parcels which the lady-help with a sour little smile drew out of a bulging string kit. The Samuel Josephs fought fearfully for the prizes and cheated and pinched one another's arms—they were all expert pinchers. The only time the Burnell children ever played with them Kezia had got a prize, and when she undid three bits of paper she found a very small rusty button-hook. She couldn't understand why they made such a fuss . . .

But they never played with the Samuel Josephs now or even went to their parties. The Samuel Josephs were always giving children's parties at the Bay and there was always the same food. A big washhand basin of very brown fruit-salad, buns cut into four and a washhand jug full of something the lady-help called "Limonadear." And you went away in the evening with half the frill torn off your frock or something spilled all down the front of your open-work pinafore, leaving the Samuel Josephs leaping like savages on their lawn. No! They were too awful.

On the other side of the beach, close down to the water, two little boys, their knickers rolled up, twinkled like spiders. One was digging, the other pattered in and out of the water, filling a small bucket. They were the Trout boys, Pip and Rags. But Pip was so busy digging and Rags was so busy helping that they didn't see their little cousins until they were quite close.

"Look!" said Pip. "Look what I've discovered." And he showed them an old, wet, squashed-looking boot. The three little girls stared.

"Whatever are you going to do with it?" asked Kezia.

"Keep it, of course!" Pip was very scornful. "It's a find—see?"

Yes, Kezia saw that. All the same . . .

"There's lots of things buried in the sand," explained Pip. "They get chucked up from wrecks. Treasure. Why—you might find—"

"But why does Rags have to keep on pouring water in?" asked Lottie.

"Oh, that's to moisten it," said Pip, "to make the work a bit easier. Keep it up, Rags."

And good little Rags ran up and down, pouring in the water that turned brown like cocoa.

"Here, shall I show you what I found yesterday?" said Pip mysteriously, and he stuck his spade into the sand. "Promise not to tell."

They promised.

"Say, cross my heart straight dinkum."

The little girls said it.

Pip took something out of his pocket, rubbed it a long time on the front of his jersey, then breathed on it and rubbed it again.

"Now turn round!" he ordered.

They turned round.

"All look the same way! Keep still! Now!"

And his hand opened; he held up to the light something that flashed, that winked, that was a most lovely green.

"It's a nemeral," said Pip solemnly.

"Is it really, Pip?" Even Isabel was impressed.

The lovely green thing seemed to dance in Pip's fingers. Aunt Beryl had a nemeral in a ring, but it was a very small one. This one was as big as a star and far more beautiful.

V

As the morning lengthened whole parties appeared over the sand-hills and came down on the beach to bathe. It was understood that at eleven o'clock the women and children of the summer colony had the sea to themselves. First the women undressed, pulled on their bathing dresses and covered their heads in hideous caps like sponge bags; then the children were unbuttoned. The beach was strewn with little heaps of clothes and shoes; the big summer hats, with stones on them to keep them from blowing away, looked like immense shells. It was strange that even the sea seemed to sound differently when all those leaping, laughing figures ran into the waves. Old Mrs. Fairfield, in a lilac cotton dress and a black hat tied under the chin, gathered her little brood and got them ready. The little Trout boys whipped their shirts over their heads, and away the five sped, while their grandma sat with one hand in her knitting-bag ready to draw out the ball of wool when she was satisfied they were safely in.

The firm compact little girls were not half so brave as the tender, delicate-looking little boys. Pip and Rags, shivering, crouching down, slapping the water, never hesitated. But Isabel, who could swim twelve strokes, and Kezia, who could nearly swim eight, only followed on the strict understanding they were not to be splashed. As for Lottie, she didn't follow at all. She liked to be left to go in her own way, please. And that way was to sit down at the edge of the water, her legs straight, her knees pressed together, and to make vague motions with her arms as if she expected to be wafted out to sea. But when a bigger wave than usual, an old whiskery one, came lolloping along in her direction, she scrambled to her feet with a face of horror and flew up the beach again.

"Here, mother, keep those for me, will you?" Two rings and a thin gold chain were dropped into Mrs. Fairfield's lap.

"Yes, dear. But aren't you going to bathe here?"

"No-o," Beryl drawled. She sounded vague. "I'm undressing farther along. I'm going to bathe with Mrs. Harry Kember."

"Very well." But Mrs. Fairfield's lips set. She disapproved of Mrs. Harry Kember. Beryl knew it.

Poor old mother, she smiled, as she skimmed over the stones. Poor old mother! Old! Oh, what joy, what bliss it was to be young . . .

"You look very pleased," said Mrs. Harry Kember. She sat hunched up on the stones, her arms round her knees, smoking.

AT THE BAY

"It's such a lovely day," said Beryl, smiling down at her.

"Oh, my *dear*!" Mrs. Harry Kember's voice sounded as though she knew better than that. But then her voice always sounded as though she knew something better about you than you did yourself. She was a long, strange-looking woman with narrow hands and feet. Her face, too, was long and narrow and exhausted-looking; even her fair curled fringe looked burnt out and withered. She was the only woman at the Bay who smoked, and she smoked incessantly, keeping the cigarette between her lips while she talked, and only taking it out when the ash was so long you could not understand why it did not fall. When she was not playing bridge—she played bridge every day of her life—she spent her time lying in the full glare of the sun. She could stand any amount of it; she never had enough. All the same, it did not seem to warm her. Parched, withered, cold, she lay stretched on the stones like a piece of tossed-up driftwood. The women at the Bay thought she was very, very fast. Her lack of vanity, her slang, the way she treated men as though she was one of them, and the fact that she didn't care twopence about her house and called the servant Gladys "Glad-eyes," was disgraceful. Standing on the veranda steps Mrs. Kember would call in her indifferent, tired voice, "I say, Glad-eyes, you might heave me a handkerchief if I've got one, will you?" And Glad-eyes, a red bow in her hair instead of a cap, and white shoes, came running with an impudent smile. It was an absolute scandal! True, she had no children, and her husband . . . Here the voices were always raised; they became fervent. How can he have married her? How can he, how can he? It must have been money, of course, but even then!

Mrs. Kember's husband was at least ten years younger than she was, and so incredibly handsome that he looked like a mask or a most perfect illustration in an American novel rather than a man. Black hair, dark blue eyes, red lips, a slow sleepy smile, a fine tennis player, a perfect dancer, and with it all a mystery. Harry Kember was like a man walking in his sleep. Men couldn't stand him, they couldn't get a word out of the chap; he ignored his wife just as she ignored him. How did he live? Of course there were stories, but such stories! They simply couldn't be told. The women he'd been seen with, the places he'd been seen in . . . but nothing was ever certain, nothing definite. Some of the women at the Bay privately thought he'd commit a murder one day. Yes, even while they talked to Mrs. Kember and took in the awful concoction she was wearing, they saw her, stretched as she lay on the beach; but cold, bloody, and still with a cigarette stuck in the corner of her mouth.

Mrs. Kember rose, yawned, unsnapped her belt buckle, and tugged at the tape of her blouse. And Beryl stepped out of her skirt and shed her jersey, and stood up in her short white petticoat, and her camisole with ribbon bows on the shoulders.

"Mercy on us," said Mrs. Harry Kember, "what a little beauty you are!"

"Don't!" said Beryl softly; but, drawing off one stocking and then the other, she felt a little beauty.

"My dear—why not?" said Mrs. Harry Kember, stamping on her own petticoat. Really—her underclothes! A pair of blue cotton knickers and a linen bodice that reminded one somehow of a pillowcase . . . "And you don't wear stays, do you?" She touched Beryl's waist, and Beryl sprang away with a small affected cry. Then "Never!" she said firmly.

"Lucky little creature," sighed Mrs. Kember, unfastening her own.

Beryl turned her back and began the complicated movements of some one who is trying to take off her clothes and to pull on her bathing-dress all at one and the same time.

"Oh, my dear—don't mind me," said Mrs. Harry Kember. "Why be shy? I shan't eat you. I shan't be shocked like those other ninnies." And she gave her strange neighing laugh and grimaced at the other women.

But Beryl was shy. She never undressed in front of anybody. Was that silly? Mrs. Harry Kember made her feel it was silly, even something to be ashamed of. Why be shy indeed! She glanced quickly at her friend standing so boldly in her torn chemise and lighting a fresh cigarette; and a quick, bold, evil feeling started up in her breast. Laughing recklessly, she drew on the limp, sandy-feeling bathing-dress that was not quite dry and fastened the twisted buttons.

"That's better," said Mrs. Harry Kember. They began to go down the beach together. "Really, it's a sin for you to wear clothes, my dear. Somebody's got to tell you some day."

The water was quite warm. It was that marvellous transparent blue, flecked with silver, but the sand at the bottom looked gold; when you kicked with your toes there rose a little puff of gold-dust. Now the waves just reached her breast. Beryl stood, her arms outstretched, gazing out, and as each wave came she gave the slightest little jump, so that it seemed it was the wave which lifted her so gently.

"I believe in pretty girls having a good time," said Mrs. Harry Kember. "Why not? Don't you make a mistake, my dear. Enjoy yourself." And suddenly she turned turtle, disappeared, and swam away quickly, quickly, like a rat. Then she flicked round and began swimming back. She was going to say something else. Beryl felt that she was being poisoned by this cold woman, but she longed to hear. But oh, how strange, how horrible! As Mrs. Harry Kember came up close she looked, in her black waterproof bathing-cap, with her sleepy face lifted above the water, just her chin touching, like a horrible caricature of her husband.

VI

In a steamer chair, under a manuka tree that grew in the middle of the front grass patch, Linda Burnell dreamed the morning away. She did nothing. She looked up at the dark, close, dry leaves of the manuka, at the chinks of blue between, and now and again a tiny yellowish flower dropped on her. Pretty—yes, if you held one of those flowers on the palm of your hand and looked at it closely, it was an exquisite small thing. Each pale yellow petal shone as if each was the careful work of a loving hand. The tiny tongue in the centre gave it the shape of a bell. And when you turned it over the outside was a deep bronze colour. But as soon as they flowered, they fell and were scattered. You brushed them off your frock as you talked; the horrid little things got caught in one's hair. Why, then, flower at all? Who takes the trouble—or the joy—to make all these things that are wasted, wasted . . . It was uncanny.

On the grass beside her, lying between two pillows, was the boy. Sound asleep he lay, his head turned away from his mother. His fine dark hair looked more like a shadow than like real hair, but his ear was a bright, deep coral. Linda clasped her hands above her head and crossed her feet. It was very pleasant to know that all these bungalows were empty, that everybody was down on the beach, out of sight, out of hearing. She had the garden to herself; she was alone.

Dazzling white the picotees shone; the goldeneyed marigolds glittered; the nasturtiums wreathed the veranda poles in green and gold flame. If only one had time to look at these flowers long enough, time to get over the sense of novelty and strangeness, time to know them! But as soon as one paused to part the petals, to discover the under-side of the leaf, along came Life and one was swept away. And, lying in her cane chair, Linda felt so light; she felt like a leaf. Along came Life like a wind and she was seized and shaken; she had to go. Oh dear, would it always be so? Was there no escape?

. . . Now she sat on the veranda of their

Tasmanian home, leaning against her father's knee. And he promised, "As soon as you and I are old enough, Linny, we'll cut off somewhere, we'll escape. Two boys together. I have a fancy I'd like to sail up a river in China." Linda saw that river, very wide, covered with little rafts and boats. She saw the yellow hats of the boatmen and she heard their high, thin voices as they called . . .

"Yes, papa."

But just then a very broad young man with bright ginger hair walked slowly past their house, and slowly, solemnly even, uncovered. Linda's father pulled her ear teasingly, in the way he had.

"Linny's beau," he whispered.

"Oh, papa, fancy being married to Stanley Burnell!"

Well, she was married to him. And what was more she loved him. Not the Stanley whom every one saw, not the everyday one; but a timid, sensitive, innocent Stanley who knelt down every night to say his prayers, and who longed to be good. Stanley was simple. If he believed in people—as he believed in her, for instance—it was with his whole heart. He could not be disloyal; he could not tell a lie. And how terribly he suffered if he thought any one— she—was not being dead straight, dead sincere with him! "This is too subtle for me!" He flung out the words, but his open, quivering, distraught look was like the look of a trapped beast.

But the trouble was—here Linda felt almost inclined to laugh, though Heaven knows it was no laughing matter—she saw *her* Stanley so seldom. There were glimpses, moments, breathing spaces of calm, but all the rest of the time it was like living in a house that couldn't be cured of the habit of catching on fire, on a ship that got wrecked every day. And it was always Stanley who was in the thick of the danger. Her whole time was spent in rescuing him, and restoring him, and calming him down, and listening to his story. And what was left of her time was spent in the dread of having children.

Linda frowned; she sat up quickly in her steamer chair and clasped her ankles. Yes, that was her real grudge against life; that was what she could not understand. That was the question she asked and asked, and listened in vain for the answer. It was all very well to say it was the common lot of women to bear children. It wasn't true. She, for one, could prove that wrong. She was broken, made weak, her courage was gone, through child-bearing. And what made it doubly hard to bear was, she did not love her children. It was useless pretending. Even if she had had the strength she never would have nursed and played with the little girls. No, it was as though a cold breath had chilled her through and through on each of those awful journeys; she had no warmth left to give them. As to the boy—well, thank Heaven, mother had taken him; he was mother's, or Beryl's, or anybody's who wanted him. She had hardly held him in her arms. She was so indifferent about him that as he lay there . . . Linda glanced down.

The boy had turned over. He lay facing her, and he was no longer asleep. His dark-blue, baby eyes were open; he looked as though he was peeping at his mother. And suddenly his face dimpled; it broke into a wide, toothless smile, a perfect beam, no less.

"I'm here!" that happy smile seemed to say. "Why don't you like me?"

There was something so quaint, so unexpected about that smile that Linda smiled herself. But she checked herself and said to the boy coldly, "I don't like babies."

"Don't like babies?" The boy couldn't believe her. "Don't like *me*?" He waved his arms foolishly at his mother.

Linda dropped off her chair on to the grass.

"Why do you keep on smiling?" she said severely. "If you knew what I was thinking about, you wouldn't."

But he only squeezed up his eyes, slyly, and rolled

his head on the pillow. He didn't believe a word she said.

"We know all about that!" smiled the boy.

Linda was so astonished at the confidence of this little creature . . . Ah no, be sincere. That was not what she felt; it was something far different, it was something so new, so . . . The tears danced in her eyes; she breathed in a small whisper to the boy, "Hallo, my funny!"

But by now the boy had forgotten his mother. He was serious again. Something pink, something soft waved in front of him. He made a grab at it and it immediately disappeared. But when he lay back, another, like the first, appeared. This time he determined to catch it. He made a tremendous effort and rolled right over.

VII

The tide was out; the beach was deserted; lazily flopped the warm sea. The sun beat down, beat down hot and fiery on the fine sand, baking the grey and blue and black and white-veined pebbles. It sucked up the little drop of water that lay in the hollow of the curved shells; it bleached the pink convolvulus that threaded through and through the sand-hills. Nothing seemed to move but the small sand-hoppers. Pit-pit-pit! They were never still.

AT THE BAY

Over there on the weed-hung rocks that looked at low tide like shaggy beasts come down to the water to drink, the sunlight seemed to spin like a silver coin dropped into each of the small rock pools. They danced, they quivered, and minute ripples laved the porous shores. Looking down, bending over, each pool was like a lake with pink and blue houses clustered on the shores; and oh! the vast mountainous country behind those houses—the ravines, the passes, the dangerous creeks and fearful tracks that led to the water's edge. Underneath waved the sea-forest—pink thread-like trees, velvet anemones, and orange berry-spotted weeds. Now a stone on the bottom moved, rocked, and there was a glimpse of a black feeler; now a thread-like creature wavered by and was lost. Something was happening to the pink, waving trees; they were changing to a cold moonlight blue. And now there sounded the faintest "plop." Who made that sound? What was going on down there? And how strong, how damp the seaweed smelt in the hot sun . . .

The green blinds were drawn in the bungalows of the summer colony. Over the verandas, prone on the paddock, flung over the fences, there were exhausted-looking bathing-dresses and rough striped towels. Each back window seemed to have a pair of sand-shoes on the sill and some lumps of rock or a bucket or a collection of pawa shells. The bush quivered in a haze of heat; the sandy road was empty except for the Trouts' dog Snooker, who lay stretched in the very middle of it. His blue eye was turned up, his legs stuck out stiffly, and he gave an occasional desperate-sounding puff, as much as to say he had decided to make an end of it and was only waiting for some kind cart to come along.

"What are you looking at, my grandma? Why do you keep stopping and sort of staring at the wall?"

Kezia and her grandmother were taking their siesta together. The little girl, wearing only her short drawers and her under-bodice, her arms and legs bare, lay on one of the puffed-up pillows of her grandma's bed, and the old woman, in a white ruffled dressing-gown, sat in a rocker at the window, with a long piece of pink knitting in her lap. This room that they shared, like the other room's of the bungalow, was of light varnished wood and the floor was bare. The furniture was of the shabbiest, the simplest. The dressing-table, for instance, was a packing-case in a sprigged muslin petticoat, and the mirror above was very strange; it was as though a little piece of forked lightning was imprisoned in it. On the table there stood a jar of sea-pinks, pressed so tightly together they looked more like a velvet pincushion, and a special shell which Kezia had given her grandma for a pin-tray, and another even more special which she had thought would make a very nice place for a watch to curl up in.

"Tell me, grandma," said Kezia.

The old woman sighed, whipped the wool twice round her thumb, and drew the bone needle through. She was casting on.

"I was thinking of your Uncle William, darling," she said quietly.

"My Australian Uncle William?" said Kezia. She had another.

"Yes, of course."

"The one I never saw?"

"That was the one."

"Well, what happened to him?" Kezia knew perfectly well, but she wanted to be told again.

"He went to the mines, and he got a sunstroke there and died," said old Mrs. Fairfield.

Kezia blinked and considered the picture again . . . a little man fallen over like a tin soldier by the side of a big black hole.

"Does it make you sad to think about him, grandma?" She hated her grandma to be sad.

It was the old woman's turn to consider. Did it make her sad? To look back, back. To stare down the years, as Kezia had seen her doing. To look after *them* as a woman does, long after *they* were out of sight. Did it make her sad? No, life was like that.

"No, Kezia."

"But why?" asked Kezia. She lifted one bare arm and began to draw things in the air. "Why did Uncle William have to die? He wasn't old."

Mrs. Fairfield began counting the stitches in threes. "It just happened," she said in an absorbed voice.

"Does everybody have to die?" asked Kezia.

"Everybody!"

"*Me?*" Kezia sounded fearfully incredulous.

"Some day, my darling."

"But, grandma." Kezia waved her left leg and waggled the toes. They felt sandy. "What if I just won't?"

The old woman sighed again and drew a long thread from the ball.

"We're not asked, Kezia," she said sadly. "It happens to all of us sooner or later."

Kezia lay still thinking this over. She didn't want to die. It meant she would have to leave here, leave everywhere, for ever, leave—leave her grandma. She rolled over quickly.

"Grandma," she said in a startled voice.

"What, my pet!"

"*You're* not to die." Kezia was very decided.

"Ah, Kezia"—her grandma looked up and smiled and shook her head—"don't let's talk about it."

"But you're not to. You couldn't leave me. You couldn't not be there." This was awful. "Promise me you won't ever do it, grandma," pleaded Kezia.

The old woman went on knitting.

"Promise me! Say never!"

But still her grandma was silent.

Kezia rolled off the bed; she couldn't bear it any longer, and lightly she leapt on to her grandma's knees, clasped her hands round the old woman's throat and began kissing her, under the chin, behind the ear, and blowing down her neck.

"Say never . . . say never . . . say never—" She gasped between the kisses. And then she began, very softly and lightly, to tickle her grandma.

"Kezia!" The old woman dropped her knitting. She swung back in the rocker. She began to tickle Kezia. "Say never, say never, say never," gurgled Kezia, while they lay there laughing in each other's arms. "Come, that's enough, my squirrel! That's enough, my wild pony!" said old Mrs. Fairfield, setting her cap straight. "Pick up my knitting."

Both of them had forgotten what the "never" was about.

VIII

The sun was still full on the garden when the back door of the Burnells' shut with a bang, and a very gay figure walked down the path to the gate. It was Alice, the servant-girl, dressed for her afternoon out. She wore a white cotton dress with such large red spots on it and so many that they made you shudder, white shoes and a leghorn turned up under the brim with poppies. Of course she wore gloves, white ones, stained at the fastenings with iron-mould, and in one hand she carried a very dashed-looking sunshade which she referred to as her *perishall*.

Beryl, sitting in the window, fanning her freshly-washed hair, thought she had never seen such a guy. If Alice had only blacked her face with a piece of cork before she started out, the picture would have been complete. And where did a girl like that go to in a place like this? The heart-shaped Fijian fan beat scornfully at that lovely bright mane. She supposed Alice had picked up some horrible common larrikin and they'd go off into the bush together. Pity to make herself so conspicuous; they'd have hard work to hide with Alice in that rig-out.

But no, Beryl was unfair. Alice was going to tea with Mrs. Stubbs, who'd sent her an "invite" by the little boy who called for orders. She had taken ever such a liking to Mrs. Stubbs ever since the first time she went to the shop to get something for her mosquitoes.

"Dear heart!" Mrs. Stubbs had clapped her hand to her side. "I never seen any one so eaten. You might have been attacked by canningbals."

Alice did wish there'd been a bit of life on the road though. Made her feel so queer, having nobody behind her. Made her feel all weak in the spine. She couldn't believe that some one wasn't watching her. And yet it was silly to turn round; it gave you away. She pulled up her gloves, hummed to herself and said to the distant gum-tree, "Shan't be long now." But that was hardly company.

Mrs. Stubbs's shop was perched on a little hillock just off the road. It had two big windows for eyes, a broad veranda for a hat, and the sign on the roof, scrawled MRS. STUBBS'S, was like a little card stuck rakishly in the hat crown.

On the veranda there hung a long string of bathing-dresses, clinging together as though they'd just been rescued from the sea rather than waiting to go in, and beside them there hung a cluster of sandshoes so extraordinarily mixed that to get at one pair you had to tear apart and forcibly separate at least fifty. Even then it was the rarest thing to find the left that belonged to the right. So many people had lost patience and gone off with one shoe that fitted and one that was a little too big . . . Mrs. Stubbs prided herself on keeping something of everything. The two windows, arranged in the form of precarious pyramids, were crammed so tight, piled so high, that it seemed only a conjuror could prevent them from toppling over. In the left-hand corner of one window, glued to the pane by four gelatine lozenges, there was—and there had been from time immemorial—a notice.

LOST! HANSOME GOLE BROOCH
SOLID GOLD
ON OR NEAR BEACH
REWARD OFFERED

Alice pressed open the door. The bell jangled, the red serge curtains parted, and Mrs. Stubbs appeared. With her broad smile and the long bacon knife in her hand, she looked like a friendly brigand. Alice was welcomed so warmly that she found it quite difficult to keep up her "manners." They consisted of persistent little coughs and hems, pulls at her gloves, tweaks at her skirt, and a curious difficulty in seeing what was set before her or understanding what was said.

Tea was laid on the parlour table—ham, sardines,

a whole pound of butter, and such a large johnny cake that it looked like an advertisement for somebody's baking-powder. But the Primus stove roared so loudly that it was useless to try to talk above it. Alice sat down on the edge of a basket-chair while Mrs. Stubbs pumped the stove still higher. Suddenly Mrs. Stubbs whipped the cushion off a chair and disclosed a large brown-paper parcel.

"I've just had some new photers taken, my dear," she shouted cheerfully to Alice. "Tell me what you think of them."

In a very dainty, refined way Alice wet her finger and put the tissue back from the first one. Life! How many there were! There were three dozzing at least. And she held it up to the light.

Mrs. Stubbs sat in an arm-chair, leaning very much to one side. There was a look of mild astonishment on her large face, and well there might be. For though the arm-chair stood on a carpet, to the left of it, miraculously skirting the carpet-border, there was a dashing water-fall. On her right stood a Grecian pillar with a giant fern-tree on either side of it, and in the background towered a gaunt mountain, pale with snow.

"It is a nice style, isn't it?" shouted Mrs. Stubbs; and Alice had just screamed "Sweetly" when the roaring of the Primus stove died down, fizzled out, ceased, and she said "Pretty" in a silence that was frightening.

"Draw up your chair, my dear," said Mrs. Stubbs, beginning to pour out. "Yes," she said thoughtfully, as she handed the tea, "but I don't care about the size. I'm having an enlargemint. All very well for Christmas cards, but I never was the one for small photers myself. You get no comfort out of them. To say the truth, I find them dis'eartening."

Alice quite saw what she meant.

"Size," said Mrs. Stubbs. "Give me size. That was what my poor dear husband was always saying. He couldn't stand anything small. Gave him the creeps. And, strange as it may seem, my dear"—here Mrs. Stubbs creaked and seemed to expand herself at the memory—"it was dropsy that carried him off at the larst. Many's the time they drawn one and a half pints from 'im at the 'ospital . . . It seemed like a judgmint."

Alice burned to know exactly what it was that was drawn from him. She ventured, "I suppose it was water."

But Mrs. Stubbs fixed Alice with her eyes and replied meaningly, "It was *liquid*, my dear."

Liquid! Alice jumped away from the word like a cat and came back to it, nosing and wary.

"That's 'im!" said Mrs. Stubbs, and she pointed

dramatically to the life-size head and shoulders of a burly man with a dead white rose in the buttonhole of his coat that made you think of a curl of cold mutting fat. Just below, in silver letters on a red cardboard ground, were the words, "Be not afraid, it is I."

"It's ever such a fine face," said Alice faintly.

The pale-blue bow on the top of Mrs. Stubbs's fair frizzy hair quivered. She arched her plump neck. What a neck she had! It was bright pink where it began and then it changed to warm apricot, and that faded to the colour of a brown egg and then to a deep creamy.

"All the same, my dear," she said surprisingly, "freedom's best!" Her soft, fat chuckle sounded like a purr. "Freedom's best," said Mrs. Stubbs again.

Freedom! Alice gave a loud, silly little titter. She felt awkward. Her mind flew back to her own kitching. Ever so queer! She wanted to be back in it again.

IX

A strange company assembled in the Burnells' washhouse after tea. Round the table there sat a bull, a rooster, a donkey that kept forgetting it was a donkey, a sheep and a bee. The washhouse was the perfect place for such a meeting because they could make as much noise as they liked, and nobody ever interrupted. It was a small tin shed standing apart from the bungalow. Against the wall there was a deep trough and in the corner a copper with a basket of clothes-pegs on top of it. The little window, spun over with cobwebs, had a piece of candle and a mouse-trap on the dusty sill. There were clothes-lines criss-crossed overhead and, hanging from a peg on the wall, a very big, a huge, rusty horseshoe. The table was in the middle with a form at either side.

"You can't be a bee, Kezia. A bee's not an animal. It's a ninseck."

"Oh, but I do want to be a bee frightfully," wailed Kezia . . . A tiny bee, all yellow-furry, with striped legs. She drew her legs up under her and leaned over the table. She felt she was a bee.

"A ninseck must be an animal," she said stoutly. "It makes a noise. It's not like a fish."

"I'm a bull, I'm a bull!" cried Pip. And he gave such a tremendous bellow—how did he make that noise?—that Lottie looked quite alarmed.

"I'll be a sheep," said little Rags. "A whole lot of sheep went past this morning."

"How do you know?"

"Dad heard them. Baa!" He sounded like the little lamb that trots behind and seems to wait to be carried.

"Cock-a-doodle-do!" shrilled Isabel. With her red cheeks and bright eyes she looked like a rooster.

"What'll I be?" Lottie asked everybody, and she sat there smiling, waiting for them to decide for her. It had to be an easy one.

"Be a donkey, Lottie." It was Kezia's suggestion. "Hee-haw! You can't forget that."

"Hee-haw!" said Lottie solemnly. "When do I have to say it?"

"I'll explain, I'll explain," said the bull. It was he who had the cards. He waved them round his head. "All be quiet! All listen!" And he waited for them. "Look here, Lottie." He turned up a card. "It's got two spots on it—see? Now, if you put that card in the middle and somebody else has one with two spots as well, you say 'Hee-haw,' and the card's yours."

"Mine?" Lottie was round-eyed. "To keep?"

"No, silly. Just for the game, see? Just while we're playing." The bull was very cross with her.

"Oh, Lottie, you *are* a little silly," said the proud rooster.

Lottie looked at both of them. Then she hung her head; her lip quivered. "I don't not want to play," she whispered. The others glanced at one another like conspirators. All of them knew what that meant. She would go away and be discovered somewhere standing with her pinny thrown over her head, in a corner, or against a wall, or even behind a chair.

"Yes, you *do*, Lottie. It's quite easy," said Kezia.

And Isabel, repentant, said exactly like a grown-up, "Watch *me*, Lottie, and you'll soon learn."

"Cheer up, Lot," said Pip. "There, I know what I'll do. I'll give you the first one. It's mine, really, but I'll give it to you. Here you are." And he slammed the card down in front of Lottie.

Lottie revived at that. But now she was in another difficulty. "I haven't got a hanky," she said; "I want one badly, too."

"Here, Lottie, you can use mine." Rags dipped into his sailor blouse and brought up a very wet-looking one, knotted together. "Be very careful," he warned her. "Only use that corner. Don't undo it. I've got a little starfish inside I'm going to try and tame."

"Oh, come on, you girls," said the bull. "And mind—you're not to look at your cards. You've got to keep your hands under the table till I say 'Go.'"

Smack went the cards round the table. They tried with all their might to see, but Pip was too quick for them. It was very exciting, sitting there in the wash-house; it was all they could do not to burst into a little chorus of animals before Pip had finished dealing.

"Now, Lottie, you begin."

Timidly Lottie stretched out a hand, took the top card off her pack, had a good look at it—it was plain she was counting the spots—and put it down.

"No, Lottie, you can't do that. You mustn't look first. You must turn it the other way over."

"But then everybody will see it the same time as me," said Lottie.

The game proceeded. Mooe-ooo-er! The bull was terrible. He charged over the table and seemed to eat the cards up.

Bss-ss! said the bee.

Cock-a-doodle-do! Isabel stood up in her excitement and moved her elbows like wings.

Baa! Little Rags put down the King of Diamonds and Lottie put down the one they called the King of Spain. She had hardly any cards left.

"Why don't you call out, Lottie?"

"I've forgotten what I am," said the donkey woefully.

"Well, change! Be a dog instead! Bow-wow!"

"Oh yes. That's *much* easier." Lottie smiled again. But when she and Kezia both had a one Kezia waited on purpose. The others made signs to Lottie and pointed. Lottie turned very red; she looked bewildered, and at last she said, "Hee-haw! Ke-zia."

"Ss! Wait a minute!" They were in the very thick

of it when the bull stopped them, holding up his hand. "What's that? What's that noise?"

"What noise? What do you mean?" asked the rooster.

"Ss! Shut up! Listen!" They were mouse-still. "I thought I heard a—a sort of knocking," said the bull.

"What was it like?" asked the sheep faintly.

No answer.

The bee gave a shudder. "Whatever did we shut the door for?" she said softly. Oh, why, why had they shut the door?

While they were playing, the day had faded; the gorgeous sunset had blazed and died. And now the quick dark came racing over the sea, over the sandhills, up the paddock. You were frightened to look in the corners of the washhouse, and yet you had to look with all your might. And somewhere, far away, grandma was lighting a lamp. The blinds were being pulled down; the kitchen fire leapt in the tins on the mantelpiece.

"It would be awful now," said the bull, "if a spider was to fall from the ceiling on to the table, wouldn't it?"

"Spiders don't fall from ceilings."

"Yes, they do. Our Min told us she'd seen a

spider as big as a saucer, with long hairs on it like a gooseberry."

Quickly all the little heads were jerked up; all the little bodies drew together, pressed together.

"Why doesn't somebody come and call us?" cried the rooster.

Oh, those grown-ups, laughing and snug, sitting in the lamp-light, drinking out of cups! They'd forgotten about them. No, not really forgotten. That was what their smile meant. They had decided to leave them there all by themselves.

Suddenly Lottie gave such a piercing scream that all of them jumped off the forms, all of them screamed too. "A face—a face looking!" shrieked Lottie.

It was true, it was real. Pressed against the window was a pale face, black eyes, a black beard.

"Grandma! Mother! Somebody!"

But they had not got to the door, tumbling over one another, before it opened for Uncle Jonathan. He had come to take the little boys home.

X

He had meant to be there before, but in the front garden he had come upon Linda walking up and down the grass, stopping to pick off a dead pink or give a top-heavy carnation something to lean against, or to take a deep breath of something, and then walking on again, with her little air of remoteness. Over her white frock she wore a yellow, pink-fringed shawl from the Chinaman's shop.

"Hallo, Jonathan!" called Linda. And Jonathan whipped off his shabby panama, pressed it against his breast, dropped on one knee, and kissed Linda's hand.

"Greeting, my Fair One! Greeting, my Celestial Peach Blossom!" boomed the bass voice gently. "Where are the other noble dames?"

"Beryl's out playing bridge and mother's giving the boy his bath . . . Have you come to borrow something?"

The Trouts were for ever running out of things and sending across to the Burnells' at the last moment.

But Jonathan only answered, "A little love, a little kindness"; and he walked by his sister-in-law's side.

Linda dropped into Beryl's hammock under the manuka-tree, and Jonathan stretched himself on the grass beside her, pulled a long stalk and began chewing it. They knew each other well. The voices of children cried from the other gardens. A fisherman's light cart shook along the sandy road, and from far away they heard a dog barking; it was muffled as though the dog had its head in a sack. If you listened you could just hear the soft swish of the sea at full tide sweeping the pebbles. The sun was sinking.

"And so you go back to the office on Monday, do you, Jonathan?" asked Linda.

"On Monday the cage door opens and clangs to upon the victim for another eleven months and a week," answered Jonathan.

Linda swung a little. "It must be awful," she said slowly.

"Would ye have me laugh, my fair sister? Would ye have me weep?"

Linda was so accustomed to Jonathan's way of talking that she paid no attention to it.

"I suppose," she said vaguely, "one gets used to it. One gets used to anything."

"Does one? Hum!" The "Hum" was so deep it seemed to boom from underneath the ground. "I wonder how it's done," brooded Jonathan; "I've never managed it."

Looking at him as he lay there, Linda thought again how attractive he was. It was strange to think that he was only an ordinary clerk, that Stanley earned twice as much money as he. What was the matter with Jonathan? He had no ambition; she supposed that was it. And yet one felt he was gifted, exceptional. He was passionately fond of music; every spare penny he had went on books. He was always full of new ideas, schemes, plans. But nothing came of it all. The new fire blazed in Jonathan; you almost heard it roaring softly as he explained, described and dilated on the new thing; but a moment later it had fallen in and there was nothing but ashes, and Jonathan went about with a look like hunger in his black eyes. At these times he exaggerated his absurd manner of speaking, and he sang in church—he was the leader of the choir—with such fearful dramatic intensity that the meanest hymn put on an unholy splendour.

"It seems to me just as imbecile, just as infernal, to have to go to the office on Monday," said Jonathan, "as it always has done and always will do. To spend all the best years of one's life sitting on a stool from nine to five, scratching in somebody's ledger! It's a queer use to make of one's . . . one and only life, isn't it? Or do I fondly dream?" He rolled over on the grass and looked up at Linda. "Tell me, what is the difference between my life and that of an ordinary prisoner. The only difference I can see is that I put myself in jail and nobody's ever going to let me out. That's a more intolerable situation than the other. For if I'd been—pushed in, against my will—kicking, even—once the door was locked, or at any rate in five years or so, I might have accepted the fact and begun to take an interest in the flight of flies or counting the warder's steps along the passage with particular attention to variations of tread and so on. But as it is, I'm like an insect that's flown into a room of its own accord. I dash against the walls, dash against the windows, flop against the ceiling, do everything on God's earth, in fact, except fly out again. And all the while I'm thinking, like that moth, or that butterfly, or whatever it is, 'The shortness of life! The shortness of life!' I've only one night or one day, and there's this vast dangerous garden, waiting out there, undiscovered, unexplored."

"But, if you feel like that, why—" began Linda quickly.

"*Ah!*" cried Jonathan. And that "ah!" was somehow almost exultant. "There you have me. Why? Why indeed? There's the maddening, mysterious question. Why don't I fly out again? There's the window or the door or whatever it was I came in by. It's not hopelessly shut—is it? Why don't I find it and be off? Answer me that, little sister." But he gave her no time to answer.

"I'm exactly like that insect again. For some reason"—Jonathan paused between the words—"it's not allowed, it's forbidden, it's against the insect law, to stop banging and flopping and crawling up the pane even for an instant. Why don't I leave the office? Why don't I seriously consider, this moment, for instance, what it is that prevents me leaving? It's not as though I'm tremendously tied. I've two boys to provide for, but, after all, they're boys. I could cut off to sea, or get a job up-country, or—" Suddenly he smiled at Linda and said in a changed voice, as if he were confiding a secret, "Weak . . . weak. No stamina. No anchor. No guiding principle, let us call it." But then the dark velvety voice rolled out:

> *Would ye hear the story*
> *How it unfolds itself . . .*

and they were silent.

The sun had set. In the western sky there were great masses of crushed-up rose-coloured clouds. Broad beams of light shone through the clouds and beyond them as if they would cover the whole sky. Overhead the blue faded; it turned a pale gold, and the bush outlined against it gleamed dark and brilliant like metal. Sometimes when those beams of light show in the sky they are very awful. They remind you that up there sits Jehovah, the jealous God, the Almighty, Whose eye is upon you, ever watchful, never weary. You remember that at His coming the whole earth will shake into one ruined graveyard; the cold, bright angels will drive you this way and that, and there will be no time to explain what could be explained so simply . . . But to-night it seemed to Linda there was something infinitely joyful and loving in those silver beams. And now no sound came from the sea. It breathed softly as if it would draw that tender, joyful beauty into its own bosom.

"It's all wrong, it's all wrong," came the shadowy voice of Jonathan. "It's not the scene, it's not the setting for . . . three stools, three desks, three inkpots and a wire blind."

Linda knew that he would never change, but she said, "Is it too late, even now?"

"I'm old—I'm old," intoned Jonathan. He bent towards her, he passed his hand over his head. "Look!" His black hair was speckled all over with silver, like the breast plumage of a black fowl.

Linda was surprised. She had no idea that he was grey. And yet, as he stood up beside her and sighed and stretched, she saw him, for the first time, not resolute, not gallant, not careless, but touched already with age. He looked very tall on the darkening grass, and the thought crossed her mind, "He is like a weed."

Jonathan stooped again and kissed her fingers.

"Heaven reward thy sweet patience, lady mine," he murmured. "I must go seek those heirs to my fame and fortune . . ." He was gone.

XI

Light shone in the windows of the bungalow. Two square patches of gold fell upon the pinks and the peaked marigolds. Florrie, the cat, came out on to the veranda, and sat on the top step, her white paws close together, her tail curled round. She looked content, as though she had been waiting for this moment all day.

"Thank goodness, it's getting late," said Florrie. "Thank goodness, the long day is over." Her greengage eyes opened.

Presently there sounded the rumble of the coach, the crack of Kelly's whip. It came near enough for one to hear the voices of the men from town, talking loudly together. It stopped at the Burnells' gate.

Stanley was half-way up the path before he saw Linda. "Is that you, darling?"

"Yes, Stanley."

He leapt across the flower-bed and seized her in his arms. She was enfolded in that familiar, eager, strong embrace.

"Forgive me, darling, forgive me," stammered Stanley, and he put his hand under her chin and lifted her face to him.

"Forgive you?" smiled Linda. "But whatever for?"

"Good God! You can't have forgotten," cried

AT THE BAY

Stanley Burnell. "I've thought of nothing else all day. I've had the hell of a day. I made up my mind to dash out and telegraph, and then I thought the wire mightn't reach you before I did. I've been in tortures, Linda."

"But Stanley," said Linda, "what must I forgive you for?"

"Linda!"—Stanley was very hurt—"didn't you realize—you must have realized—I went away without saying good-bye to you this morning? I can't imagine how I can have done such a thing. My confounded temper, of course. But—well"—and he sighed and took her in his arms again—"I've suffered for it enough to-day."

"What's that you've got in your hand?" asked Linda. "New gloves? Let me see."

"Oh, just a cheap pair of wash-leather ones," said Stanley humbly. "I noticed Bell was wearing some in the coach this morning, so, as I was passing the shop, I dashed in and got myself a pair. What are you smiling at? You don't think it was wrong of me, do you?"

"On the *con*-trary, darling," said Linda, "I think it was most sensible."

She pulled one of the large, pale gloves on her own fingers and looked at her hand, turning it this way and that. She was still smiling.

Stanley wanted to say, "I was thinking of you the whole time I bought them." It was true, but for some reason he couldn't say it. "Let's go in," said he.

XII

Why does one feel so different at night? Why is it so exciting to be awake when everybody else is asleep? Late—it is very late! And yet every moment you feel more and more wakeful, as though you were slowly, almost with every breath, waking up into a new, wonderful, far more thrilling and exciting world than the daylight one. And what is this queer sensation that you're a conspirator? Lightly, stealthily you move about your room. You take something off the dressing-table and put it down again without a sound. And everything, even the bed-post, knows you, responds, shares your secret . . .

You're not very fond of your room by day. You never think about it. You're in and out, the door opens and slams, the cupboard creaks. You sit down on the side of your bed, change your shoes and dash out again. A dive down to the glass, two pins in your hair, powder your nose and off again. But now—it's suddenly dear to you. It's a darling little funny room. It's yours. Oh, what a joy it is to own things! Mine—my own!

"My very own for ever?"

"Yes." Their lips met.

No, of course, that had nothing to do with it. That was all nonsense and rubbish. But, in spite of herself, Beryl saw so plainly two people standing in the middle of her room. Her arms were round his neck; he held her. And now he whispered, "My beauty, my little beauty!" She jumped off her bed, ran over to the window and kneeled on the window-seat, with her elbows on the sill. But the beautiful night, the garden, every bush, every leaf, even the white palings, even the stars, were conspirators too. So bright was the moon that the flowers were bright as by day; the shadow of the nasturtiums, exquisite lily-like leaves and wide-open flowers, lay across the silvery veranda. The manuka-tree, bent by the southerly winds, was like a bird on one leg stretching out a wing.

But when Beryl looked at the bush, it seemed to her the bush was sad.

"We are dumb trees, reaching up in the night, imploring we know not what," said the sorrowful bush.

It is true when you are by yourself and you think about life, it is always sad. All that excitement and so on has a way of suddenly leaving you, and it's as though, in the silence, somebody called your name, and you heard your name for the first time.

"Beryl!"

"Yes, I'm here. I'm Beryl. Who wants me?"

"Beryl!"

"Let me come."

It is lonely living by oneself. Of course, there are relations, friends, heaps of them; but that's not what she means. She wants some one who will find the Beryl they none of them know, who will expect her to be that Beryl always. She wants a lover.

"Take me away from all these other people, my love. Let us go far away. Let us live our life, all new, all ours, from the very beginning. Let us make our fire. Let us sit down to eat together. Let us have long talks at night."

And the thought was almost, "Save me, my love. Save me!"

. . . "Oh, go on! Don't be a prude, my dear. You enjoy yourself while you're young. That's my advice." And a high rush of silly laughter joined Mrs. Harry Kember's loud, indifferent neigh.

You see, it's so frightfully difficult when you've nobody. You're so at the mercy of things. You can't just be rude. And you've always this horror of seeming inexperienced and stuffy like the other ninnies at the Bay. And—and it's fascinating to know you've power over people. Yes, that is fascinating . . .

AT THE BAY

Oh why, oh why doesn't "he" come soon?

If I go on living here, thought Beryl, anything may happen to me.

"But how do you know he is coming at all?" mocked a small voice within her.

But Beryl dismissed it. She couldn't be left. Other people, perhaps, but not she. It wasn't possible to think that Beryl Fairfield never married, that lovely fascinating girl.

"Do you remember Beryl Fairfield?"

"Remember her! As if I could forget her! It was one summer at the Bay that I saw her. She was standing on the beach in a blue"—no, pink—"muslin frock, holding on a big cream"—no, black—"straw hat. But it's years ago now."

"She's as lovely as ever, more so if anything."

Beryl smiled, bit her lip, and gazed over the garden. As she gazed, she saw somebody, a man, leave the road, step along the paddock beside their palings as if he was coming straight towards her. Her heart beat. Who was it? Who could it be? It couldn't be a burglar, certainly not a burglar, for he was smoking and he strolled lightly. Beryl's heart leapt; it seemed to turn right over, and then to stop. She recognized him.

"Good evening, Miss Beryl," said the voice softly.

"Good evening."

"Won't you come for a little walk?" it drawled.

Come for a walk—at that time of night! "I couldn't. Everybody's in bed. Everybody's asleep."

"Oh," said the voice lightly, and a whiff of sweet smoke reached her. "What does everybody matter? Do come! It's such a fine night. There's not a soul about."

Beryl shook her head. But already something stirred in her, something reared its head.

The voice said, "Frightened?" It mocked, "Poor little girl!"

"Not in the least," said she. As she spoke that weak thing within her seemed to uncoil, to grow suddenly tremendously strong; she longed to go!

And just as if this was quite understood by the other, the voice said, gently and softly, but finally, "Come along!"

Beryl stepped over her low window, crossed the veranda, ran down the grass to the gate. He was there before her.

"That's right," breathed the voice, and it teased, "You're not frightened, are you? You're not frightened?"

She was; now she was here she was terrified, and it seemed to her everything was different. The moonlight stared and glittered; the shadows were like bars of iron. Her hand was taken.

"Not in the least," she said lightly. "Why should I be?"

Her hand was pulled gently, tugged. She held back.

"No, I'm not coming any farther," said Beryl.

"Oh, rot!" Harry Kember didn't believe her. "Come along! We'll just go as far as that fuchsia bush. Come along!"

The fuchsia bush was tall. It fell over the fence in a shower. There was a little pit of darkness beneath.

"No, really, I don't want to," said Beryl.

For a moment Harry Kember didn't answer. Then he came close to her, turned to her, smiled and said quickly, "Don't be silly! Don't be silly!"

His smile was something she'd never seen before. Was he drunk? That bright, blind, terrifying smile froze her with horror. What was she doing? How had she got here? the stern garden asked her as the gate pushed open, and quick as a cat Harry Kember came through and snatched her to him.

"Cold little devil! Cold little devil!" said the hateful voice.

But Beryl was strong. She slipped, ducked, wrenched free.

"You are vile, vile," said she.

"Then why in God's name did you come?" stammered Harry Kember.

Nobody answered him.

XIII

A cloud, small, serene, floated across the moon. In that moment of darkness the sea sounded deep, troubled. Then the cloud sailed away, and the sound of the sea was a vague murmur, as though it waked out of a dark dream. All was still.

Permissions Acknowledgements

'The Contessina' by Elizabeth Bowen reproduced with permission of Curtis Brown Group Ltd, London, on behalf of the Literary Executors of the Estate of Elizabeth Bowen.

'A Summer Cold' by A. A. Milne reproduced with permission of Curtis Brown Ltd, London, on behalf of The Estate of the late Lesley Milne Ltd. Copyright © The Estate of the late Lesley Milne Ltd, 1920.

MACMILLAN COLLECTOR'S LIBRARY

Own the world's great works of literature in one beautiful collectible library

Designed and curated to appeal to book lovers everywhere, Macmillan Collector's Library editions are small enough to travel with you and striking enough to take pride of place on your bookshelf. These much-loved literary classics also make the perfect gift.

Beautifully made, every Macmillan Collector's Library book adheres to the same high production values. Each hardback features gilt edges, a ribbon marker and cloth binding, and every paperback has a bespoke illustrated cover.

Discover a new and exciting anthology or cherish your favourite classic stories with this elegant collection.

**Macmillan Collector's Library:
own, collect, and treasure**

Discover the full range at
panmacmillan.com/mcl